HORSEY MERE

A DI Tanner Mystery

- Book Five -

DAVID BLAKE

www.david-blake.com

Proofread by Jay G Arscott

Special thanks to Kath Middleton

Published by Black Oak Publishing Ltd
in Great Britain, 2020

Disclaimer:
These are works of fiction. Names, characters, businesses, places, events and incidents are either the products of the author's imagination or used in a fictitious manner. Any resemblance to actual persons, living or dead, or actual events is purely coincidental.

ISBN: 9798671354720

DEDICATION

For Akiko, Akira and Kai.

BOOKS BY DAVID BLAKE

CRIME FICTION
Broadland
St. Benet's
Moorings
Three Rivers
Horsey Mere

CRIME COMEDY
The Slaughtered Virgin of Zenopolis
The Curious Case of Cut-Throat Cate
The Thrills & Spills of Genocide Jill
The Herbaceous Affair of Cocaine Claire

SPACE CRIME COMEDY
Space Police: Attack of the Mammary Clans
Space Police: The Final Fish Finger
Space Police: The Toaster That Time Forgot
Space Police: Rise of the Retail-Bot
Space Police: Enemy at the Cat Flap
Space Police: The Day The Earth Moved A Bit

SPACE ADVENTURE COMEDY
Galaxy Squad: Danger From Drackonia

ROMANTIC COMEDY
Headline Love & Prime Time Love

SHORT STORY COLLECTION
Fish Fingered

"For all that is in the world, the lust of the flesh, and the lust of the eyes, and the pride of life, is not of the Father, but is of the world."
1 John 2:16

- PROLOGUE -

Saturday, 31st October

SAM LEWIS LET his bicycle crash down onto a grass verge before stepping up onto the carpark's low wooden boundary fence. There he teetered for a moment, his arms helping to find his balance, before standing tall, staring out at the wide expanse of water before him.

Finding what he was looking for, the single Hawthorne tree that clung to the edge of Horsey Mere, he turned his head into the brisk, cold wind, still blowing hard from the night before. As his sun-bleached hair whipped wildly about his head, he caught sight of his two friends, pedalling hard over the carpark towards him.

'Hurry up you two! It'll be dark soon!'

'All right, all right,' moaned Tom, the tallest of the three. 'Keep your hair on.'

Leaving them to follow, Sam jumped off the barrier, straight into a run.

When he was about twenty metres from the tree he stopped, catching his breath whilst staring up at its tangled web of lifeless branches, watching them being tussled and bent by the unrelenting wind.

He wasn't prepared to go any further. Not on his own he wasn't.

When his two friends finally appeared, one on each side, both breathing hard as they leaned over on their knees, he heard the voice of Jason, the smallest and youngest.

'Are you sure it's hers?'

'I reckon. You can see the stone slab, just under the roots. C'mon, I'll show you.'

Proceeding with more caution, the three boys edged themselves towards the tree's ancient base, doing their best to ignore the anguished sound of branches creaking and groaning above their heads. Once there, they squinted down through the rapidly diminishing light.

Lying at their feet was the first layer of the tree's complex system of tangled roots, the earth that had nurtured them for countless generations having been washed away by three days of torrential rain.

'That's it, there!' Sam exclaimed, pointing down at a broken mud-covered slab of stone, the exposed tree roots surrounding it like the bars of a rusty cage.

His two friends crouched down to take a closer look.

'The tree must have grown over the top of it,' observed Jason, reaching out with his hand to touch the slab before pulling it away.

'There's an engraving as well,' added Sam. 'I haven't been able to make the name out, but the date's pretty clear.'

'November 23, 1637,' Jason read aloud. 'It must be hers.'

Sam stood up to place his hands squarely down on his hips. 'We'll know for sure when we get it out.'

Tom took to his feet to stare over at him. 'You what?'

'When we get it out,' Sam repeated. 'We'll be able to see what's underneath.'

'I'm not sure I want to see what's underneath!'

'We'll be able to wash the mud off in the water as well, to see what the name says.'

'You're seriously telling me that you want us to remove a stone that had been deliberately placed over the grave of a 17th Century witch?'

'Why not?'

'On Halloween?'

'Oh, I get it now. You're scared.'

'Damned right I am! You do know *why* they placed stones like this on top of witches' graves, and not standing upright beside them, like most normal people's?'

Sam shrugged.

'To stop them rising from the dead.'

'Oh, come on.'

'I'm being serious.'

'Well, if that's the case, we're too late. The stone's already been broken.'

'But it hasn't been moved yet, at least not by a human's hand.'

'Maybe *she* broke it, trying to get out,' muttered Jason, standing up to join his two older friends.

The three boys stopped where they were to stare down, eyes wide, mouths open.

'Anyway, as I said,' continued Tom, swallowing, 'it's getting dark. I think we should be heading back.'

'We're here now,' said Sam. 'We may as well at least *try* to pull it out. For all we know, it's not even hers; just some four-hundred-year-old dead guy's.'

'If it was a gravestone, it would have *two* dates on it, not just one.'

'But if we can prove it's hers, we're definitely going to get in the papers. We might even get paid for the story, especially if we can sell it to the nationals. I mean, it's not as if anyone else has been able to find the final resting place of Elizabeth Craddock.'

As the other two considered that for a moment, Sam drove home his advantage. 'One thing I do know; if we don't, someone else will.'

'All right,' Tom agreed, with obvious reluctance, 'but if we see her remains climbing out, then I'm off!'

'I think we can all agree on that.'

Having made the collective decision, the three teenagers each took a step forward, before coming to a grinding halt.

'Are we sure about this?' questioned Tom, unable to keep his eyes off the stone, and the tangle of roots growing over it.

Before anyone had a chance to reply, a savage gust of wind tore over the water, blasting into them like a sledgehammer. As the branches above their heads shook with demonic rage, they felt the ground lift up beneath their feet, sending all three of them flying over backwards.

With the wind disappearing through the branches, into the ever-darkening landscape beyond, the boys were left staring through their knees at the stone slab they'd only moments before been about to try and wrestle out from the ground. Before them, rising up between the two broken halves were a pair of skeletal feet, its toes deformed, twisted and bent.

There they remained, staring at the feet, unable to speak, hardly daring to breathe.

It was only when they saw one of the toes twitch that Jason began to scream.

- CHAPTER ONE -

'WHAT'VE WE GOT?' called Tanner, raising his voice above the noise of the bitterly cold north-easterly wind that whipped continuously around his head.

Up ahead on the path, lit by Tanner's and Jenny's powerful torches, walked the ghostly figure of Norfolk Constabulary's Medical Examiner, Doctor Iain Johnstone.

'Photic retinopathy!' he called back, lifting a hand to shield his eyes from the beams. 'At least, I will if you keep shining those damned things into my face.'

Apologising, Tanner and Jenny lowered their torches to focus them on the grassy path ahead.

'Apart from that,' Johnstone continued, stopping in front of the two detectives, 'I think you've had a wasted journey.'

'Not a body then?'

'Oh, it's a body alright, but I suspect it may be a little past its sell by date to be a police matter.'

'Sorry?'

'I think it's the skeletal remains of Elizabeth Craddock, a woman who passed away some four-hundred years ago.'

Tanner exchanged an intrigued glance with Jenny, before turning back to ask, 'How can you be so sure?'

'Because, Detective Inspector Tanner, I have over twenty-five years' experience of dealing with such matters, although, in this particular case, having her name and the date of her death marked on an overlying gravestone probably helped a little.'

After offering Tanner and Jenny a rare self-amused smirk, Johnstone continued. 'Anyway, I think it's something for a team of local historians to get their teeth into, as opposed to Norfolk's finest.'

'Don't I know that name from somewhere?' enquired Jenny, with a sagacious frown. 'Elizabeth Craddock? Wasn't she supposed to have been the last witch to have been tried and hanged in these parts?'

'I've got no idea, but it would certainly explain the position of the body. She'd been buried vertically, head facing down inside what must have been quite a deep shaft.'

'And that means she was a witch, does it?' queried Tanner.

'That's how they buried them,' Jenny replied. 'Presumably, to prevent them from rising from the grave. The idea was that if they were buried head down and started to try and tunnel their way out, they'd end up in the depths of hell; at least that was the thinking at the time. They'd also place a heavy stone slab over the top of them, just to be on the safe side.'

Tanner gave her a sideways glance. 'I'd no idea you knew so much about witches.'

Jenny shrugged. 'Well, I used to be one, you see,' she continued, in a matter-of-fact tone of voice, 'but there's not much demand for them these days, so I joined the police instead.'

With both Tanner and Johnstone casting a wary eye over her, she let out a heavy sigh. 'Good grief. I'm joking! We learnt about them at school.'

'That's a relief,' muttered Tanner, glancing over at Johnstone. 'I'm not sure being married to a witch would have looked good on my CV.'

'Yes, of course. I heard you two were getting hitched. So...when's the big day?'

'17th January,' Jenny replied, smiling at Tanner, before thinking to add, 'but we haven't sent out the invitations yet.'

'Don't feel you need to include me.'

'You're already on the list,' Tanner responded.

'Oh! Well, thank you very much. Does, er, Forrester know?'

'We felt we had no choice but to tell him.'

'And what did he say – about you two working together?'

'We knew we wouldn't be able to continue when we made the decision.'

'I see. So, which one of you is going to be leaving us?'

'That'll be me,' Jenny replied, half raising her hand.

'Any idea what you'll be doing instead.'

'Not yet, no, but at the moment, I can't think beyond the wedding.'

'No doubt something will come to mind. Anyway,' Johnstone continued, glancing back over his shoulder, 'I'd better be off. Feel free to take a look at the remains, but as I said, I'm fairly sure they're more of archaeological interest than anything else.'

- CHAPTER TWO -

Sunday, 8ᵗʰ November

TANNER FINISHED WATCHING an old wooden motorboat chug slowly past from the warmth of their cabin's bed, before returning his attention back to the newspaper article he'd been reading.

'They're still going on about our local MP, Patrick Hopkins,' he called out to Jenny, sitting up at the table in their old wooden yacht's cockpit, under which one of only two electric heaters was positioned.

'What was that?' she asked, with an obvious lack of interest.

'The Norfolk Herald. They're saying that he's a direct descendant of Matthew Hopkins.'

'Sorry, who?'

'The Witchfinder General, from the 17th Century. He was the one who supposedly tried and hanged Elizabeth Craddock. I mean, it's just ridiculous.'

'Then why are you reading it?'

It was a good question, and had he not just finished his last book, he probably wouldn't have been.

'Well, I suppose it's quite entertaining.'

'That's probably why they write it.'

'They're saying that now Elizabeth Craddock's body has been exhumed, her spirit is free to seek revenge on all those who'd accused her of witchcraft, including their descendants, which is why they've been going on about our local MP.'

'I'd have to agree with you. That does sound a little far-fetched.'

'A little?'

'But I don't suppose it does any harm.'

'Unless your surname just happens to be Hopkins, and you're the MP for Norfolk.'

'Yes, well, I'm sure he must be used to people making stuff up about him. I can't imagine he'd take it seriously. He probably hasn't even read it. Anyway, why don't you come up here and help me with the invitation list.'

'For what?'

'Er, the wedding, remember?'

'Oh, yes, of course. I'd almost forgotten about that.'

'Do please tell me you're joking.'

'Of course I am,' Tanner replied, dragging himself out of bed to make his way up the companionway steps.

Popping his head out into the cockpit, he caught Jenny's eye. 'Whose wedding was it again?'

'That's really not very funny. Now, sit down and make yourself useful.'

'Right, what do you want me to do?' he replied, doing as he was told.

'We need to make a final decision on some of these names. Then we need to email out the invitations.'

'Email, really?'

'Why not?'

'But it's just so last Tuesday. Why can't we use WhatsApp instead?'

'I'm not having this discussion with you again.'

'But it would be so easy. All we'd have to do is set

up a group, invite everyone we know, and then ask who wants to come.'

'I know how WhatsApp works.'

'Then why can't we use it?'

'As I tried to explain to you last night, because it's a wedding, not a barbecue!'

'Yes, but only because we're having it in January.'

'Are you deliberately trying to wind me up?'

'Only a little,' Tanner replied, with a mischievous grin.

'Well don't. You've no idea how stressful this is.'

'Which is another perfect excuse to use WhatsApp, don't you think?'

'No, I don't think. Besides, I don't know anyone else whose used it to organise a wedding.'

'That's probably because they don't know what WhatsApp is.'

'Er, I don't mean to be rude, but *you* didn't know what WhatsApp was until I told you. And that was only about two weeks ago.'

'At least I'd heard of it before then.'

'And that's the other reason we're not going to – because not everyone does.'

'Only because they don't know what a great means of communication it is. If we send out an email, telling them about it, whilst also mentioning the fact that we'll be using it to organise our wedding, I'm sure they'd be happy to download the app. Once they have, it won't take them long to get the hang of it.'

'You're still winding me up, aren't you?'

He offered her a guilty smile. 'I'm sorry. How about using Snapchat instead?'

'We don't have time for this. We should have had these invitations out weeks ago. Now, let's focus, shall we?'

'Right. You have my full and undivided attention.'

With the distant sound of Tanner's phone ringing from somewhere down in the cabin, Tanner got back up to his feet.

'Hold on, I'd better get that.'

Jenny let out a world-weary sigh.

Ducking back down to find the phone hiding under his pillow, recognising the number, he called up, 'It's work, I'm afraid.'

'Can't you leave it? I mean, it's not as if we're on duty.'

'Which means it must be important.'

'Go on then,' Jenny bemoaned, 'but if we don't get these invitations out soon, we'll be the only two people going.'

- CHAPTER THREE -

IN THEIR OFFICIAL capacity as members of Norfolk's CID, Detective Inspector John Tanner and Detective Sergeant Jenny Evans stood just inside the doorway of a gloomy, well-proportioned wood-panelled study. On the far wall hung a portrait of Paddy Ashdown, a former Liberal Democrat leader, scowling down at them from his lofty position above an old pedestal writing desk. In the centre of the room, a Persian rug had been rolled back to reveal a dark wooden floor, where a five-pointed star had been drawn using dusty white chalk. Positioned at the end of each point was a delicate glass sphere, about the size of a large jam jar, and in the centre was a chair, toppled over on its side.

But Tanner and Jenny had hardly noticed any of those things. From the moment they'd entered the room, their eyes had been transfixed by what was hanging from a rope looped around a thick brass hook in the ceiling, tied off to an old wrought iron radiator screwed down to the floor.

It was the body of a man, senior in years, wearing an unfashionable pair of brown corduroy trousers together with a colourful argyle-patterned cardigan.

Seeing their resident medical examiner standing inside the five-pointed star, hands clasped behind his back as he too stared up at the body, Tanner caught his attention to watch him step his way carefully over towards them.

'I understand it's our local MP,' commented Dr Johnstone, pushing his glasses up the ridge of his nose.

'Patrick Hopkins,' Tanner confirmed, unable to take his eyes from the body's purple bloated face. 'We were only just talking about him when we got the call.'

'Nothing bad, I hope?'

Forcing himself to look away, Tanner glanced briefly at Johnston before staring down at the floor. 'It was in relation to the stories the Norfolk Herald had been writing.'

'You mean all that Witchfinder General nonsense?'

'We were saying that we doubted he'd have allowed himself to be affected by it. Looks like we were wrong.' Tanner returned his attention to the medical examiner. 'Assuming he did this to himself, that is?'

'I'll have a better idea when I get him back to the lab, but from what I can see so far, it does look that way, even down to his missing finger.'

'His finger is missing?' Tanner queried, searching the body's hands to find a bandaged bloody stump.

'Well, not missing, exactly. It's in one of the glass balls on the floor. It would appear that he'd cut it off, sometime before making the decision to hang himself.'

'But – for what possible reason?'

'I've no idea.'

Having had his attention drawn to the glass ball in question, Tanner glanced briefly around at the others. 'And what's in the rest, dare I ask?'

'Fortunately, nothing as gruesome. A hair sample, nail cuttings, saliva and some blood. I'm presuming they all belong to him, but I'll leave that for forensics to confirm.'

'Any ideas about the five-pointed star?'

'I could be wrong, but as with the glass balls, I think that's one for you to work out.'

'Fair enough.' Tanner glanced round at his fiancée. 'Jenny?'

'Who, me?' she replied, with a clear note of surprise. 'How should I know?'

'You said you studied witchcraft at school.'

'Er, I said I learnt about witches during History class, which is hardly the same thing. And as far as I can remember, that didn't cover the use of five-pointed stars, or why a member of Parliament would place various pieces of his body into glass jars before hanging himself. They probably did that in Chemistry, or maybe Home Economics.'

'So that's a no, then?'

Jenny shrugged. 'Maybe he was a man-witch and was trying to cast a spell to protect himself from Elizabeth Craddock's vengeful spirit, but it went a bit wrong and he ended up hanging by his neck from the ceiling. Or I suppose it could have been that he was a keen sailor, and just got carried away when practicing his knots.'

Tanner narrowed his eyes at her.

'What?'

'Looks like I'd better leave you two to it,' Johnstone remarked, turning away. 'Oh, before I go, I believe the young man who found the body is still waiting to give a statement, at least he was about half an hour ago.'

'Any idea where he is?' asked Tanner, glancing out the way they'd come in.

'He was out in the hall. Not sure now though.'

- CHAPTER FOUR -

STEPPING OUT INTO the hall, they were shown into the kitchen by a uniformed police constable. There they found a scruffy-looking young man with an unshaven face, still wearing his coat.

'Sorry to have kept you,' Tanner began, pulling out his ID. 'I'm Detective Inspector Tanner. This is my colleague, Detective Sergeant Evans. Norfolk Police.'

'Russell Dewhurst,' the man replied, pushing himself up from an old kitchen chair. 'I'm a reporter for the Norfolk Herald.'

'Oh, really!' came Tanner's surprised response, leading him to exchange a curious glance with Jenny. 'We've been told you found the body?'

'I did.'

'May we enquire why it was that you were here?'

'I'd arranged to interview Mr Hopkins a few days ago.'

'At his house?'

'Here, yes,' Dewhurst confirmed. 'He told me to come round at four o'clock.'

'Was there anyone else here, when you arrived?'

'Nobody, no.'

'Then I must admit to finding myself more than a little curious to know how you got in, if the only person who could have come to the door was otherwise engaged?'

'It was open.'

'Oh, right. I assume you rang the doorbell before stepping inside?'

'Of course!'

'And when there was no reply, finding the door open, you decided to take a look around?'

'I thought he'd simply left it open for me, to save him having to come to the door.'

'You thought that was likely, did you?'

The young journalist shrugged back a response.

'And when you came in, how did you know where to find him?'

'It was the only room with a light on.'

'His study door was open again, was it?'

'Well, no. I saw the light under the door, so I knocked and pushed it open to find him – to find him...'

The young man stopped mid-sentence.

'You said that you work for the Norfolk Herald?' continued Tanner.

'That's right.'

'Freelance?'

'Full time.'

'I don't suppose it was you who came up with that ridiculous story that he was a descendant of the Witchfinder General, and that the vengeful spirit of Elizabeth Craddock was walking the earth, searching for his soul?'

The journalist's eyes fixed themselves on Tanner's.

'It was my story, yes.'

With Tanner glaring at him, the young man continued.

'I'm sorry about what's happened, but I was only doing my job.'

'Your job being to make up malicious stories about public figures without a care in the world as to how they may affect the people they're written about?'

'It wasn't made-up,' Dewhurst declared, taking a defensive stance. 'At least, not the part about him being a descendant of the Witchfinder General.'

'I see. So you have actual proof, do you?'

'We traced his family all the way back to the 17th Century. That's what the interview was going to be about.'

'Did he know that, before agreeing to see you?'

'Well, no, but he must have had some idea. We'd been running the story for over a week. I admit, at first it was pure conjecture, that he was related, being that he had the same surname, but then we found the proof.'

'And what was that?'

'His family tree. Look, I'll show you.'

With seeming frantic urgency, the young man swung a rucksack off his shoulder to begin rifling through its contents.

Fishing out a rolled-up piece of paper, he held it out for the DI to take, but Tanner only stared down at it with dismissive disdain.

'It proves I didn't make it up,' Dewhurst continued, his voice unwavering.

'To be honest, Mr Dewhurst, I'd only be interested in reviewing that document if it turns out that Patrick Hopkins's death was anything but how it appears. Saying that, the coroner may think differently, as may the victim's family, should they feel they have sufficient grounds to sue; either yourself, or the newspaper you work for.'

The reporter's face remained unmoved.

'On what possible grounds could they sue?'

'Well, I'm no lawyer, but they'd probably start with character defamation, possibly even libel, especially if that document you're holding proves to be nothing more than a pack of lies. And don't forget public perception, of course. When word gets out that one of your sordid little stories has directly led to the death of someone who, by all accounts, was a much liked and highly respected member of our community, don't be surprised if your advertisers come to the collective decision that their money is better spent elsewhere.'

Seeing how Dewhurst's face had finally begun to show at least some signs of remorse, Tanner concluded his little speech. 'Goodnight, Mr Dewhurst.' Turning to lead Jenny out, he glanced back over his shoulder. 'Sleep well.'

- CHAPTER FIVE -

HEADING BACK TO the study, they entered to find Dr Johnstone taking notes in the corner.

'How's it all going?' Tanner enquired, his eyes immediately drawn back to the body, still hanging from the ceiling.

'Ah, yes,' the medical examiner exclaimed, glancing up. 'Forensics have pointed out something of particular interest.'

'Which is?'

'The stool.'

Realising it wasn't where it had been before, on its side, under the body, Tanner raised an eyebrow. 'It hasn't been stolen, has it?'

'Most amusing,' Johnstone muttered, as he headed over to the corner of the room where a number of items had been neatly piled up inside labelled tamper-proof evidence bags.

Lifting one with the stool inside, he returned to place it upright, directly under the body's feet.

'As you can see,' he continued, 'it's not quite high enough to have done the job.'

He was right. The gap between the MP's feet and the top of the stool was too great for him to have been standing on it before kicking it over, even if he'd been balancing on his tiptoes before doing so.

'So, someone did that to him?' said Jenny, gazing up at the man with a wistful expression.

'It looks that way.'

'Any idea if he was dead before being strung up?' questioned Tanner.

'From what I can tell, he was alive, but I'll have a better idea when I get him back to the lab.'

Tanner glanced down, first at the stool, then at the five-pointed star and the macabre glass balls that were still surrounding it. 'I suppose he could have been drugged. Did anyone find any chalk, by any chance?'

'Not that I'm aware of. I didn't see any on his hands, either.'

Jenny caught Johnstone's eye. 'How about on the finger that was severed?'

'Good question!'

As Johnstone picked his way over to the glass jar under discussion, Tanner smiled to himself as he took in his fiancée. The question she'd posed provided him with yet another instance, one of many recently, which made him realise just how much he was going to miss having her by his side.

'There's definitely a residue of something on this one,' he heard Johnstone mutter.

Tanner returned his attention to the medical examiner to find him holding the severed finger up to the light. 'Chalk?'

'It looks like it.'

'If it is, it would mean he'd drawn the five-pointed star before cutting it off.'

'Unless that's what someone wants us to think,' commented Jenny.

'Anyway,' Tanner continued, turning his head to the door where they'd come in. 'I suppose we'd better have another chat with that journalist friend of ours.'

Jenny followed his gaze. 'I think he's gone. At least, I thought I heard someone leave.'

'Not to worry. We know where to find him. Any idea when you'll be able to have the post-mortem results for us?'

Johnstone glanced down at his watch. 'Probably not until tomorrow afternoon.'

'OK, but if you could let us know anything sooner, it would be appreciated.'

Seeing him nod, Tanner turned to Jenny. 'I'd better give Forrester a call. He's going to be none too pleased to hear that our local MP's been murdered. That much I do know.'

- CHAPTER SIX -

Monday, 9th November

'IF I COULD have everyone's attention,' came DCI Forrester's voice, booming over the heads of Wroxham Police Station's staff as they assembled themselves in front of him.

After waiting a moment for their various muted conversations to subside, Forrester continued.

'I'm sure you've all heard by now that the body of our local MP, Patrick Hopkins, was found yesterday. We believe he died on Saturday evening, sometime between the hours of nine o'clock and twelve. For reasons DI Tanner is about to cover, we are treating this as a murder investigation. He'll also be highlighting some disturbing items found at the scene, all of which will need to be taken into consideration. Before he does, I just wanted to say a few words.

'I knew Patrick,' he continued, his voice taut with emotion. 'He was a good man, one who was remarkably popular within the Broads' community, for a politician, at least. He had the rare ability to win people over, even those who didn't share his political views, which I'd have to say would include myself. Obviously, the fact that he was a politician will mean that there must be any number of people who've harboured ill feelings towards him. But as its unlikely they'd have done so to the point of wanting him dead, I'd advise you to look at those who'd have the most to gain from him not being around anymore, especially in light of the fact that there will now have to be a by-election.

'Anyway, that's enough from me. DI Tanner will be the senior investigating officer. Before I hand you over, I'm sure I don't need to remind everyone that you'll need to treat everything you see and hear with the strictest confidence. If I hear of anyone so much as saying hello to a journalist, as and when they all start to show up, you'll have me to answer to. I hope that's understood.'

With everyone nodding, Forrester stepped to the side to let Tanner take centre stage.

'Good morning. As DCI Forrester mentioned, I'd like to start by going over some of the more unusual aspects surrounding Mr Hopkins death.'

Tanner turned to face the whiteboard behind him.

'As you can see from the photographs, whoever killed him went to some lengths to make it appear that he took his own life. The body was found hanging by a rope looped over a hook in the ceiling before being tied off to a wall-mounted radiator. There were no signs that the victim had been bound in any way, or that he'd been killed beforehand. The only way we knew that the scene had been staged was because the stool found lying underneath him was too low for his feet to have reached, making it impossible for the victim to have kicked it over. We're still awaiting the full results from the post-mortem, but for now we're working under the assumption that he must have been drugged before being hauled up.

'The other unusual aspects involve what you've no doubt already seen. Forensics believe that the five-pointed star was drawn by the victim, at least one day before he was found. These very singular glass balls you can see, positioned at the end of each point, contained samples from different parts of his body: hair, blood, saliva, nail clippings. The last one contained the index finger of his left hand.'

Tanner allowed the expected flutter of remarks to circle the room before continuing.

'However, they can't find any evidence to suggest that any of those items were placed there by anyone other than the victim himself, even the finger, which our medical examiner believes was removed at least twenty-four hours before the victim died. So, although he may not have taken his own life, something had clearly been going on beforehand.

'That leads me to who we found lurking at the scene, Mr Russell Dewhurst, a reporter for the infamous Norfolk Herald. He's the person responsible for the recent stories centred around Elizabeth Craddock, the alleged 17th Century witch whose remains were found a couple of weeks ago at Horsey Mere, which I'm sure you've already heard about. He's also the one who wrote that Patrick Hopkins was a direct descendent of the person considered to have tried and hanged Craddock, the self-proclaimed Witchfinder General, Matthew Hopkins. Our current thinking is that although the stories they've been publishing, about how the unearthing of Craddock's body had freed her spirit to seek vengeance on the descendants of those who'd had her tried and hanged as a witch, were beyond ridiculous, we can only assume Patrick Hopkins had decided to take them at face value. As well as the five-pointed star and the glass balls, we also found a book at the scene about witchcraft which, although new, showed signs that it had been read, at least in part.

'Returning to the reporter, according to him, he'd

arranged to interview Patrick Hopkins at four o'clock yesterday evening. His statement says that he arrived to find the front door open. When nobody answered, he let himself in. Unfortunately, he was allowed to leave the scene before we realised that Patrick Hopkins's death wasn't as it first appeared. Our first job is to therefore question him again. We need to know his whereabouts during the days leading up to Hopkins's death. When we spoke, he said he'd brought with him documented proof that the victim was who he'd been claiming, a direct descendant of Matthew Hopkins. I'd be very curious to see that document. More importantly, I'd like to know where he got it from. DI Cooper, I'll leave that with you.'

Seeing him nod, Tanner added, 'And make sure to get his prints and DNA to see if they match anything found at the crime scene.'

'DS Gilbert, I'd like yourself and DC Beech to start taking a look into Patrick Hopkins life. He may have been a popular MP, but that doesn't mean he didn't have enemies. We need to know who they might be, and which of them are most likely to have gained from his death.

'Meanwhile, DS Evans and I are going to start piecing together Hopkins's movements over the last week or so, our first stop being to work out where he bought the book on witchcraft from.'

- CHAPTER SEVEN -

PARKING HIS SLEEK but somewhat dated Jaguar XJS in Stalham High Street, a pretty market town to the north of Horning, Tanner stepped out to begin staring about.

'What was it called again?' he asked Jenny, as she emerged from the car.

'Tarragon,' she replied, closing her notebook. 'It should be up here on the left somewhere.'

With Jenny leading the way, they were soon standing outside a small glass-fronted shop with a window display featuring a wide assortment of colourful items including books, CDs, candles, jewellery, crystals, and what Tanner assumed to be wind chimes, all set against a backdrop of intricately designed wall hangings and woven tapestries.

'I guess it's some sort of new age spiritualist shop,' commented Tanner, his eyes jumping from one item to another.

'Something like that,' Jenny agreed. 'Look, there's that book we found at Hopkins's place.'

'I recognise those glass balls as well. Let's have a look inside, shall we?'

Pushing open the door to the sound of a small bell tinkling above their heads, they crept their way into a cosy quiet shop, decorated in a similar fashion to the window display outside.

'Let me know if I can be of any help,' came a

woman's voice, thick with a foreign accent from somewhere over to the right.

Glancing around, Tanner saw an attractive middle-aged woman with dark skin and deep penetrating eyes smiling over at him from behind a counter, her hand resting on a large open book.

'If you can,' came Tanner's reply, wandering over whilst fishing out his ID. 'Detective Inspector Tanner and Detective Sergeant Evans. Norfolk Police.'

To Tanner's surprise, the lady didn't seem at all fazed by the sudden arrival of two police inspectors, and simply laid a leather bookmark over the page she must have been reading before closing it.

'How can I help?'

With the unnerving feeling that she'd somehow been expecting them, Tanner cleared his throat. 'There's a book in your shop window about witchcraft.'

'Nature's Guide,' she responded, still smiling.

'That's the one. We were just wondering if you keep records of who you've sold copies to?'

'Only if they'd placed an order.'

'And has anybody?'

'Not recently,' she replied. 'Maybe it would be easier, Mr Tanner, if you were to simply ask me who it was that you are looking for?'

With an unsettling sense of exposed vulnerability, as if the woman was reading his mind as easily as the book lying on the counter before her, Tanner glanced briefly over at Jenny. 'I don't suppose you have a picture of the victim we could show to Mrs...?

'Matar. Janna Matar.'

Leaving Jenny to dig out her phone, Tanner returned his attention to the lady. 'Are you the owner?'

'I am.'

'How's business?' he asked, glancing around.

'Improving, thankfully.'

Tanner raised a discreet eyebrow, wondering how much worse it could have been before, given the fact that the shop was deserted.

'How long have you been here for?'

'About a year.'

'I suppose it takes a while to become established.'

'I've been told that a successful retail business is mainly about choosing the right location.'

'And this is, is it?'

'I've lived here most of my life,' she replied, with an amused smile, 'so I have a good knowledge of the area. We'll be OK.'

'Where were you before?'

'I moved here from Iraq back in 2003, shortly after the war started.'

Remembering who it was who'd started the war in question, a prickle of guilt had Tanner moving the subject along.

'Well, no doubt business will pick up.'

'Contrary to appearances, we have been quite busy recently, probably thanks to what was found over at Horsey Mere; that and all the related news stories.'

'I assume you're referring to the ones featured in the Norfolk Herald?'

'Well, we do get that particular publication, but I was thinking more about the local news in general.'

Interrupting their conversation, Jenny cleared her throat to pass Tanner her phone.

Seeing she'd managed to find a headshot of the deceased MP, Tanner showed the image to the shop's owner.

'I don't suppose you recognise this man?'

Leaning forward to squint at the image, the lady replied, 'He was in here a few days ago.'

'Do you know who he is?'

'I don't know his name; if that's what you mean?'

'You don't recognise him from anywhere?'

'Apart from having seen him here, I don't, but your question makes me think I should.'

'His name's Patrick Hopkins,' Tanner replied, studying the woman's face.

'I'm sorry,' she shrugged. 'Is he someone famous?'

'He's our local MP, Mrs Matar, or at least he was.'

'I'd no idea!'

Tanner narrowed his eyes at her. 'So, you haven't been reading what's been written about him recently in the Norfolk Herald?'

'We may have the paper delivered, Mr Tanner, but that doesn't mean we have to read it.'

'I assume you didn't know that he was found dead yesterday, either?'

'Again, no.'

'But he was in here, though?'

'As I said.'

'And he bought a copy of that book, the one in the window?'

'On my recommendation.'

'Why would you recommend that book in particular?'

'Because he was asking if I had any books about witchcraft.'

'Is that the only one you have?'

'We keep quite a few, but that's the most popular.'

'Did he buy anything else?'

'I seem to remember he bought a box of our glass Witch Balls as well, another popular product.'

'What would they have been for?'

'Traditionally, their purpose is to provide protection.'

'Protection? From what?'

'A malevolent curse.'

'And how are they supposed to do that?' questioned Tanner, with a dismissive snort.

The woman stared over at him as if he was a child arriving for his first day at school. 'The person seeking to create a spell of protection would have to place an item from their person inside the ball. A lock of hair, a piece of skin, nail clippings, that sort of thing.'

'I see. I don't suppose you have any idea why someone would go to the extreme lengths of cutting off a body part?'

The lady paused before answering. 'It is one of Nature's many laws, Mr Tanner. The greater the sacrifice, the greater the reward.'

'Which means?'

'The more a person is willing to give up, the more they can expect in return. In this instance, if someone was looking to invoke a spell of protection, the greater their sacrifice, the more powerful the spell.'

'And you believe all that stuff, do you?'

'It's not what *I* believe, Mr Tanner,' the lady replied, her deep-set eyes penetrating his.

'What about five-pointed stars? What are they used for?'

'Normally as apotropaic charms, again helping to ward off evil forces.'

At that moment, the sound of crashing glass exploded into the shop.

Launching himself at the door, Tanner pulled it open just in time to see a scrawny teenager, his head covered by a light grey hoodie, pelting away down the narrow high street, nearly knocking an elderly lady to the ground as he went.

A quick glance over his shoulder confirmed what he thought had happened. Something had been thrown through the shop's window, leaving a gaping jagged hole and a million shards of razor-sharp glass hanging off the items on display.

Seeing Jenny emerge from the shop behind him, Tanner called out, 'Get uniform down here. I'm going after him.' With that, he sprinted away, leaving Jenny calling after, 'John, wait! Come back!'

- CHAPTER EIGHT -

SPRINTING AFTER THE hooded youth, as fast as his forty-something year-old body would allow, Tanner was almost relieved to see him jump into a grubby non-descript white van parked at the far end of the high street.

A hand on either knee, Tanner gasped at the air as he watched the van disappear in a cloud of noxious diesel smoke, all the while attempting to make out the number plate. But like his general level of fitness, his eyes weren't what they used to be either.

Cursing the day he turned forty, he pulled himself up before turning to jog his way back at a more leisurely pace.

Arriving to find a small group of people had gathered outside, with Jenny busy helping the owner to lift out some of the larger items from what was left of the window display, Tanner dug out his ID to hold up to the crowd.

'Did anyone see who did this?'

With a policeman arriving at the scene, the crowd quickly began to disperse, leaving a shrunken old lady with her hand raised half in the air.

Tanner stepped over towards her.

'I don't suppose you saw his face?'

'Well, yes and no,' the lady replied. 'It all happened so quickly. He nearly ran straight into me.'

'Did you recognise him? Was he from around

here?'

'I'm sorry, I don't know. They all look the same these days, don't you think? Especially as they all wear those horrible hoodie-type things pulled up over their heads. I can't stand them. They should be banned, that's what they should be.'

'I'd have to agree,' Tanner responded, 'but unfortunately, there's no law to stop people from wearing them, more's the pity.'

Tanner was about to give up with the witness when she piped up with, 'He had red hair, if that helps; and a decidedly mean look in his eyes.'

'I'll make a note of that, thank you.'

Turning away, he checked the surrounding buildings for any signs of a CCTV camera. Spying one two shops down, facing towards them, he turned his attention back to the broken window to find Jenny staring over at him with an obvious smirk.

'I assume he got away?'

'He had a van parked down the road.'

'Did you get the number plate?'

Tanner shook his head.

'Oh well, never mind. Whoever it was, they threw this.'

She was holding out a hefty-looking rectangular object wrapped in newspaper.

'Without unwrapping it, I'd say it's a brick,' Jenny continued. 'The newspaper is the front page of today's Norfolk Herald. The headline's been circled in red.'

'Dare I ask what it says?'

'Witch's curse causes MP's death.'

'Oh for Christ's sake!' Tanner moaned. 'I suppose the article was written by that idiot reporter we met yesterday, no doubt before he found out that Hopkins had been murdered.'

'I can't see from here. Not without unwrapping it.'

'OK, well I suggest we let forensics do that. Hopefully they'll be able to pull something off it. There's a CCTV camera pointing this way, which might help us as well.'

Looking over to see Mrs Matar, the shop's owner, carefully unhooking one of the windchimes, Tanner sought to garner her attention. 'I'm sorry about all this.'

'Hardly your fault.'

'Are you OK?'

'A little shaken, but I'll be fine.'

'Has anything like this happened before?'

'Well, no, but I'm not too surprised. In the material world in which we live, spiritual matters are rarely understood, which does tend to leave a vacuum often filled by fear. Hatred tends to be an unfortunate by-product. To be honest, at this time I'm more concerned about having my stock taken.'

'Well look, don't worry. We'll help with having your window boarded up and replaced. I assume you have insurance?'

'I let my daughter deal with all that sort of thing.'

'Is she around?'

'She's at college; but should be back soon.'

Tanner returned his attention to Jenny.

'Did you call the station?'

Jenny nodded. 'They're sending Higgins and another PC.'

'OK, good. I suggest we stay here until they arrive. We can get them to help tidy up a little and arrange for the window to be boarded up. Maybe you can take some pictures, for the benefit of the insurance company?'

'No problem,' she replied, pulling out her phone.

'Whilst you do that, I'd better give the office a call, to see how they've been getting on in our absence.'

- CHAPTER NINE -

TAKING HIMSELF AWAY from the shop, Tanner put a call through to the office.

'Vicky, it's Tanner. I assume you heard what happened?'

'Someone put a brick through a shop window?'

'The one we just happened to be in at the time.'

'Did you catch the culprit?'

'Unfortunately not. He was too fast, and I'm far too old. Anyway, we found out that Patrick Hopkins had been there a few days ago. It was where he got the book on witchcraft from, along with the glass balls. The owner said he bought them for protection.'

'Protection from what?'

'Presumably from the curse he must have believed Elizabeth Craddock had placed on him.'

'He'd been reading the Norfolk Herald then?'

'Believing it as well. Apparently, five-pointed stars have a similar purpose, at least that's what the woman who owned the shop said.'

'Are you thinking of her as a possible suspect?'

'Who, the shop's owner? To be honest, I wasn't, but only because she didn't seem to have a clue who Hopkins was.'

'Or maybe that's what she wanted you to think.'

'It's possible, I suppose,' mused Tanner, 'but some sort of motive would be useful. I don't think it's normal for shop owners to go around killing their customers, unless they forgot to pay for the items they were seen walking out with.'

'But it does make sense though, that whoever killed him knew his state of mind; that he was in fear of his life to the extent that he was drawing five-pointed stars on the floor whilst removing various parts of his body to stick them inside glass jars. Maybe she knew exactly who he was when he came into the shop,' Vicky continued, 'and decided to tell someone, someone who *did* have a motive for wanting him dead?'

'One of her customers?'

'I was thinking more along the lines of one of Hopkins's political rivals. We managed to find out that he had quite a few. The last election was a particularly sordid affair. He eventually won the seat from Michael Drummond, but not after a bitterly fought campaign, one which ended with Drummond suing Hopkins for character defamation.'

'Who won that?'

'The court went with Hopkins, stating Drummond wasn't able to prove what his opponent had said wasn't true.'

'Remind me who Michael Drummond is again?'

'He was the Foreign Secretary for the last government.'

Tanner thought for a moment. 'I don't suppose we know if he'll be running in the expected by-election?'

'I've no idea, but I wouldn't be surprised.'

'OK, then I suggest we keep him in mind. If he does put his name forward, and the investigation is still open, I think he'd be worth having a chat with. Have you been able to find out anything else about Hopkins?'

'Only that he was in the Army.'

'How long ago was that?'

'About twenty years.'

'OK, keep digging. How's Cooper been getting on?'

'He's out having a chat with that reporter. Before I forget, he asked me to tell you that he found out who did the research into Patrick Hopkins's ancestry. It was a retired history professor called Francis Bamford. It's become something of a specialty for him. He's even got a website offering his services.'

'I suppose we'd better make a note to see him at some stage,' Tanner replied, without much enthusiasm.

'I think we may want to meet with him a little sooner than that. I Googled his name quickly. He used to be married but they divorced about five years ago.'

'Uh-huh,' said Tanner, hoping that wasn't it.

'Apparently, his wife ran off with someone else.'

'Is this leading somewhere, Vicky?'

'You'll never guess who that someone else was?'

'You're right, I won't.'

'Our recently deceased MP, Patrick Hopkins.'

'OK, now you've got my attention.'

'It doesn't end there,' Vicky continued. 'His estranged wife ended up being killed in a car crash, about a year after the divorce. Hopkins was behind the wheel but survived with nothing but a few cuts and scratches. He'd apparently been drinking, but not enough to put him over the limit. The accident happened only a few months after the General Election, when he was voted in as Norfolk's new MP. Professor Bamford made a lot of noise in the national press afterwards, calling him a murderer and saying that he should resign.'

'Sounds like he was still in love with his wife.'

'And blamed Hopkins for her death, as well as for being the one who'd lured her away from him.'

Tanner paused for a moment. 'I think he's just moved up to the top of a rather slim pile of suspects. Can you send me over his contact details?'

'I already have.'

- CHAPTER TEN -

BACK AT THE shop, Tanner found Jenny inside, now helping the owner to store away the items they'd rescued from the shop's window display.

'Unfortunately, Ms. Matar,' he called out, 'we're going to have to go.'

'OK,' she replied, glancing up. 'Thanks for all your help.'

'Sorry again for what happened, but there will be a couple of police constables arriving shortly. I'll tell them to give you a hand to get the window boarded up, and with anything else you need.'

With Jenny joining him, they were about to head out when Tanner turned back. 'One more thing, Ms. Matar. You mentioned earlier that you keep records of people who've placed orders for books.'

'Yes, but only until they've picked up the order. Then I throw them away.'

'So you don't keep a customer database, or anything?'

'You'd be better off asking my daughter about that sort of thing.'

'And you both live here, do you?' asked Tanner, fishing out one of his business cards.

'We have a small flat upstairs which we share with my mother.'

'Your mother is upstairs?'

'She is, but don't worry. She wouldn't have heard anything. Her hearing went a long time ago.'

Tanner stepped over to her with his card. 'Perhaps you could ask your daughter to give me a call at some stage?'

'Of course. I'll ask her when she gets back.'

Seeing them turn to leave, Ms. Matar called out, 'Thank you again, oh, and by the way, congratulations!'

With the shop door closed, Tanner and Jenny exchanged a similar confused look.

'Did you tell her about us?' Jenny questioned.

'I thought you must have?'

'Not me.'

Tanner glanced down at her hand. 'She must have seen your ring and was congratulating you.'

'It sounded more like she was congratulating both of us.'

With a squad car pulling up on the curb, Tanner changed the subject.

'Anyway, I just got off the phone with Vicky.'

'Any news?'

'She told me that Cooper's having another chat with our reporter friend from the Norfolk Herald. He found out who they used to investigate Hopkins's ancestry. It was a retired history lecturer by the name of Professor Bamford, who has some interesting history of his own.'

'What's that?'

'I'll tell you on the way.'

'I take it that means we're going to see him?'

Tanner nodded. 'Vicky's just sent me over his address.'

- CHAPTER ELEVEN -

BOUT AN HOUR later, Professor Francis Bamford was leading Tanner and Jenny down the narrow dark hall of a modest bungalow with white pebble-dashed walls and an overgrown garden.

Ushering them into a dusty living room with the strong whiff of damp in the air, the tired-looking grey haired old man turned to ask, 'Can I get either of you anything to drink? A coffee, perhaps?'

'We're fine, but thank you,' Tanner replied, as Jenny and himself perched themselves on the edge of a faded old sofa to begin staring around at a floor littered with hefty books and unruly piles of dog-eared academic journals.

'Sorry it's a bit of a mess,' he said, levering himself down into an armchair that creaked under his weight. 'Now, what can I do for you? I'm not in any trouble, I hope?'

'Not at all,' began Tanner, focussing his attention of the man's sagging grey face. 'We wanted to talk to you about your work involving genealogy.'

'Oh, right!' the professor chirped, his whole face brightening. 'Would it be for one of you?'

'Er – neither of us, no, but it *is* what you do, for a living?'

'I'd probably describe it more as a hobby than an actual job.'

'But you do get paid for it?'

'I suppose it depends on who the client is. I do seem to end up doing quite a few for free, although mainly for friends and family members.'

'How about newspapers?'

'Newspapers?'

'The Norfolk Herald, for example?'

The professor took a moment to take Tanner in before answering.

'I assume you're referring to the one I did recently for the Hopkins family.'

'We are.'

'OK, well, no. I'd never done one for a newspaper before, or any organisation for that matter, but the manner which that one came about was particularly unusual.'

'Go on.'

'Well,' the professor began, sitting back in his chair to gaze up at the ceiling. 'I seem to remember I was visiting the archaeological dig where the remains of Elizabeth Craddock were being exhumed. Fascinating stuff! Anyway, when I was there, I found myself talking to a young man who began asking me about the history of witchcraft in the area, currently quite a popular theme. I think he was a little surprised to discover that East Anglia was the epicentre of witch-hunting, in England at least, thanks largely to the work of one man, Matthew Hopkins, the self-proclaimed Witchfinder General. He was responsible for more people being tried and hanged for witchcraft in England than during the previous hundred years.

'Anyway, he went on to ask me about our MP, Patrick Hopkins; whether it was possible that there could be a family connection.'

'And what did you say?'

'I said that it was possible, of course, but highly

unlikely. The name Hopkins means "son of Hob", which in turn is a shortened version of the name Robert, of which there were quite a few.'

'But you agreed to carry out the research?' asked Tanner, endeavouring to move the conversation along.

'I knew it would be a challenge, but I did, yes.'

'Did you know that he was a reporter?'

'He did mention something about it, but neglected to tell me that he worked for the Norfolk Herald. Had I known that, I'd have *never* agreed. Having my name associated with such a publication is hardly beneficial to my reputation.'

'That aside for now,' continued Tanner, 'what did you discover?'

'Well, the whole thing proved far harder than I thought, involving numerous trips to various graveyards. I even had to make a journey to France! But I was eventually able to trace his ancestral link all the way back to Matthew Hopkins.'

'And then you sold that information to the Norfolk Herald?'

'I'd been contracted by them to undertake the research, so naturally I passed on my findings.'

'Despite knowing what sort of a newspaper it was, and that they'd already been writing stories that he was indeed a blood relative of the Witchfinder General?'

'A contract is a contract, inspector, and as they paid half my fee upfront, I felt I had little choice. To be quite honest,' the professor continued, crossing his legs, 'I really don't see what any of this has to do with the police.'

'Haven't you seen the news?'

'Not today, no. Why?'

'Because, Professor Bamford, the person whose

ancestry you were so diligently researching has turned up dead.'

'Patrick Hopkins is *dead*?' the man asked, sitting forward.

'His body was found in his study yesterday evening, hanging by the neck. There was a five-pointed star drawn on the floor and various parts of his body had been placed into so-called "Witch's Balls", apparently in a misguided attempt to ward off a curse Elizabeth Craddock had placed on Matthew Hopkins and his alleged descendants, all according to your client, the Norfolk Herald.'

'But – I'd no idea. How could I have known he'd take it all so seriously?'

'Anyway, no doubt you'll be relieved to learn that he didn't take his own life.'

'I thought you said he hanged himself?'

'I said he was found hanging, Professor. I didn't say anything about him doing it to himself.'

'You mean, he was murdered?'

'It would appear so.'

'Good God!'

'May I ask if you knew him at all?'

'Who? Patrick Hopkins? I met him once, at a fund-raising dinner, about five years ago, but I can't say I knew him.'

'How about your wife?'

After holding Tanner's gaze for a moment, the professor looked away.

'I take it she did know him?' questioned Tanner.

The professor remained motionless for a moment before returning his gaze to Tanner.

'My wife left me for him, but I assume you already knew that. But I didn't lie to you just now. I did only meet him once, at that fund-raising dinner. My wife was seated next to him. It was obvious they were getting on well together, but I had no idea that they'd started to see each other. The first I knew about it was when she announced out of the blue that she was leaving me. I spent the next two years desperately hoping she'd come back, and then – and then...'

As tears began threatening the corners of his eyes, Tanner couldn't help but feel sorry for him.

'...she was killed in a car accident,' Tanner concluded, 'with Hopkins behind the wheel.'

A sterile silence fell over the room, eventually broken by Tanner.

'Professor Bamford. Can you tell us your whereabouts yesterday evening?'

'I – I was here, but you can't honestly think I would be capable of doing such a thing?'

'Can anyone verify that – that you were here?'

'No, but -'

'I'm afraid we'll need to collect a sample of your DNA and fingerprints. Would you like to come to the station to do that, or would you prefer us to send someone over?'

'But I -'

'I think we'd better send someone over,' Tanner said, glancing over at Jenny.

'Right, we'd better be on our way. Thank you for your time, professor. Oh, and if you have any plans for any more trips away, I'm afraid you're going to have to cancel them.'

- CHAPTER TWELVE -

I T WAS ONLY ten past four in the afternoon when they left the professor's house, but with the clocks having gone back two weeks before, daylight had already slipped away, and they found themselves emerging into a cold and uninviting darkness.

'Did you believe any of that?' questioned Jenny, as they opened the Jag's long heavy doors to ease themselves down into its sumptuous cream leather seats.

'What, you mean that he was at the archaeological dig when a reporter just happened to start up a conversation with him about Elizabeth Craddock and the whole Witchfinder General thing? And how that led directly to him picking up a commission to delve into the ancestry of the very man who'd not only run off with his wife, but had effectively killed her as well?'

'That's the one.'

'Not really. I think it's far more likely that he was the one who approached The Norfolk Herald, probably after seeing what they'd started writing about Patrick Hopkins. You never know, it could have been him who gave them the idea for the story in the first place.'

'And the validity of his research?'

'Who knows. I wouldn't be surprised if he just made up the whole thing to slurry Hopkins's name.

As to whether or not he had a hand in his death, we'll have to wait and see what forensics comes up with.'

Half an hour later, driving through Wroxham on their way to the police station, they were met by the sight of a solitary news van parked on the curb opposite, the name BBC East lit up by the car's headlights.

'Does that mean they've found out Patrick Hopkins was murdered?' questioned Jenny, peering out through the windscreen.

'If they knew that, there'd be standing room only!'

Slowing the car to make the turning into the station, it was only after he'd narrowly avoided running over a cameraman when he realised something was amiss. The carpark was virtually empty.

'Where on Earth is everyone?'

'Forrester's still here,' Jenny observed, nodding over at his BMW.

'But nobody else. There aren't even any squad cars.'

Parking up, they ignored the questions being thrown over to them by the journalist standing by the side of the road to hurry in through the main entrance.

Finding the office to be as deserted as the carpark, Tanner left Jenny beside her desk, tasked with the job of finding someone to collect the professor's prints and DNA, whilst he headed over to have a chat with Forrester.

'Sorry to bother you,' he said, after rapping his knuckles on the door.

'Ah, Tanner! I was wondering when you'd be back.'

'I have got the right time?' Tanner asked, glancing down at his watch. 'It is only twenty to five?'

'I think so, yes, why?'

'I was just wondering where everyone was?'

'Oh, I see what you mean. Believe it or not, they're all out. The phone's been ringing off the hook since you left.'

Tanner raised a curious eyebrow. 'What's been going on?'

'I reckon it's that bloody newspaper again.'

'The Norfolk Herald?'

'The one and only. Did you see their front page today?'

'Only in part. It was wrapped around the brick thrown through that shop's window we were at earlier.'

'Now why doesn't that surprise me. It would seem that their wholly inaccurate report of Patrick Hopkins's death, that he killed himself thanks to a witch's curse, has ignited what can only be described as a wave of xenophobic racism in the area.'

'Racism?'

'I'm not sure what else to call it. There have been on-going reports that gangs of white males are roaming the streets, accusing even the most vaguely looking foreign woman of being part of some sort of witch's coven, making them out to be somehow responsible for Patrick Hopkins having killed himself.'

'But he didn't, though.'

'I'm fully aware of that, thank you, Tanner, but they don't know that, do they.'

'Then don't you think we should tell them?'

'What, that a Member of Parliament has been murdered? Jesus Christ! There's already one van parked outside. Can you imagine what would happen when the news gets out that he was?'

'But you're going to have to tell them at some point.'

'I am?'

'Aren't you?'

Forrester thought for a moment before shunting his chair back to stand up and lumber his way over to his window. There he used his fingers to pry open the blinds, just enough to peer out at the carpark, and the BBC East news van nudged up on the curb opposite.

'To be honest, I'm not sure which is worse. Having a bunch of racist yobs hurling abuse at our ethnic minority, or the nation's media descending upon us, all set to start spreading rumours about who they think is responsible for Hopkins's murder. I seem to remember the last time that happened was on my predecessor's watch, leading to an innocent man being beaten to death, closely followed by the DCI's dismissal.'

Forrester had a point, and Tanner took a moment to be grateful for not having to be standing in his shoes.

With Forrester not saying any more, Tanner eventually asked, 'What are you going to do?'

'Unfortunately, I'm not sure I have much choice. It will be worse if we're caught attempting to cover it up. Anyway,' he sighed turning around to head back to his desk, 'no doubt it can wait till the morning. How've you been getting on?'

'I think we have a potential suspect.'

'That sounds encouraging. Go on.'

'We've just got back from speaking with Professor Francis Bamford. He's the person who The Norfolk Herald commissioned to undertake research into Patrick Hopkins's ancestry. It turns out that his wife left him to marry Hopkins, who then was killed in the car crash, when Hopkins was behind the wheel.'

'Now that *is* interesting.'

'So I wouldn't be at all surprised if he simply made

up the ancestral connection to the Witchfinder General thing as a way of getting back at him, maybe even deciding to go one step further.'

'I assume you've asked him to stay put for now?'

'As well as arranging to have his prints and DNA collected, yes sir.'

'And if nothing comes from that?'

'Vicky is still looking into Patrick Hopkins's past, at least she was supposed to be, and the last thing I heard, Cooper was chatting to that reporter from The Norfolk Herald, but as neither of them are here, I've yet to get any feedback as to how either have been getting on.'

'Yes, well, as I said, we've had numerous calls concerning anti-social disturbances. You should count yourself lucky that I haven't sent you and Jenny out as well.'

'I appreciate that, sir, but I need my team focussed on solving the murder of Patrick Hopkins, not wandering around the Broads doing their best to protect our ethnic minority from a bit of verbal abuse.'

'A young girl was savagely beaten, Tanner! Another was shoved into the river. She very nearly drowned!'

Tanner glanced down at the floor. 'I'm sorry, I didn't know.'

'Whether you like it or not, it's CID's job to occasionally assist uniformed officers with less serious offences, as you well know. That's especially true in a small community such as ours.'

'Of course, but we still have a murder to solve.'

'Our priority is to protect those in our community who are still alive, Tanner, not those who are already dead!'

'Absolutely, sir, although I'm not sure the national

press will see it that way, not when they find out what really happened to our local MP.'

'All the more reason to not tell them,' Forrester mused.

'Unless Cooper already has.'

'Why would he have done that?'

'He *was* interviewing that reporter today, from the Norfolk Herald, wasn't he? I can't believe he wouldn't have mentioned the fact that Hopkins *hadn't* taken his own life.'

A grim shadow fell over Forrester's face. 'I'd not thought of that,' he said, taking himself back to the window.

'To be honest, sir, I hadn't either, else I'd have advised him not to mention it.'

'I don't suppose there's any chance that he didn't?'

'I think that's probably a little unlikely, sir.'

'Shit!' Forrester cursed, levering the blinds open again.

An uncomfortable silence followed, broken by the blinds being snapped shut.

'Then it looks like we've been left with little choice. I'll release a statement first thing tomorrow. No doubt we'll have to follow that up with a press conference. Between now and then, it would be helpful to have a suspect in custody, so if you and Jenny could make sure to get the prints and DNA of that professor of yours over to forensics before end of play today, even if you have to do it yourselves, that would be appreciated.'

- CHAPTER THIRTEEN -

Tuesday, 10th November

THE FOLLOWING AFTERNOON, Tanner was standing shoulder to shoulder with Forrester outside the police station. With Tanner having just finished giving a few awkward remarks in support of what Forrester had already said, they were now attempting to field a barrage of questions being hurled at them from over a dozen frenzied reporters, whose numbers had continued to grow since Forrester had issued a press release earlier that morning.

Since their meeting the day before, the situation had grown steadily worse, with more reports coming in of foreign looking women being racially abused, sometimes assaulted, along with a variety of shops and homes being targeted by white hooded youths throwing bricks wrapped in despicable messages of hate. The situation had become so bad, Forrester had been left with little choice but to call for a support unit from HQ in Norwich.

As a reporter shouted out if they thought the murder of Patrick Hopkins had anything to do with the discovery of Elizabeth Craddock's remains, the blast of a siren made them all turn around with a collective start.

Charging down the already congested road

towards them was a fire engine, its roof lights flashing, forcing cars that had already been struggling to navigate themselves around the assortment of badly parked news vans to find a space to pull over.

With the fire truck left to inch its way past, together with the sound of another fast approaching, Forrester took advantage of the distraction to tell Tanner to head inside and find out what was going on.

Doing so, Tanner had only just made it through the main entrance when he met Jenny, hurrying out the other way.

'Someone's petrol bombed Tarragon!'

'Tarragon?' Tanner questioned.

'The shop we were at yesterday,' Jenny replied, nudging past.

'Jesus Christ!' Tanner exclaimed, spinning on his heel to hurry after.

With the second fire engine roaring up the road towards them, they clambered into Tanner's XJS, heading for the exit. There they were forced to stop as the monstrously proportioned truck began bullying its way past the scores of cars, all doing their best to give it the room it needed to squeeze itself through.

Pulling out behind it, they followed in silence, heading north towards the market town of Stalham.

It wasn't long before they saw an ominous plume of thick black smoke rising vertically up into the windless grey autumnal sky.

Ten minutes later they were turning into the very same high street they'd been driving along just the day before. Jolting the car up onto the curb about halfway down, they leapt out to begin pelting along the pavement, heading for a crowd of people beyond which Tanner could see two firefighters, each grappling with the end of a rubber hose as they attempted to control the jet of water that blasted out from its end.

With their elbows out, they forced their way through the crowd to come face to face with someone they instantly recognised; PC Higgins, on his own, doing his best to keep the many on-lookers at a safe distance.

'Is anyone inside?' called Tanner, staring up at the shop to see flames rising from the nearest upstairs window.

'No idea,' came Higgins's flustered response. 'I've only just got here myself.'

Tanner glanced back at the building, just in time to see a shadowy figure, tugging at the base of the furthest window, its glass black with soot. Seeing a fireman who appeared to be directing operations beside one of the trucks, Tanner launched himself towards him. Forced to shout above the noise of the engine, he pulled out his ID to point up at the window. 'There's someone trapped up there!'

'We know!' replied the man, shoving him back, just as the end of an aluminium ladder came flying around from the other side of the truck, missing Tanner's head by inches.

Retreating to where Jenny was helping Higgins to push the crowd back, Tanner looked on as the firefighter carrying the ladder dropped one end down onto the pavement before pushing the other high into the air. The moment its top met the wall above, he scrambled up. Within seconds he was screaming at the figure inside to stand back, before bringing a hand-held axe crashing against the frame.

First through the jagged glass opening came a wall of smoke, black as the night, followed by the head of the shop's owner, her face contorted as she choked on the noxious fumes.

In one swift movement, the fireman flung her over his shoulder, as if she weighed no more than a bag of flour, before carrying her down to safety.

Tanner was about to head over to see if she was OK, when he saw the fireman drop her into the arms of a waiting paramedic before turning on his heel to charge back up the ladder. Reaching the top, instead of helping someone else out, he levered himself over the ledge to disappear inside.

With Tanner's eyes glued to the window, a relieved gasp rose up from the crowd as the fireman's head re-appeared, this time with a silver-haired old lady draped over his shoulder, her thin brown limbs hanging loose about him like a broken puppet.

Waiting with his breath held as the fireman stepped cautiously out through the window to place a tentative foot on the first rung of the ladder, Tanner hurried over to where the paramedics were lifting the first rescued victim into the back of an awaiting ambulance.

'Is she alright?' he asked the nearest, glancing down at the woman's face.

'Hopefully,' came the paramedic's terse response. 'But it's too soon to know.'

Tanner stepped back as the fireman returned. Waiting for him to ease the silver-haired woman down, he caught his eye to ask, 'Was there anyone else inside? A young girl?'

'I looked, but I only found the old lady,' the fireman replied, his face glistening with sweat.

Tanner turned to glance back at the shop to find no less than three hoses were now playing over the building. As he looked on, the sound of slipping roof tiles was followed by the sight of the entire roof caving in on itself, sending smoke and dust billowing out through the windows at the top.

As the crowd stepped back in fear of the entire shop collapsing, Tanner hoped to God that the fireman was right, and that the owner's daughter wasn't trapped inside. If she was, he knew there'd be little hope she'd be found alive.

- CHAPTER FOURTEEN -

Monday, 16ᵗʰ November

THE WEEK RUMBLED along in a similar vein, with xenophobic racist abuse going hand in hand with the occasional violent attack, leaving the staff at Wroxham Police Station exhausted and Tanner unable to make any sensible progress towards finding out who was responsible for the murder of the former MP, Patrick Hopkins.

Meanwhile, half the nation's press remained camped outside, all reporting the same news whilst Forrester was left on the receiving end of daily calls from a despairing Superintendent Whitaker, each one becoming increasingly irate, demanding news and more importantly, results!

With the weekend offering little respite, come Monday morning Tanner was called into Forrester's office for an update.

'Right,' Forrester began, scowling over as Tanner crept in to take a cautious seat. 'Where are we?'

Tanner lifted one leg over the other. 'We had a challenging weekend, sir.'

'I'm well aware of that!'

'Well, sir,' Tanner continued, glancing down at the front of the desk. With nothing having changed since their meeting on Friday, he was unsure what else to say. 'As you know, neither Professor Bamford's prints nor his DNA were found in Patrick Hopkins's study, or anywhere inside his house, which means that although he has motive, we've got no evidence to place him at the scene.'

'Did you take a look into that journalist, as per my instructions; the one who said he found the body?'

'Russell Dewhurst,' Tanner clarified. 'We've been able to prove that he was inside the study, but he'd already admitted as much. But we've been unable to find any evidence to suggest that he'd been anywhere near the body, and we can't find a single motive for him wanting Hopkins dead. In fact, I'd say the opposite was probably true.'

'So you're telling me that not a single thing has happened since Friday?'

'Not at all, sir. Three Arabian girls were beaten up on Saturday night, another on Sunday morning, and two more shops have had their windows smashed.'

Forrester's face darkened. 'I meant in relation to the murder of Patrick Hopkins, as you well know!'

'I'm sorry, sir, but I've been so focussed on attempting to keep the peace, as ordered, I've hardly had a chance to think about it.'

'Isn't it possible for you to do two things at the same time?'

'Not according to my ex-wife.'

'Then you'll have to start learning how, won't you?'

'Yes, sir, but in fairness, I'm not sure what else we can do. We can't just magically pull a suspect out of a hat.'

'Haven't forensics been able to come up with anything else?'

'They have, sir, yes, in the form of multiple sets of prints and DNA, none of which can be found on the police national database.'

'Have you made an effort, at least, to find out who

they all belong to?'

'Well, one was the cleaner.'

'And the others?'

'From what we can work out, the only other people who'd entered his house during the last three months were delivery drivers, mainly for his weekly grocery shop.'

'Have you been able to identify them?'

'Some, but not all. The supermarket he used don't keep records of who delivers what to where, at least not accurate ones, and those we were able to identify said they'd only take his shopping through to the kitchen, never the study.'

'What about Hopkins's background?'

'Vicky and Sally have been doing their best to look into it, but considering he was a Member of Parliament, they've found remarkably little. Since leaving the Army, he'd been a model tax paying citizen. He hadn't been involved in a single scandal, at least none that had been reported, he hardly drank, didn't do drugs, and had no obvious interest in either women or men, of any age. The only vice he seemed to have was gambling.'

'Couldn't that have led to something? An unpaid dept to a local criminal?'

'He'd only ever bet on cricket matches, and only up to a maximum of ten pounds.'

'Then why bother mentioning it?' Forrester said, raising his voice.

Tanner shrugged. 'I was simply endeavouring to illustrate just how little we've been able to find on him, sir.'

'Do you have *any* good news for me?'

'Yes, sir. Janna Matar, the owner of the shop that was petrol bombed last week; she's been given the all-clear. Her daughter is picking her up from Wroxham

Medical Centre this morning.'

'That's something, I suppose.'

'And apart from their grandmother, nobody else has died.'

'Any luck finding out who did it?'

'We have a partial CCTV facial image of the person who put the brick through the window, but nothing showing who threw the petrol bomb. From witness statements, all we know is that both were of a similar height and build, and each wore the same coloured hoodies, so there's every chance it's the same person.'

'But you don't know who?'

'Cooper's been dealing with it, sir.'

'Of course.'

Forrester let out a heavy sigh. 'OK, well, if that's it.'

A knock at the door had Jenny stepping inside.

'Sorry to bother you,' she began, glancing first at Forrester, then Tanner, 'but the date for the by-election has been announced.'

'When for?' asked Forrester, sitting up.

'On the 10th December, about three weeks from now.'

'Have any candidates come forward?'

'Three so far,' she replied, opening up her notebook. 'Susan Sutton for Labour, Michael Drummond, Conservative, and Nick Carter, the new leader for the British National Union party.'

'Well, Michael Drummond's fairly well known, being that he used to be the Foreign Secretary. He lost his seat to Patrick during the last election. From what I remember, he wasn't too happy about it either.'

'I assume it's OK for us to have a chat with him?'

Forrester paused before answering. 'I suppose you'll have to, but you must tread carefully, Tanner. He may not be a member of the Cabinet anymore, but he must still have all the associated connections. He was also well known for his temper. If you even so much as hint at the idea that he may have had anything to do with this, without some sort of credible evidence to back it up, I can easily imagine him coming down on us like a tonne of bricks. Even if you do find something on him, you *have* to run it by me first, before you either say or do anything. Is that understood?'

'Of course, sir.'

'I mean it! I'm not losing my job over this.'

'If we find anything, I'll run it by you first, sir,' Tanner repeated, doing his best to sound like he meant it.

Forrester studied Tanner's face for a moment, before turning his attention back to Jenny.

'Who were the other two again?'

'Susan Sutton and Nick Carter,' Jenny replied, referring back to her notes.

'I can't say I've heard of the first one, but the name Nick Carter rings a bell.'

'He's got form, sir. GBH, back in 2016.'

'And he's still allowed to run for election?'

'Once someone's been released from prison, there's nothing to stop them, no matter what crime they were convicted of.'

Forrester gave Jenny a look of horrified incredulity. 'Are you sure about that?'

'It came up in my sergeant's exam. Technically, he'd have even been able to stand if he was still in prison, as long as his sentence was less than a year.'

'Good God! And was it?'

'It was only six months.'

Forrester shook his head. 'Well, as they say, you learn something new every day. At least we should still have his prints and DNA on file. See if we do, then I suggest you get them over to forensics to see if they match anything found at the scene. I don't suppose you have any idea if he knew Patrick Hopkins?'

'I've yet to look, sir.'

'OK, that's fine,' Forrester replied, before turning his attention back to Tanner. 'When you go and see him, I suggest you keep him in mind for this recent spate of racist attacks. As the latest leader of the British National Union, I wouldn't be at all surprised if he's the one who's been behind it all.'

- CHAPTER FIFTEEN -

'SORRY TO BOTHER you,' said Tanner, holding his ID up to the heavily made-up face of a rake thin middle-aged woman, bearing down at him from the steps of an imposing Tudor mansion. 'We're looking for Mr Michael Drummond.'

'May I ask what it's concerning?' the lady questioned, glowering down at his ID with a look of unimpressed disdain.

'We understand he's running in the forthcoming by-election?'

'I believe he is, although, I must admit, I'd no idea it was against the law.'

'Er, it's not, Ma'am.'

'Well, thank God for that!' she said, her voice dripping with condescending sarcasm. 'I thought you'd come to read him his rights.'

Tanner forced a thin smile over at her. 'If we could just have a word?'

'You still haven't told me what it's about; unless you're offering to hand out leaflets?'

'It's concerning Patrick Hopkins. The MP found dead in his study last week.'

'And what's that got to do with my husband?'

'We don't know yet, that's why we'd like to talk to him.'

'If you must,' she huffed. 'He's in the conservatory. Follow me, I'll take you through, but if you could wipe your feet first,' she added, bringing her eyes down to stare at their shoes, in much the same way she'd been looking at their IDs, 'we've only just had the floor polished.'

'Darling, it's the police,' the lady announced, having led Tanner and Jenny through an immaculately presented stately home, one which bore a greater resemblance to a museum than a family residence.

'For me?' came the reply from a handsome blue-eyed man in his senior years, peering over the top of a copy of the Financial Times.

'No, the dog,' came the woman's belligerent response.

On the marble floor, beside the wicker armchair the man was reclined on, the floppy ears of a sleeping black Labrador pricked up in the air.

'Don't worry, Charlie,' muttered the man, leaning over to give the dog's head a comforting pat. 'She's only joking.'

'Right then,' the lady continued, clasping her hands together. 'If I may, I'll leave the four of you to it.' With that, she spun around to head back out the way she'd come.

Waiting for her to leave, Tanner turned to face the man. 'Mr Michael Drummond?'

'I'm not sure who else you'd be expecting,' the man replied, folding up his newspaper to stand up from the chair.

'Detective Inspector Tanner. This is my colleague, Detective Sergeant Evans. Norfolk Police.'

'So, what's all this about?'

Ignoring the question, Tanner took a moment to glance around. 'Nice place you have here.'

'Thank you, although I can't say it was my choice.'

'Your wife's?'

'I inherited it. It's been in the family for years. Far too big for my liking. There are only so many bedrooms a man needs, don't you think? The cleaners alone cost me a small fortune.'

'Is it just the two of you?'

'And Charlie, of course.'

Hearing his name, the dog lept to his feet to begin wagging its tail, gazing up at his master with a look of doleful expectation.

Drummond beamed a loving smile at him before leaning over to flatten down his ears with his hand. 'I'll take you for a walk later. Now, lie down, there's a good boy.'

Surprisingly, the dog instantly did as he was told.

'We just have a few questions concerning Mr Patrick Hopkins,' Tanner interrupted.

'The late MP? Why, what about him?

'We understand you knew him?'

'Well, yes, but I doubt I was the only one.'

Tanner took a moment to consider how to best frame his next question.

'I was wondering if you'd be able to describe your relationship with him?'

'You mean, were we having a secret extra-marital gay love affair together?'

'Er, I actually meant something more along the lines of how you two got on, in more general terms, but if you were, we'd certainly be interested to find out more.'

'We were political rivals, inspector.'

'Sorry, does that mean you didn't?'

Drummond locked his arms over his chest to take up a defiant stance. 'Have you seriously come all the way over here to accuse me of murdering Patrick Hopkins?'

'Not at all, Mr Drummond, we're simply speaking

to everyone who we believe may have had a motive for having done so.'

'I see. May I be so bold as to ask what you think my motive would have been? Revenge for having lost to him in the last election, or maybe to trigger a by-election, so giving me a one-in-three chance of winning my seat back?'

'People have murdered for less, Mr Drummond, I can assure you.'

'People with only half a brain, perhaps.'

Tanner decided that a change of tack was probably in order. 'Can you think of anyone who may have wished him harm?'

'You mean, apart from me?'

Tanner responded with an unamused smile.

'Nobody specific springs to mind, inspector,' Drummond continued, adopting a more serious expression, 'but in such politically charged times, frankly, it could have been anyone.'

The man was right, of course, but that was of little use to Tanner.

'Just for the record, Mr Drummond, may I ask when you saw Mr Hopkins last?'

'God knows!'

'Any chance you could be a little more specific?'

'Whenever the last election was.'

'You haven't seen him since?'

'Not that I'm aware of. Is there anything else?'

'Just one more thing. I don't suppose you can tell us where you were on Saturday, 7th November, between the hours of nine and twelve in the evening?'

'I think we were at a wedding,' he replied, raising his eyes briefly up to the glass ceiling, before bringing them to bear on the phone he'd fished out from a pocket. 'Yes, we were. My niece's.'

'Whereabouts was that?'

'Warwick Castle.'

'I assume you'll be able to provide us with a list of people who could verify that?'

'Probably over a hundred,' Drummond replied, attaching something akin to a victorious grin.

'Did you stay overnight?'

'In a nearby hotel. It was called the Castle Arms, or something similar. The wife will know.'

Making sure Jenny had made a note of that, Tanner returned his attention to the former Foreign Secretary standing before him.

'OK, well, I think we have everything we need,' said Tanner, nodding over at Jenny, 'for now at least. If we could just arrange a suitable time for us to collect a sample of your fingerprints and DNA, your wife as well, we'll be on our way.'

'I'm sorry, but what possible reason could you have for wanting those?'

'I'm afraid it's standard procedure; to collect samples from anyone we consider to be a suspect.'

'You *still* think I killed him?'

'Either you or your wife.'

'Despite everything I've told you?'

'I suppose that depends if you've been telling the truth.'

'I see. So now you're accusing me of lying.'

'Sorry, forgive me, Mr Drummond. I thought you were a politician, or at least you used to be.'

- CHAPTER SIXTEEN -

'WHAT A DELIGHTFUL couple,' commented Jenny, the moment they were outside on the drive listening to the front door being slammed shut behind them.

'That's the British elite for you.'

'Could his wife have been any more sarcastic?'

Tanner couldn't help but smirk at the comment as they began making their way over towards his car.

'She'd certainly give you some competition,' he eventually replied.

Jenny glanced over at him from the corner of her eye, before facing forward again to mutter, 'She wouldn't stand a chance.'

'I think you're right!' Tanner laughed, catching the determined look on her face.

'Anyway,' Jenny continued, 'what did you make of all that? Did you think he was telling the truth?'

'It's always difficult to tell with politicians. We'll need to check his alibi. I must admit, it did seem incredibly convenient to have been attending a wedding the very weekend his former political rival was hanged by the neck until dead.'

'How about what he was saying about motive?'

'You mean his remark about murdering Hopkins to give him nothing more than a one-in-three chance of winning the by-election?'

'That's the one.'

'As I said to him back there, people have done far worse for considerably less. Maybe he's been told that if he can bring the district back under Conservative control, he'd be guaranteed to get his old job back. Who knows where he thinks he'll be able to go from there. I learned a long time ago to never underestimate the lengths the rich and shameless would go for the acquisition of power. From what I can make out, they're basically brought up to believe that it's their God-given right to be in control. That's why so many of them go into politics.'

'But he'd still need to win.'

'I've heard you say yourself that Norfolk has traditionally been a safe seat for the Conservatives, and that the only reason Hopkins won before was thanks to a wave of people voting Lib Dem in the last election. No doubt he'd be able to turn on the charm as well; when the time comes.'

'How about the wife?'

'She's probably more of a suspect than he is. Imagine her thinking she'd married into money and power, with all the social advantages that came with it, only to find her husband being booted out of Government to end up kicking around at home with nothing better to do than to pat his dog on the head whilst poring over the Financial Times; and that reminds me.'

Reaching the car, Tanner turned to stare back at the enormous Tudor mansion, how its square patterned shapes of gleaming black beams stood out against the pristine white walls, and how perfectly trimmed the hedgerows were that led up to its grandiose entrance. 'As soon as we get back to the station, I want us to start looking into their finances. His remark about the number of cleaners they need makes me think they could be having money troubles.

I mean, it must cost a small fortune to keep it looking like this. If the money hasn't been coming in from a position in Government, maybe it hasn't been coming in from anywhere.'

'Maybe he's been spending his time investing in the stock market, hence his choice of newspaper.'

'Perhaps unwisely,' Tanner added, raising an eyebrow at Jenny as they both heaved open the Jag's doors.

Before ducking inside, Jenny caught Tanner's eye. 'Do you think there will be any repercussions?'

'From what?'

'From you having just accused the former Foreign Secretary of having murdered his main political rival, and lying about it in the process?'

'Did I?' mused Tanner, gazing up towards the slate grey sky above.

'A tiny bit,' Jenny replied, smiling.

Tanner shrugged. 'I suppose I may have done. I'd better let Forrester know to brace for impact when we get back to the office.'

- CHAPTER SEVENTEEN -

BACK AT THE station, leaving Jenny at her desk, Tanner made his way over to Forrester's office.

'Sorry to bother you again,' he said, having rapped his knuckles on the door. 'Just to let you know that we're back from having spoken with Michael Drummond.'

Forrester cast a wary eye up at his senior DI. 'Dare I ask how it went?'

'He said he and his wife were attending a wedding at the time of Hopkins's murder, but we'll have to see.'

'I was more interested to know if you were able to conduct the interview without managing to upset the man?'

'Well, sir,' began Tanner, as he shifted from one foot to the other, 'towards the end, I must admit he did seem to have reached the frankly bizarre conclusion that I'd accused him of having murdered his former political rival.'

'Please God, tell me you're joking!'

'In my defence,' Tanner continued, 'it does tend to be a little difficult to make enquiries into someone's relationship with a recent murder victim, including how they got on, when they last saw each other, where they were at the time of the person's death, and if they'd be happy to provide samples of their prints and

DNA, without giving them the impression that you think they may have had something to do with it.'

'I take it that means you did?'

'Perhaps a little.'

Forrester let out a world-weary sigh.

'Anyway,' Tanner continued, thinking it was probably best to move the subject along, 'I'd mark both him and his wife down as definite suspects, for the time being at least.'

'OK, but under absolutely no circumstances is the press allowed to find out that we're considering them.'

'Yes, sir.'

'And the second we find something that proves beyond all reasonable doubt that they had nothing to do with it, you're to let them know, and I don't mean by email.'

'Absolutely, sir.'

'After having deleted every shred of any personal information we've managed to collect in the process.'

'Of course, sir.'

Forrester took a moment to study Tanner's expression, as if searching for even the vaguest sign that he wasn't taking the situation with the utmost seriousness. But Tanner had the sort of chiselled face which could often prove difficult to read. Eventually, he returned his attention back to his monitor. 'So anyway, what's your next step?'

'I've asked Jenny to arrange for someone to collect samples of their prints and DNA. Then I need to get Vicky and Sally to start a background check. I'm especially interested in their finances. They've got quite a place out there. It looks like it's just stepped off the front page of Country Life. And as Mr Drummond has effectively been unemployed since the last election, I'm certainly curious to know how they've been able to afford to keep it that way.'

'And then?'

'Then we're going to head over to see the second candidate, Susan Sutton.'

'She's nobody famous, is she? Not some former A-list celebrity with about three million followers on Twitter?'

'Er, no sir. I think she uses Instagram.'

'I was being serious, Tanner.'

'I'm sorry, sir. She's nobody famous, although she is reported to be quite active on Parenting Portal.'

'You're kidding?'

'I'd never joke about Parenting Portal, sir.'

Forrester glared over at him. Even though he knew he was joking, it was impossible to tell. 'Your endless sarcasm really isn't appreciated, Tanner.'

'Sorry, sir.'

'Anyway, you'd better be off, but again, *please* be careful with this Sutton woman. I'd really prefer not to have to arrive at work tomorrow to find a group of disgruntled placard-wielding parents lining the road outside, demanding my resignation.'

'Don't worry, sir. Even if they wanted to, I'm not sure there's any room.'

- CHAPTER EIGHTEEN -

'I'M TOLD YOU wanted to see me,' came the voice of a flustered-looking woman, marching into the meeting room Tanner and Jenny had been shown into a few minutes earlier.

'Susan Sutton?' Tanner enquired, digging out his ID.

'I am.'

'Detective Inspector Tanner and Detective Sergeant Evans. Norfolk Police.'

'Right, yes, and...?' she replied, her eyes dancing between the two of them.

'Sorry to bother you. It's about Patrick Hopkins.'

'Oh, right. Sorry, I wasn't expecting that. I heard what happened, of course.'

'We were just wondering if you knew him at all?'

'Only from what I'd seen of him on TV.'

'You'd never actually met him?'

'Not that I'm aware of.'

'Or had any contact?'

'Again, no, why?'

Tanner took a moment to choose his next words very carefully. As far as he could tell, with her unkempt mess of dark red hair, flushed cheeks, creased clothes and poorly made-up face, she looked almost exactly like the permanently stressed-out mum he could imagine spending half her life logging into Parenting Portal, ready to organise an angry protest march at the click of a mouse button.

'We're in the process of following standard police practice,' he eventually began, 'in order to establish a list of all those who knew Mr Hopkins; family, friends, business acquaintances and in your case, political rivals.'

'Oh, I see. Well, to be honest, I'm not sure I fall into any of those categories. As I said, I'd never met the man before, nor had any communication with him, so I could hardly be described as either a friend or a business acquaintance. I don't think I can be considered a political rival either, being that I only made the decision to put my candidature forward when the by-election was announced.'

'With regret, we also have to consider all those who are likely to gain from his death as well.'

The woman squared herself up to Tanner.

'Are you suggesting that I killed him for a chance of becoming Norfolk's next MP?'

'It's absurd, I know,' Tanner replied, with a smile of self-reproach. 'But, unfortunately, with a case as serious as this, we have no choice but to leave no stone unturned.'

The woman relaxed her stance a little. 'Fair enough, I suppose. So, what do you want to know?'

'You've already answered the first question, thank you. All we need to know now is your whereabouts at the time of his death, and to then arrange a suitable time to collect a sample of your fingerprints and DNA.'

Sensing she was about to protest the necessity of such a requirement, Tanner thought to add, 'But only to allow us to eliminate you from our enquiries.'

Sutton remained silent for a moment. 'Would I need to come to the station?'

'We can send someone around here, if you prefer,

or to your home. It's entirely up to you.'

Tanner could almost see her weighing up the options.

'Judging by how many TV news vans are currently parked outside Wroxham Police Station,' she eventually replied, 'I think it would be best if they could come to my house.'

'That's no problem at all. And your whereabouts at the time in question?'

'Sorry, yes, of course,' she began, digging out her phone. When was it again?'

'The evening of Saturday, 7th November, between nine o'clock and twelve.'

'Right. I can't see anything, so I must have been at home.'

'Would anyone be able to vouch for you?'

'Only my husband, I'm afraid.'

'That's absolutely fine.' Seeing Jenny close her notebook out of the corner of his eye, Tanner clasped his hands together to offer the lady a pleasant smile. 'Thank you for your cooperation, Mrs Sutton. We won't take up any more of your time.'

Outside the modern office building they'd had the meeting in, they made their way over the packed carpark, searching for Tanner's car.

'You see,' Jenny teased, wrapping her arm around Tanner's, 'you *can* be nice.'

Tanner snorted back a response. 'Don't worry. It won't happen again. Although, in fairness, I was struggling to find a reason for her to have had a hand in it.'

'She did seem to lack motive,' agreed Jenny.

'Anyway, let's keep her on the list for now and wait to see if forensics are able to come back with anything. Meanwhile, I suggest we get back to the office to help Vicky and Sally with their background check into the Drummonds.'

'What about the third candidate, Nicholas Carter?'

'I think he can probably wait till tomorrow,' Tanner replied, glancing down at his watch. 'Out of the three of them, I'd say he has the least to gain from Hopkins's death. I mean, I can't see him winning the election. This may be a right-wing borough, but it's not *that* right-wing.'

- CHAPTER NINETEEN -

Tuesday, 17th November

WITH HIS HEAD leaning forward, Dr Samuel Atterbury shuffled his way along the well-trodden grass path that clung to the banks of Horsey Mere. Up ahead was the Hawthorne tree where what they believed to be the remains of Elizabeth Craddock had been found about three weeks before, instantly becoming the focal point of excitement for Norfolk's archaeological community and beyond.

The site was of particular interest to the doctor, mainly because his consultancy firm had been fortunate enough to win the bid to excavate the site. The other reason was that he knew this would be his very last project. Retirement loomed dark on the horizon, and there was nothing he could do about it. Plagued in his later years by hyperkyphosis, the medical condition that had curved the top of his spine, turning him into what was commonly known as a hunchback, it had been many years since he'd been able to take part in the more physical aspects of the profession he'd devoted the entirety of his adult life to. Over time, his role had gradually eroded, leaving him working more as a glorified lab assistant than anything else, and even that had become a challenge.

Knowing it would be his final project, his last chance to make his mark in the world of archaeology, the moment he'd heard the news that they'd won the contract he made the decision that he would oversee the excavation himself, no matter how challenging it would be. Even if he wouldn't be able to stay all day, he felt that as long as he could put a few hours in, preferably being the first one to arrive on site each morning, it would be enough. Being early was no great hardship, at least not from having to get up before dawn to do so. These days he'd find himself wide awake by five o'clock, no matter what day of the week it was.

Already physically exhausted, he took a moment to catch his breath. Lifting his head as high as the curvature of his spine would allow, he did his best to gaze ahead, attempting to see how far he had to go. Through twisting tendrils of early morning mist, he could just about make out the orange netting they'd used to mark out the site's boundaries. He wasn't even halfway.

Unsure if he'd be able to go any further, he checked the time on his watch. It was nearly quarter to eight. His excavation team would be arriving any minute. He knew what would happen if they found him stranded on the path like this. They'd use it as an excuse to send him back to the lab. Knowing them, they may even call for an ambulance.

Allowing his head to roll forward again, he locked his jaw together and took a few deep revitalising breaths before forcing himself to continue.

Ten minutes later, struggling for air as beads of sweat dripped from the end of his nose, he finally allowed himself to stop. Somehow he'd managed to reach the base of the tree at the furthest end of the site. At his feet was the edge of a deep black muddy trench. This was the first of three they'd dug and was far deeper than normal. With Elizabeth Craddock's remains having been buried vertically, down a long deep shaft, they'd had no choice but to keep going until they'd reached her skull. The dig had been made more challenging by the ancient tree that had grown over the site. With it being of special interest, they'd been unable to secure permission to have it taken down, forcing them to work around its complex system of roots, as best they could.

He remained there for a moment; his head leaning forward with his chin resting unnaturally against the top of his rib cage. As he caught his breath, he relived the moment they'd uncovered the heavily corroded steel nail that had been hammered through the poor woman's jaw, hopefully after her death. They knew this was something that used to be done to women believed to have been witches, to prevent them from uttering spells from inside the grave. It was one of many macabre pieces of evidence that had led them to believe that the remains were indeed that of Elizabeth Craddock, the 17th Century woman whose capture, trial and execution as Norfolk's last known witch had been so famously documented in local history.

The distant rumble of a car heading down Horsey Road made him realise just how quiet it was. There wasn't so much as a breath of air. He couldn't even hear the sound of birds singing from the surrounding marshes as he had on previous mornings.

Out of the corner of his eye he saw the headlights of the car he'd heard turn off the road, into the carpark. Curious to know who'd arrived, he tilted his head to the side to try and see. The sudden crack of a branch above made his whole body jump with a start.

As it did, something soft touched the top of his ear. Twisting violently around, his hand stabbed blindly at the air above. Becoming dangerously un-balanced, he placed a foot behind him, to stop himself falling back into the trench. But it came down on its very edge, the soft mud immediately giving away underneath. Desperate to stop himself going over he reached out with a hand, searching for something, anything to grab hold of to stop him. When his wrist knocked against something hard, his fingers clamped themselves around it, just in time to stop him from toppling over.

As he hung, half-suspended in the air, the heel of one foot digging into the edge of the trench, the other suspended underneath, he glanced up to see what it was that his hand had taken hold of.

Above him, hanging by her neck, was the body of a naked young woman, her skin dark and smooth, her eyes bulging as they stared down into his. The moment he realised that he'd taken hold of her ankle, he cried out in terror as his hand instinctively let go.

- CHAPTER TWENTY -

A
N HOUR AND a half later, Tanner and Jenny stood with their hands buried deep inside their coat pockets, just outside a line of blue and white Police Do Not Cross tape that had been hastily strung up around the area encircling the tree at Horsey Mere. From the carpark behind them came intermittent voices from a gathering crowd, carried over towards them on a brisk autumnal breeze. An ominous rumble of thunder had Tanner glancing over his shoulder, where a bank of thick black clouds could be seen, rolling in from the North Sea less than a mile beyond.

Returning his attention to the scene, he called over to their medical examiner, who they could see standing on some of the various aluminium platforms that had been placed around the trench, directly beneath the body of a dark-skinned girl hanging from the tree.

'Good morning, doctor. Do you have anything for us?'

Seeing Johnstone beckon him over, with Jenny requesting to remain where she was, Tanner ducked under the tape to begin using the steel platforms as stepping-stones to where Johnstone was standing.

'It's definitely not suicide,' the doctor eventually replied, as Tanner approached.

Reaching the body, Tanner stopped to stare up at

it. 'I didn't think it was. Not with her being stripped like this.'

Johnstone followed his gaze. 'I don't think that's as relevant as you might think. It's surprisingly normal for suicide victims to remove their clothes before taking their own lives, especially in the case of teenagers.'

'And is she?'

'Is she what?'

'A teenager?'

'Not sure. She's not old, I know that much.'

'I don't suppose anyone's been able to find her clothes, or some form of identification?'

'Not that anyone's told me, but the jewellery she's wearing should help to give you an idea as to who she is. She also has a tattoo.'

Taking it in turns to step around the body, Johnstone brought Tanner's attention to a small but very singular symbol located at the top of her thigh.

Tanner pulled out his phone to take a picture, before pulling up the image to enlarge it. The tattoo consisted of circle in the middle, with two more on either side, each of which was eclipsed.

'Pagan?' posed Johnstone.

'Who knows,' Tanner mused, putting the phone away to glance around at the scene. 'Any idea who found the body?'

'A local archaeologist, apparently. His team found him lying at the bottom of the trench.' Johnstone pointed down at the hole they were standing beside which was as wide as it was deep. 'He must have fallen when he found her.'

'What was he doing so close?' questioned Tanner, staring down.

Johnstone shrugged. 'Maybe he was trying to get her down?'

'Maybe he was the one who strung her up!' Tanner exclaimed, glancing around. 'I don't suppose you know if he's still here?'

'I heard he was taken to Wroxham Medical Centre.'

'OK, I suppose we'll have to catch up with him there. Do you have anything else for me?'

Johnstone pivoted around to gesture at the large body of water that made up Horsey Mere. 'I'll need to take a sample, but I'd say there was a good chance she'd been in the water, before she was hanged.'

Tanner raised an eyebrow. 'Well, she can't have been having a swimming lesson, not in the middle of November.'

'Assuming the mud on her heels matches the mud down there,' said Johnston, pointing at two parallel lines coming out of the water, 'I'd say she'd been thrown into the mere before being dragged out again, possibly by the same rope that's now around her neck.'

'Are you suggesting that she may have been drowned?'

'No, she was definitely hanged. I think someone was probably attempting to get rid of any physical evidence before doing so, either that or they were trying to find out if she could swim.'

Tanner gave the doctor a confused look, leading Johnstone to draw in an impatient breath. 'I believe it used to be one of the more popular methods to identify if someone was a witch; to see if they floated.'

Tanner balked at the suggestion. 'You're saying someone killed her because they thought she was a witch?'

'All I'm saying is that judging by the chosen location, and all the recent talk in the press, I wouldn't be as surprised as perhaps I would normally be.'

Tanner realised the doctor had a point. With everything that had been going on recently, maybe this was the next inevitable step.

'Anyway,' Johnstone continued, glancing over Tanner's shoulder at the horizon beyond, 'I'd better get back to work. Looks like there's a storm coming.'

- CHAPTER TWENTY ONE -

RETURNING TO WHERE Jenny stood waiting, her shoulders hunched over with her face nuzzled down inside her coat's high collar, he saw her lift her head to call out, 'What did he say?'

'Nothing good.'

'Not suicide?'

Tanner shook his head. 'He thinks she was thrown into the mere before being hanged.'

'Any thoughts as to why?'

'The most obvious would be to help remove any incriminating evidence, but Johnston had another theory.'

'Which was?'

'With everything that's been going on recently, he suggested it may have been to see if she'd sink or swim.'

'You mean, as a way of finding out if she was a witch?'

Tanner raised an eyebrow. 'It took me longer to get there than that, but yes, something along those lines.'

Jenny held up the police tape for him to duck under.

'Any idea who she is?'

'Not yet, but that reminds me.'

Retrieving his phone, he held it out to show her the picture he'd taken.

'She had this tattooed on her hip. Any ideas?'

'It's the Triple Moon,' came Jenny's immediate response. 'I hate to say it, but the symbol has a strong association with witchcraft.'

'In what way?'

'It's supposed to represent the three phases of womanhood; maiden, mother and crone.'

'And that's witchcraft, is it?'

Jenny shrugged. 'It was one of a number of symbols women used to denote that they practiced it.'

'I can't imagine why they'd have wanted anyone to find out, knowing what would happen if they were caught.'

'Probably to make a living. Many considered them to be the spiritual healers of the day, certainly more so than their local vicar.'

As they began traipsing their way back along the now well-trodden grass path, Jenny asked the question that was now weighing on Tanner's mind.

'Do you think she was killed because someone thought she was a witch?'

Tanner paused before answering. 'I think, with all these recent attacks, the motivation was more likely to have been racial, using witchcraft as an excuse to justify their actions.'

'So, she was hanged because of the colour of her skin?' Jenny asked, her voice incredulous.

'You don't have to go very far back in history to find such horrific practices to have been commonplace. I remember reading somewhere that the last documented case was in the eighties.'

'But that was in America, surely?'

'Probably, but how many people do you think have been stabbed or beaten to death, right here in the UK, for the same reason? It may not be an on-going problem here in Norfolk, but in London it's a different story.'

As they neared the end of the path, Tanner cast his eyes into the crowd being kept behind the carpark's low wooden boundary by three uniformed officers, each wearing a yellow high-visibility jacket.

With his eye fixed on a particular individual, Tanner leaned his head in towards Jenny. 'You know that old saying, that a criminal always returns to the scene of the crime?'

'You mean the one used as a standard plot device for your typical 1980s TV detective series, the ones where everyone used to wear shoulder-pads and drive around in cars very similar to yours?'

'That's the one.'

'I'm aware of it.'

'Well, don't look now, but you see that young man with the red hair, standing just the other side of the barrier?'

'You mean, the short skinny guy?'

'Uh-huh.'

'What about him?'

'If I'm not very much mistaken, he's the guy I chased the other day. The one who threw that brick through the shop window.'

'I thought you said you didn't see his face.'

'I didn't, but he has the same build, he's wearing a light grey hoodie, and the hair colour is certainly right.'

As Tanner said that, the young man seemed to realise he'd become the centre of their attention as they saw him look casually away, as if something had caught his eye off in the distance. A moment later he glanced back, before shuffling slowly around to begin nudging away from them, back through the crowd.

'It must be him,' Tanner announced, breaking into an unexpected run.

With Jenny lurching after him, it wasn't long

before they reached the edge of the carpark, only to find the young man had disappeared.

'He couldn't have gone far,' said Tanner, stepping up onto the barrier, scanning his eyes over the crowd before taking in the vehicle-strewn carpark beyond.

A second later, his eyes were drawn by the sound of a car door being slammed, followed by the heavy churn of a diesel engine. When he saw a familiar white van nudge itself out from behind someone's SUV, he brought Jenny's attention to it before diving into the crowd, pushing and shoving his way through to emerge out the other side to see the van turn right onto the road.

Launching into a sprint, he raced over the carpark, heading for his car, just as the van roared into life, leaving a horizontal plume of noxious grey diesel smoke trailing in the air behind.

Reaching his car, Tanner jumped inside to start the engine. With Jenny joining him a second later, he slipped the car into gear before spinning the wheels on the loose gravel surface, heading for the exit.

The moment the tyres bit into the road's hard asphalt surface, Tanner buried the accelerator deep into the plush cream-coloured carpet whilst taking a firm grip of the car's smooth black leather steering wheel.

'Hold on,' he called over to Jenny, as the car's automatic gearbox clicked down two notches before leaping into life.

With the roar of its massive twelve-cylinder engine growing louder by the second, tearing around the first bend they caught a glimpse of the van ahead, before watching it disappear behind the hedgerow hugging the next.

Forced off the throttle to take the corner, Tanner accelerated hard out, only to be met by another bend in what was an otherwise empty road.

Tanner continued pushing the car hard along the twisting winding road until a T-junction appeared directly in front of them.

Bringing the car to a juddering halt, Tanner looked first left then right. 'Did you see which way he went?'

'I didn't,' came Jenny's honest reply.

'How about a number plate?'

'Not a chance.'

'Shit!'

They sat there in silence for a moment, trying to decide what to do.

'Well,' began Tanner, 'there's no point asking anyone to keep an eye out for a man in a van, especially as it's white.'

'So, what next?'

'If Johnstone is right, and that girl back there was murdered, then it's a whole new investigation, one that I'm not sure I'm too keen to take on, not if Forrester wants me to stay on the Hopkins case.'

As a car appeared in his rear-view mirror, realising he'd stopped in the middle of the road, Tanner indicated left, checked the road ahead and pulled out.

'Er...you do realise that the station is back that way?' mentioned Jenny, glancing behind them.

'I'm not going back, at least, not yet.'

'But...aren't we supposed to let Forrester know that we have another murder investigation on our hands?'

'We don't know that, at least not officially, and we won't until Johnstone comes back with the post-mortem results. So, between now and then, I think it's safe for us to stay focussed on the Hopkins case.'

- CHAPTER TWENTY TWO -

'**T**HIS BETTER BE good,' muttered a disgruntled looking Nick Carter, after a couple of larger than average men had shown Tanner and Jenny into one of two offices inside an old lopsided portacabin, located at the far end of Lowestoft Family Fun Beach. 'I'm exceptionally busy at the moment.'

'We won't take up much of your time,' Tanner promised, as Jenny and himself took the seats being offered to them in front of the most rudimentary of desks. 'Nice place you have here,' he added, in a disingenuous tone.

'Unlike some, I don't waste my money on plush offices,' Carter replied. 'I don't appreciate having to pay the extortionate business rates either, that seem to creep up every year without anyone being able to see the benefit. Anyway, that's something I'll be changing when I win the election. Did you know I was running?' he added, his irritated frown transforming into an affable enough smile.

'We did,' Tanner replied. 'By the sound of it, you seem to fancy your chances.'

'Have you seen the competition?' Carter laughed. 'Some Etonian twat and a stressed-out menopausal mum. Personally, I think I stand *every* chance of winning. I wouldn't be standing if I didn't.'

'I suppose not,' Tanner replied. 'May I ask what

made you decide to?'

The large stocky man took a moment to tug down at the lapels of the shiny blue suit that he looked as if he'd been stuffed into. 'I think it's fairly obvious that people are ready for a change, and by that I mean a *real* change, not just some idiot using the word because that's what they think people want to hear, when in fact they really mean just more of the same. The trouble with the country is quite obvious. Everyone knows it, it's just that nobody's got the guts to do anything about it.'

'Too many foreigners?'

'Too many people,' Carter corrected. 'Our country's seemingly permanent open-door immigration policy is bringing our great nation to its knees.'

'You're saying that it has nothing to do with the colour of people's skin?'

'The British National Union are as much against Europeans as we are the Asians and blacks.'

'But you do think that anyone who isn't both British and white should...what's the phrase again: go back to where they came from?'

'It would be a start,' Carter retorted, offering both Tanner and Jenny a lurid smile.

'And I suppose your plan to encourage them all to pack up and leave is through the use of intimidation and violence?'

'Er, no, Mr Tanner. I plan to get rid of them all by becoming the MP for Norfolk, hence the reason for launching my campaign.'

'Presumably, that means you've had nothing to do with the recent spate of racist motivated attacks?'

'Ah, I see. That's why you're here.'

'If you could answer the question.'

'I didn't, no. But if I had, would you seriously

expect me to sit here and openly admit to it?'

Tanner took a moment to dig out his own little-used notebook.

'I've been told you've served time at her Majesty's pleasure.'

'Yes, and...?'

'For grievous bodily harm.'

'Some guy tried to get off with my wife, so I hit him.'

'You put him in hospital.'

'The guy had a weak jaw.'

'Which you broke in three places, along with his nose and half his teeth.'

Carter shrugged. 'My dad would always tell me that if you hit someone, make sure they don't get up again. He'd then offer me a practical demonstration.'

'I'm amazed you survived to tell the tale.'

'Yes, well. I made sure to listen to his second lesson.'

'And what was that?'

'To duck!' he grinned, presenting them with two near perfect rows of unnaturally white teeth.

'From your story, I take it that you're married?'

'Divorced. The bitch ran off with someone when I was inside.'

Tanner smiled. 'Ironic, don't you think?'

'What is?'

'That you got yourself locked-up for protecting her good name, only for her to leave you when you were.'

Carter shrugged. 'That's life, I suppose.'

'May I ask what you do?'

Carter leaned back in his chair. 'You mean, apart from running for election?'

'Apart from that, yes.'

'A bit of this, a bit of that. You know.'

'I'm afraid I don't.'

From the way Carter was eyeing him up, it was clear that he was trying to decide just how much he should be telling the two police officers sitting directly in front of him.

'If you must know,' he eventually said, 'I own all the amusements along the Family Fun Beach. I've also got a couple of pubs, about two dozen houses and a hotel.'

Tanner raised an eyebrow. 'Sounds like you keep yourself busy.'

'I work hard, Mr Tanner. I always have.'

'No doubt helped by a large inheritance,' Tanner jibed, deliberately trying to provoke him.

'Sadly, no. My mum died giving birth to me. After that, my dad rose to the dizzying heights of becoming an unemployed alcoholic. His idea of hard work was to beat the shit out of me as often as he could. I was forced to work the rides here when I was still at school, just to make enough money for us to eat. When he eventually died of alcohol poisoning, I was left with nothing more than a pile of unpaid bills. So no, Mr Tanner, this did *not* come easy!'

'You must subsequently have a very low opinion of all those people who come into the UK looking for free government handouts.'

'Did you really come all the way over here to ask if I'm the one behind the recent racist attacks?'

'Not only that.'

'Then what else?'

'We'd also like to talk to you about Norfolk's former MP, Patrick Hopkins.'

'What about him?'

'We were wondering if you knew him?'

'Only in the same way that most people did.'

'So, you didn't?'

'Not personally, no.'

'Do you know how he died?'

'I heard he went mad and hanged himself. Something to do with a witch's curse.'

Tanner smiled. 'I take it you read the Norfolk Herald?'

'Doesn't everyone?'

'You'd not heard that he'd been murdered?'

Tanner watched as the man's eyes shifted between his own and Jenny's.

'It's not a trick question, Mr Carter.'

'OK, yes, I did know that, obviously.'

'Why obviously?'

'Because it's been all over the news, but to be honest, I preferred the story in the Norfolk Herald; that he'd been cursed by Elizabeth Craddock, the 17th Century witch who his direct descendant, Matthew Hopkins, is said to have tried and hanged. It was even more entertaining than hearing that he'd been murdered.'

'You don't sound very upset, Mr Carter. To be honest, you sound rather pleased.'

'Why should I be upset? As I said, I didn't know the man. On top of that, if someone hadn't gone and killed him, I wouldn't have the chance I have today; to become Norfolk's next MP.'

'Which leads to my next question.'

'I suppose you'd like to know where I was at the time of his death.'

'If you could be so kind.'

'You'd better tell me when that was then, hadn't you.'

'Sorry, I thought you'd have known.'

'Why? Because you think I was there at the time?' Tanner smiled.

'Well, unfortunately for you, I wasn't.'

'I see. May I ask how you know you weren't, being

that I've yet to say when he was, and as I don't believe we ever released that particular piece of information to the press?'

'It doesn't matter when it was. As I've said before, I didn't know the man. Subsequently, I'd have had no reason to have murdered him.'

'OK, just for the record, we believe he was killed on Saturday, 7th November, sometime between nine and twelve in the evening.'

'If it was a Saturday, then I'd have been down the pub.'

'Would you mind checking?'

'I don't need to. I always go down the pub on Saturday night.'

'Fair enough. Which one?'

'The Fisherman's Arms, along the Parade. It's my local. I also just happen to own it, of course.'

Tanner closed his notebook to stand up. 'Thank you for your time, Mr Carter. I think that will be all for now.'

Seeing them about to leave, the man almost looked disappointed.

'Don't you want me to come down to the station?'

Tanner gave him a look of surprised confusion. 'We're not arresting you, Mr Carter, at least, not yet.'

'But – don't you need my prints and DNA?'

'I'm pleased to say that we already have them on file, but thanks anyway.'

'Then how about a statement?'

Tanner stood behind his chair to face him. 'Is there some particular reason why you want to come down to the station with us?'

'Under normal circumstances I wouldn't, of course, but given the fact that I've just started my election campaign, and with about half the nation's press parked outside, I was just thinking that it would probably provide an excellent opportunity for a bit of free publicity, don't you think?'

'To be seen being led inside Wroxham Police Station?'

'Well, maybe not if I was being frog-marched in wearing handcuffs, although even then I doubt it would do any harm. You know what they say, there's no such thing as bad publicity.'

'I'm not sure they had being arrested for murder in mind when they came up with that.'

'Ah, yes, but I'm not though, am I.'

'Not *yet* you're not.'

'I think it would also present an excellent opportunity to remind everyone to vote for me. I could wear my rosette; maybe give out a few leaflets. Speaking of which...' Diving into one of the desk drawers, he pulled out a handful of the ones he must have had in mind. 'Here,' he continued, standing up to hold them out.

Amused by the bare-faced cheek of the man, Tanner stared down at them for a moment before curiosity got the better of him. Taking them, he kept one for himself before handing the rest to Jenny.

'Maybe you could pass some on to your colleagues?'

'Tell you what, Mr Carter, if you give us a few more, I'll get everyone to start taking them door-to-door for you.'

It took a full moment for Carter to realise Tanner was joking.

'You nearly had me there for a moment.'

'You had me when you handed over the leaflets,' Tanner replied, unable to prevent the corners of his mouth from lifting. 'Tell you what, I'll leave some out in reception for you.'

'That's very kind. Thank you.'

'Along with an equal number from the other candidates, of course. I'd hate for anyone to think that we were being politically biased.'

With Carter returning a thin smile, Tanner and Jenny turned to make their way out.

Passing through the door, Jenny stopped dead in her tracks. Turning to face Tanner, she brought his eyes down to one of the leaflets, a finger pointed at a person pictured on the back.

After exchanging a surprised glance, Tanner turned to step back inside the office.

'Sorry, Mr Carter, but before we go, you wouldn't happen to know who this young man is?'

Screwing up his eyes to see who the detective inspector was referring to, Carter returned a look of parental pride.

'That's my son, Roy. He's one of my most ardent supporters.'

'I don't suppose you know where we could find him, by any chance?'

Carter's eyes narrowed.

'I'm afraid I don't.'

'How about an address?'

'Why the sudden interest?'

'We just want to have a chat with him, that's all.'

'About what?'

'Oh, you know, this and that.'

'I can assure you that whatever it is that you *think* he's done, he didn't.'

Tanner smirked. 'And you know that for a fact, do you?'

'He knows not to do anything stupid, not when I'm running for election.'

'Are you sure about that?'

Tanner saw a cloud of doubt roll over Carter's face.

'Anyway, I'm hardly going to tell you where he

lives now, am I.'

'No, well, fair enough. We can find out easily enough. Thanks again for your time, Mr Carter, and for the leaflets as well. Surprisingly informative. Oh, and when you do speak to him, if you could let him know that we'd like a word, I'd be most grateful.'

- CHAPTER TWENTY THREE -

THE MOMENT THE portacabin door closed behind them, Tanner handed the leaflet back to Jenny with a grateful smile. 'Well spotted, Jen.'

'It wasn't difficult,' she replied. 'He's the only one on there with bright red hair.'

'But even so, I doubt most people would have thought to look, myself included.'

Stepping over the overgrown yard where they'd found Carter's run-down mobile office, Tanner gazed up at the intricate framework that made up an enormous rollercoaster ride they could see looming up before them.

'So, he owns that, does he?'

'Along with all the others,' added Jenny.

'I can't say I'd be too keen to have a go,' Tanner continued, noting how the entire structure seemed to be leaning to one side. 'It looks like it's about to collapse at any moment.'

'Funny you should say that,' commented Jenny, reaching her fiancé's somewhat dated Jaguar XJS, 'but that's exactly how I feel every time I'm about to climb into your car.'

Tanner gave her a look of unamused nonchalance before tugging open the door. 'I suppose we'd better head back to the office, but I'm going to give them a call first. Now that we know who he is, I think Cooper needs to have Carter's son picked up as a priority.'

Leaning against the car, Tanner pulled out his phone to put a call through.

'Vicky, hi, it's Tanner. I was trying to get hold of Cooper?'

'He's just popped out for something to eat. Can I help?'

'When he comes back, can you tell him that I think we've managed to work out who was responsible for throwing that brick through the window of that shop we were at, probably for setting fire to it as well.'

'Anyone I know?'

'We think it's Nick Carter's son, Roy. Jenny spotted a picture of him on the back of his election leaflet. I think he needs to have a word with him, sooner rather than later. And maybe you could ask Sally to drop whatever she's doing to start running a background check on him? But make sure to agree it with Cooper when he gets back. I don't want him thinking I'm treading on his toes. It is supposed to be his investigation, after all.'

'No problem,' Vicky replied. 'How'd you get on at Horsey Mere this morning?'

Tanner had almost forgotten about the girl they'd found hanging by her neck only an hour or so before.

'Nothing good, I'm afraid.'

'You better know that Forrester's been asking after you.'

Tanner glanced down at his watch to find it was later than he'd thought.

'If he asks again, tell him that we're on our way back now.'

Ending the call, Tanner climbed inside the car to join Jenny.

'I assume Forrester's been wondering where we are?'

'Only a little. He'd have called if he was really

concerned.'

With the engine started, Tanner rumbled the XJS slowly over the yard's uneven surface, heading for the road running parallel with the beachfront. As he waited for a gap in the traffic, he heard Jenny ask, 'What did you make of Nick Carter?'

'He's a cheeky sod, I know that much; asking us to hand out his leaflets like that.'

'Did you think he was telling the truth; that he didn't know Patrick Hopkins?'

Tanner thought back to the way Carter seemed to have done little to hide the fact that he was anything but delighted by the news of Hopkins's death.

'To be honest, I've no idea.'

With the road clear, Tanner pulled out to begin following the beachfront, occasionally glancing out of the window at the various rides and amusements.

'So, he owns all this, does he?'

'Apparently.'

'Well, if that's true, I'd be hard pressed to believe that he wasn't having constant run-ins with the local council about them all. Half the rides look like they should be given a public health warning, the other half look like they'd come down in a stiff breeze.'

Hearing his phone ring, he dug it out to glance down at the screen.

'It's the office,' he said. 'Probably Forrester, wondering where we are.'

'Shall I answer it for you?'

'If you could,' Tanner replied, passing it over. 'Just tell him I'm driving.'

A moment later he heard Jenny say, 'Oh, hi Vicky. We thought you were Forrester.'

Silence followed, before Jenny eventually glanced over at Tanner to say, 'Really? What had he been brought in for?'

Straining his ears to hear what was being said on the other end of the line, he heard Jenny eventually say, 'OK, I'll let him know. We'll be there in about half an hour, traffic depending.'

With Jenny ending the call to pass the phone back, Tanner was left to ask, 'What did she say?'

'You'll never guess who they've just arrested. The very man we were about to start a regional search for.'

'Nick Carter's son?'

'The one and only. He was caught spraying some sort of race-related graffiti over a bus stop.'

- CHAPTER TWENTY FOUR -

HAVING SUCCESSFULLY MANAGED to avoid any interaction with the dozen or so reporters crowding the entrance to Wroxham Police Station, Tanner and Jenny passed quickly through the reception area, into the main office.

With his coat thrown over his chair, Tanner made a bee-line for the kitchen, desperate to grab a coffee before having to update Forrester. As he hurried inside, he nearly walked straight into DI Cooper, coming out the other way, a mug of steaming coffee held at the end of each arm.

Apologising, Tanner stepped to one side to catch Cooper's eye. 'Did you get my message, about Nick Carter's son, that we think he's the guy who threw the brick through that shop window?'

'I'm just about to interview him.'

'Oh, right. I don't suppose you'd mind if I joined you?'

Cooper hesitated. 'Er...' he began, glancing down at the mugs held at the ends of each arm. 'Well, I was going in with Vicky.'

'I'm sure she won't mind. I'm keen to have a word with him about the murder at Horsey Mere.'

Cooper looked up at him with a start, confusion knitting his brow. 'What murder?'

'The girl found hanging there.'

'Oh, right, sorry. I thought we all assumed it must

have been a suicide, being that we'd not heard anything.'

'Well, it's not official, but I suspect that's what Johnstone's report will say. I was about to go in and tell Forrester.'

'You mean...he doesn't know?'

It was Tanner's turn to hesitate. 'Well, I've yet to get the chance to tell him. We left the scene to head straight over to Lowestoft, to interview Nick Carter. That's when we found out about his son.'

'So, who's going to be leading the investigation into the girl at Horsey Mere?' questioned Cooper, with a look of hopeful expectation.

It was obvious what he was thinking; no doubt something similar to what Tanner had been. He knew that there was no way he'd be able to head-up two murder investigations, especially when the girl's murder had the potential to be just as high-profile as the MP's, perhaps more so. After all, when was the last time someone had been lynched in the UK, and an attractive young woman at that? But Tanner still had grave doubts that Cooper was ready to take the lead on any murder investigation, let alone one where every move was being scrutinized by the nation's press.

'That's going to be up to Forrester,' he eventually replied.

'Hadn't you better tell him then, that you think she'd been murdered?'

'Of course, but I'd rather do that when I have a potential suspect, which is why I'm keen to talk to Roy Carter.'

'What makes you think he had anything to do with it?'

'Apart from the colour of the girl's skin, we saw him at the scene, hiding in the crowd. And when we spotted him, he took off.'

'Right, but that hardly means he did it though, does it.'

'It doesn't mean he didn't, either.'

'I still think you should tell Forrester, before speaking to Carter.'

'There's not a lot we can do until we hear back from the post-mortem. There's also the possibility that Roy Carter knows who the girl is as well.'

Cooper gazed over towards the cluster of desks under the whiteboard where Vicky was sitting.

'Tell you what,' Tanner continued, 'if we interview Roy Carter together, I'll recommend to Forrester that you be given the lead on the girl's murder. How about that?'

'As the SIO?'

Tanner hesitated. He still hoped to be able to oversee the investigation, but knowing it wouldn't be his call, he thought it was safe enough to agree. 'As the SIO, but I can only make the recommendation. It will be up to Forrester to decide.'

Cooper studied Tanner's face for a moment. 'OK, agreed. But I'm to lead the interview.'

'Fine by me.'

'Let me tell Vicky, then I suggest we head inside. He's already waiting for us with his solicitor.'

'Oh, right, er, hold on. Let me just grab myself a coffee. I'll be with you in a sec.'

- CHAPTER TWENTY FIVE -

SEATED AROUND THE small rectangular table pushed up against the wall of the windowless interview room, with the formalities out the way, Cooper opened the file he'd brought in with Tanner to kick off the proceedings.

'Mr Carter, I was hoping you'd be able to explain to us what you were doing earlier today at the bus stop outside the Fenwick Estate?'

The skinny young lad pulled up the sleeves of his light grey hoodie, as if preparing himself for a fight.

'You know what I was doing, else I wouldn't be 'ere, would I?'

'For the benefit of the recording.'

Carter gazed thoughtfully up at the ceiling for a moment before smirking back at Cooper. 'I was expressing myself through the medium of paint.'

'According to the arresting officer, you were scrawling out the words "Bitches Go Home" with a spray can.'

Carter leaned forward with a sneer; his freckly white forearms covering the table. 'I fought coppers was educated, like?'

'I'm not sure what that has to do with you vandalising a bus stop.'

'It's just that the *cunt*stable who arrested me couldn't 'ave been able to read, else he'd 'ave known that I didn't write Bitches Go Home.'

'I see. So, what did you write then?'

'Witches Go Home,' he sneered. 'The B was crossed out.'

With that he sat slowly back in his chair whilst drawing his lumpy red lips back over his heavily pock-marked face.

Cooper turned his attention back to the file.

'On Monday, 9th November, you were also witnessed throwing a brick through the window of a shop called Tarragon on Stalham High Street.'

'Yeah? Who says?'

Cooper paused for a moment as he fished out a piece of paper from the file to place in the middle of the table. 'Apart from the old lady who you ran straight into when fleeing the scene, the whole thing was caught by a nearby CCTV camera.'

As Carter and his solicitor took a moment to stare down at the grainy colour image being presented to them, Cooper continued. 'For the benefit of the recording, the suspect is being shown a still camera image of a man bearing a striking resemblance to the suspect, who appears to be in the process of throwing a brick through a shop window on the date in question.'

'That could be anyone,' Carter rebutted, shoving the picture away.

'But it isn't, though, is it?'

'Well, good luck proving that in court.'

'When combined with what you were brought in here today for, plus the eye witness at the scene who, by the way, is *very* keen to testify, and the fact that this is hardly the first time you've been caught vandalising public property, we think we have every chance of a conviction.'

'OK, so maybe I did throw a brick through some bitch's – sorry – witch's shop window. So what?'

'Unfortunately, for you at least, your choice of wording, that of "Bitches Go Home", even if you put a line through the B to replace with a W, along with the act of throwing a brick through the window of a non-British national's shop, both fall under the category of being a Hate Crime. As your solicitor will no doubt be able to confirm, under the Public Order Act 1986, such a charge carries a maximum sentence of up to seven years.'

'You must be 'av'n a laugh!'

'Then there's the fact that only one day later, the very same shop was petrol bombed. I don't suppose you know anything about that, do you?'

'Only that it weren't me.'

'I see,' Cooper responded. 'May I ask why you have a can of petrol in the back of your van?'

'Why d'ya fink?

'If I knew why, I wouldn't be asking.'

'In case I run out, you moron.'

'In case you run out of what?'

'Are you deaf as well as stupid?'

'Sorry, I must have miss-heard you. You're saying that you keep a can of petrol in the back of your van in case you run out, when the vehicle in question runs on diesel?'

A surge of blood flooded the young man's face.

'I assume you do know that a diesel engine can't run on petrol?'

Carter squirmed briefly in his seat, before his eyes flashed with inspiration. 'I didn't say it was for the van, did I.'

Cooper raised a questioning eyebrow.

'I do some gardening jobs on the side, like. It's for my lawnmower; and a strimmer.'

'I see. But we didn't find either a lawnmower or a strimmer in the back of your van. Only one ten-litre

111

can of petrol.'

'I use my dad's. Actually, no, I hire them.'

His face flushed again.

'I don't suppose you'd be able to make up your mind.'

'I hire them, when I can't use my dad's.'

Cooper rolled his eyes whilst shaking his head. 'Anyway, I'm please to say that it doesn't matter what you claim to have used the petrol for. Do you know why?'

The young man shrugged.

'Because our forensics department are able to match different types of petrol, and we've just sent them a sample of yours. If it turns out to be the same as what was used for the petrol bomb, given the fact that someone died in the fire, you'll be looking at a charge of manslaughter, which will make seven years look like a walk in the park.'

By the time Cooper had finished, the young man had broken off eye contact to stare down at his hands that were now clasped together on top of the table.

'Then there's the girl found hanging by her neck at Horsey Mere, of course.'

'You can't pin that on me!' he blurted, his hands separating into fists.

'You know about that, do you?'

Once again, the youth looked flustered. 'It was in the papers, wasn't it?'

'I doubt it. She was only found this morning.'

'Then I must've 'eard about it on the radio.'

As the young man's eyes darted from one DI to the other, it was Tanner's turn to step in.

'What I think we'd both like to know is what you were doing there, only a couple of hours after the girl's body was found?'

'But – I – I wasn't.'

'What were you hoping to see?'

'I just told you. I wasn't there.'

'Er, yes you were. I saw you, and you saw me, just before you drove off in that white van of yours.'

With Carter closing his mouth to return his attention back down to his hands, Tanner continued.

'We'd also like to know who the girl is, the one you were trying to gawp at, along with everyone else?'

'How should I know?'

'So, you admit to being there?'

'When did I say that?'

'Just now.'

The skinny youth was beginning to look increasingly agitated.

'No I didn't!'

'I just asked if you knew the girl you were gawping at. You said you didn't, which implies that you knew who I was talking about. If you hadn't been there, you wouldn't have.'

'But – I – I wasn't!' the young lad replied, his eyes darting around the room, as if searching for a way out.

'That's not what you said just now.'

Carter turned to send his solicitor a look of imploring desperation.

'Detective Inspector, you can't keep badgering my client like this, purely in an attempt to provoke some sort of emotive response.'

'I'm not trying to provoke an emotive response,' Tanner replied, 'I'm trying to find out what he was doing at the scene of a young girl's murder.'

'Well, he says he wasn't there.'

'That's as may be, but I know he was because I saw him with my own two eyes, as did the detective sergeant who was with me.'

Drawing strength from having his solicitor stand

up for him, Carter spat back with, 'Even if I was, so what?'

'I'd just like to know what you were doing there, that's all?'

'Same thing as everyone else.'

'But you knew her, right?'

'I'd never seen her before in my life.'

'How can you be so sure? I mean, you couldn't have seen her face. You must have been a good hundred metres away. Don't tell me you brought binoculars.'

'I know, cus I don't hang out with foreigners.'

Barely drawing breath, Tanner changed the subject.

'Where were you last night, between the hours of nine and twelve?'

Momentarily stuck for words, Carter eventually managed to splutter out, 'I – I was down the pub, with my mates.'

'No doubt they'll be able to verify that?'

'I don't see why not.'

'Which pub?'

'It was The Fisherman's Arms.'

'Really? That's interesting. Was your dad there as well?'

'What makes you say that?'

'He does own it, doesn't he? At least, that's what he told us when we spoke to him this morning.'

Carter hesitated. 'I – I'm not sure. He could have been. I didn't see him.'

'Does he know you're here?'

The freckle covered youth stared back down at his hands, squirming again in his seat.

'I can't imagine he'll be too pleased when he finds out you are, not when he's trying to become Norfolk's next MP.'

'You're not gonna tell him, are you?' the lad asked, glancing up.

'I can't see any reason why we'd need to, unless, of course, we don't feel you've been entirely honest with us, and we need him to clarify some of your answers.'

Leaving Carter to return to staring down at the table, Tanner clapped his hands together to give Cooper a triumphant smile.

'Anyone fancy another coffee?'

- CHAPTER TWENTY SIX -

WITH THE INTERVIEW suspended, Tanner left Cooper to grab himself a coffee whilst he headed in to see Forrester.

'Sorry to bother you, sir,' he began, having rapped his knuckles on the door, 'but I thought I'd better give you a quick update.'

Forrester stared up from his monitor. 'I was about to send out a search party. Where the hell have you been?'

'We were called from home in the early hours to attend the scene of the body found at Horsey Mere. Then we had to drive over to Lowestoft to interview the third candidate for the by-election, Nick Carter. By the time we'd got back, his son had been arrested for vandalism, so I went straight in to interview him with Cooper.'

'OK, fair enough. So, what's the story with the girl? I understand she hanged herself.'

'She was found hanging, sir, yes.'

'But it *was* suicide, though?'

'I must admit, I thought it was, but by the time I left, Dr Johnstone seemed to be leaning more towards the idea that someone may have had a hand in it.'

'You're telling me she was *murdered?*'

'Well, he wasn't certain,' Tanner lied, 'and obviously he won't know until he's completed the post-mortem.'

'But that was his initial thought?'

'As I said, it's what he was leaning towards.'

'And you're only telling me this now, at, what...half-past three in the afternoon?'

'I know, sir,' Tanner replied. 'Sorry.'

'*Sorry?*' Forrester repeated, his eyes boring into Tanner's.

'But the good news is,' Tanner continued, his eyes momentarily distracted by a purple vein he could see pulsating over Forrester's forehead, one he'd never noticed before, 'is that we already have a suspect in custody.'

Forrester continued to glare at Tanner for a moment longer before his eyes began to narrow. 'I take it that means you're proceeding on the basis that she *was* murdered?'

'Er...'

'Even though, less than thirty-seconds ago, you were telling me that you didn't think she had been, and that we needed to wait for Dr Johnston's post-mortem?'

'Well, sort of, sir, yes. You see, I recognised someone in the crowd of on-lookers, where the girl had been found. It was the same man who'd been caught on CCTV, throwing a brick through that Tarragon shop window, who we also suspect had thrown the petrol bomb, killing the owner's mother, trapped upstairs. It turns out that he's Nick Carter's son, and is one of the British National Union's most ardent supporters.'

'And what's the BNU got to do with the girl at Horsey Mere?'

'It was the colour of her skin, sir.'

Cursing, Forrester shoved his chair back to lumber his way over to the window. There he stood for a few moments, staring out in silence at the still growing crowd of reporters lining the pavement outside.

'Do you think he did it?' Forrester eventually asked.

'Nick Carter's son? Well, sir, I don't think it's much of a step from petrol bombing a shop, knowing a family of non-British nationals are trapped upstairs, to stringing one up by the neck.'

'I assume you haven't told the press about this, given that you've only just told me?'

'The only other people who know are Jenny and Cooper, sir.'

'Well, that's something, I suppose. If that lot gets wind of this, all hell's going to break loose.'

More silence followed, before Forrester eventually turned to head back to his desk.

'I don't suppose there's been any progress with regard to Patrick Hopkins?'

'We went to see the Labour party candidate yesterday, Susan Sutton.'

'And?'

'She seems to lack motive, being that she only had the idea to run for election after Hopkins died. At least, that's what she said.'

'This was the Parenting Portal woman, wasn't it?'

'It was, sir, yes.'

'I hope you were nice to her?'

'More so than usual,' came Tanner's honest reply. 'Jenny arranged to have her DNA and prints collected yesterday evening. Assuming nothing matches what's been found at Hopkins's house, I'd be happy for us to cross her off the list.'

'What about Nick Carter? You said you spoke to him earlier.'

'Oh, he definitely needs to remain a suspect, sir. I've rarely met someone quite so cocky. He lied to us, straight off the bat, saying that he didn't know Patrick Hopkins had been murdered. He also denied knowing him which, again, I found very hard to believe, given his line of work.'

'And what's that?'

'Amongst other things, he owns all the rides and amusements along the Lowestoft Family Fun Beach, most of which look as if they're about to collapse. I can't imagine he hasn't had the council on his back about them. I can only assume that the only way he's been able to stop them all from being closed down is by bribing someone fairly high up. When you combine that with the fact that he's done time for GBH, and that he seems adamant that he's going to win the election, I wouldn't put it past him for having been the one who strung up the former MP, maybe even for no other reason than to trigger a by-election.'

Planting his elbows firmly on the desk, Forrester steepled his fingers together. 'If you're saying Nick Carter is a candidate for having murdered Patrick Hopkins, and his son is under suspicion for murdering a foreign girl, then I assume you're about to tell me that the two cases are connected?'

'In this instance I'm actually not, sir, no.'

Forrester raised a curious eyebrow.

'It's just that I can't see anything to connect the two, other than one suspect is the son of the other. I'm fairly sure that Patrick Hopkins was killed for political gain, either by Michael Drummond, his wife, or Nick Carter, whereas the girl found at Horsey Mere was more likely to have been murdered for no other reason than the colour of her skin.'

'Do we know who she is yet?'

'Not yet, sir, no. But if Roy Carter did kill her, I don't think it will be long before we find out. The guy's already climbing the walls, and we've only just started questioning him.'

'How long until we have to charge him?'

Tanner had completely forgotten about the time issue, that they only had twenty-four hours from the time of his arrest before having to either charge him or to let him go.

'I'd need to check the arrest report,' he replied. 'I think he was brought in at around lunchtime today.'

Forrester glanced down at his watch. 'So, not all that long then, given the circumstances.'

'Unfortunately not, sir. It's a shame he was picked up for vandalising a bus stop before we had a chance to build a case against him for the more serious charges.'

'Well, it can't be helped, I suppose.'

'And I still have the Hopkins case to work on.'

'Then you'll have to make the girl at Horsey Mere your priority, for the time being at least.'

'I was actually wondering how you'd feel about giving Cooper the lead.'

'On Hopkins or the girl?'

'The girl, sir. I was thinking that as he's already leading the investigation into the racial attacks, it would make sense for him to carry that forward into the girl's murder; assuming she was, of course.'

'With you overseeing?'

'I was actually thinking he could be the senior investigating officer, sir.'

'Is he ready for that?'

'If it's as straight forward as I think it is, and we already have the culprit in custody, then he should be.'

'And what if it isn't as straight forward as you think it is, and the whole thing goes tits up?'

'Then I'd have to step in.'

Forrester checked his watch again.

'What's your next step with the Hopkins case?'

'To see if forensics have been able to match any of the DNA samples and prints we've been sending over to them.'

'And if they don't?'

'We still need to push on with the various suspects' background checks, looking for some sort of a connection. But it's going to take time, sir. I mean, we only found out who the by-election candidates were yesterday, and if I have to oversee an investigation into the Horsey Mere girl as well, then it's going to take even longer.'

'Then I suppose I have no choice but to make Cooper the SIO.'

'With me ready to step in, should I need to,' supplemented Tanner.

Forrester let out a heavy sigh. 'OK, very well. I suppose you'd better send him in.'

'Yes, sir,' Tanner replied, turning to head out.

Reaching the door, he glanced back to add, 'Maybe you could ask him to contact Dr Johnstone's office, to see if there's any chance of him being able to come back to us with a post-mortem report on that girl before end of play today, even if it's only an interim one?'

Seeing Forrester pick up a pen, Tanner thought to add, 'And then to chase forensics for the results from the petrol we found in the back of his van. If it's the same as was used on the shop, I think we'd be able to charge him with arson, possibly manslaughter as well.'

'We'd need more than just the petrol to make that stick,' commented Forrester, scribbling away.

'True, but if nothing else, it would at least help us to convince the local magistrate that we need an extension. It would also keep the pressure on him.

Oh, and then he needs to ask them to see if they can find any evidence that the girl had been in his van. If they can, then I think it's a done deal.'

Forrester looked up from his notes with a nervous expression. 'Look, Tanner, you may as well take the lead on this one as well. I'm sure Cooper's keen, but I need someone who knows what they're doing.'

'And that's me, is it?' Tanner joked.

'Well, it's more you than Cooper, that much I do know.'

- CHAPTER TWENTY SEVEN -

I T WASN'T UNTIL gone ten o'clock that evening when Tanner and Jenny finally emerged out into the police station's cold and distinctly uninviting carpark.

With a ripple of flash photography reminding them that there were still over a dozen reporters camped outside, they hurried over to Tanner's car, doing their best to avoid being either filmed or photographed as they did.

'Don't they have homes to go to?' commented Jenny, levering herself into the seat to close the door.

'Hotel rooms, more likely,' Tanner replied, starting the engine before leaning forward to crank the heating up.

'I suppose there will be even more of them when they find out what happened to that poor girl.'

'No doubt, but with any luck, we'd have been able to charge Roy Carter by then.'

'Do you think that's likely?'

Tanner glanced over his shoulder to reverse out from the parking space. 'I suppose it depends on what forensics come back with, but we should have a pretty good idea by tomorrow if it's him.'

Jenny waited for him to finish reversing before asking something she'd been meaning to since his meeting with their DCI.

'You never told me how Cooper took the news that

Forrester wasn't going to make him the SIO.'

'Better than I was expecting,' Tanner replied, facing forward to begin heading for the exit. 'To be honest, I think he was secretly relieved. I still don't think he's ready. I'm not sure he does, either.'

Gently nudging a cameraman out of the way, Tanner pulled out onto the road.

'Do you think that newspaper article we found will be of any use?' asked Jenny, staring out at the various houses flickering past. 'The one Vicky found showing Nick Carter shaking hands with Patrick Hopkins?'

'If nothing else, it proves Nick Carter was lying; that he did know the former MP.'

'Unless he'd simply forgotten about it. I mean, it was written over five years ago.'

'I'm not sure someone like Nick Carter is the sort of person who'd forget something like that, not after he'd spent the next three months bragging about it to all his friends. I also think it's interesting that Hopkins was given the task of opening some dodgy-looking theme park ride. I'd have thought that sort of thing would have been left to the local mayor to deal with.'

Silence followed as Wroxham's streetlights disappeared, leaving them following the Jag's headlights, sweeping over the hedge-lined road ahead.

'Anyway,' Tanner eventually continued, 'we'll have to keep digging into his background, but at least we know we're not wasting our time.'

Jenny glanced down at her watch. 'You do realise that this is yet another night we're not going to have time to spend planning our wedding?'

'Yes, I know. Hopefully, we'll be able to take some time off at the weekend.'

'What, with a double murder on our hands?'

'Well, we'll have to see. I'm still confident that we'll be able to get at least one of them wrapped up by then.'

- CHAPTER TWENTY EIGHT -

Wednesday, 18ᵗʰ November

AT WORK THE following morning, Tanner had already drained two mugs of coffee before the anticipated emails finally began coming through, first from the medical examiner's office, then forensics.

Printing them off, he spent five minutes reading through each before taking them over to Cooper. Ten minutes after that, they were knocking on Forrester's door.

'Good morning, sir,' Tanner began, leading the way inside. 'We've had some positive news back from both Dr Johnstone and forensics on the girl found at Horsey Mere.'

Forrester looked up at them from a file on his desk. 'Go on.'

'The post-mortem report confirms the girl *was* murdered. She'd been hit over the head, dragged over grass and mud, and half-drowned, all before being hanged by the neck until dead.'

'And that's good news, is it?'

'Only when the forensics report is taken into consideration, the part relating to Roy Carter's van. Traces of the victim's DNA were found in the passenger seat.'

Forrester leaned forward, a hint of a smile playing

126

over his lips.

'Anything else?'

'The petrol we found in the back of the van; it was the same as was used to burn down that shop.'

'I meant in relation to the crime scene at Horsey Mere. Has any trace of our suspect been found there?'

'They haven't come back to us on that yet.'

'Have you chased them?'

'Well, no, but in fairness, it's been the site of a major archaeological dig for a good few weeks now. As the body was only found yesterday, I think they're going to need more time.'

'OK, but it's still worth giving them a call, just as a reminder. What about from the body itself?'

'Nothing's come up at all, I'm afraid. I'm sure that's why she was stripped and thrown into the water. Her killer must have known that doing so would go a long way to removing any evidence.'

'And the rope that was used to haul her up?'

'Again, nothing.'

Forrester leaned back in his chair. 'So we don't have anything that directly links Roy Carter to the scene.'

'Not yet, sir, no, but I'm confident forensics will come up with something, eventually.'

'But we can hardly go ahead and charge him with her murder on the vague hope that they might, though, can we?'

'Maybe not, sir, but at least we have enough to get an extension to keep hold of him. Hopefully, that'll give them enough time to find something. It will also give us more time to spend with him in the interview room.'

Forrester returned to sitting back in his chair. 'Are we any closer to finding out who the girl is?'

'I'm still hoping we'll be able to get him to tell us,

especially now we know she was in his van.'

'I wouldn't be so sure. Not if his solicitor has anything to do with it. Nobody's been reported missing, have they?'

'Not yet.'

'We could hold a press conference,' proposed Cooper. 'To ask if anyone knows who she is.'

'If we could keep this between ourselves,' said Forrester, shifting uncomfortably in his chair, 'for the time being, at least.'

'But it's already in the news, sir.'

'That she'd been murdered?'

'That she'd been tried and hanged as a witch.'

Forrester let out a breath. 'I assume you're referring to the Norfolk Herald?'

'I am, sir, yes.' Cooper replied. 'The other newspapers have hardly given it a mention.'

'There's a copy of it on my desk; if you'd like to see it?' offered Tanner, with an amenable smile.

'I think I'd rather be beaten about the head with a cricket bat, thank you very much.'

'Does that mean you don't, sir?'

'Of course it means I don't, you bloody idiot!'

'Sorry, sir.' Tanner apologised, doing his best to suppress a smirk. 'I wasn't sure.'

- CHAPTER TWENTY NINE -

L EAVING FORRESTER'S OFFICE, after a brief discussion as to how best to approach their second day with Roy Carter, Tanner and Cooper headed for the interview room, only to have their attention caught by the duty sergeant, PS Taylor, bursting in through the reception's double doors.

'A couple's just come in,' he began, catching Tanner's eye. 'They say their daughter's gone missing.'

Tanner stopped dead in his tracks.

'Right!' he exclaimed, peering over the sergeant's shoulder, trying to catch a glimpse of them. 'I suppose I'd better have a word. Cooper, why don't you get started on that extension application.'

'You don't want me to crack on with Carter?'

'Not on your own, no.'

'I could go in with Vicky?'

'I'd rather we wait until we know if their missing daughter is our murdered girl. If we can go back in with her identity, with everything else we've found out, it may be enough to pull a confession out of him.'

With Cooper agreeing, albeit reluctantly, Taylor led the couple into the station's second interview room, leaving Tanner hurrying back to his desk.

Printing off a selection of the photographs to show them, he was shadowed by a growing sense of dread.

If the couple's missing daughter was their murdered girl, and she hadn't simply run off with her boyfriend, then there was every chance he was about to find himself sitting across a table from them, staring into their eyes as he told them that their daughter was dead.

As he searched for the file on his computer, haunting memories of the night he'd found the body of his own daughter came flooding back. With the thoughts came a familiar surge of unwelcome emotion, slamming against the wall he'd built up over the years to help keep them at bay.

Shaking his head clear, he re-focussed on the delicate task at hand. *Hopefully, it won't be her*, he thought to himself, but his gut-feeling told him otherwise.

- CHAPTER THIRTY -

'MR AND MRS Chadha?' Tanner enquired, entering the room. 'Have I pronounced that correctly?'

'You have,' replied the husband, in what sounded more like a polite reply than an honest one.

Taking the already half-filled out Missing Person's report from the duty sergeant, Tanner presented the nervous looking couple with a comforting smile. 'May we get you anything to drink? A tea or a coffee, perhaps?'

The man glanced briefly at his wife, standing beside him, before looking back. 'We're fine, thank you.'

Dismissing Taylor, Tanner offered them a seat whilst taking one for himself.

'I understand your daughter is missing.'

'Anya, yes.'

'How old is she?'

'Seventeen.'

'When was the last time you saw her?'

'Monday evening.'

'Where was that?'

'At home. She said she was going out to see a friend.'

'Did she say who?'

'A girl called Zara. Zara Haddad.'

Tanner made a note of the name.

'I assume you've checked to see if she's there?'

'I called them this morning.'

'And she hadn't been?'

'Not even on the first night. Zara said she hadn't even said she would be. That's when we decided to come here.'

'Is there anyone else she could be staying with? A boyfriend, perhaps?'

Both parents looked utterly appalled by the idea.

'Nothing like that, no!' came Mr Chadha's curt, dismissive response.

'Sorry, of course,' Tanner apologised, taking a moment to continue filling out the form. He knew from personal experience that just because they didn't know anything about a boyfriend, didn't mean she didn't have one.

'Does she have her own phone?'

'She does.'

'I take it you've tried calling?'

'Messaging as well.'

'OK, well, it's possible that she's simply lost it, or maybe the battery ran out.'

'Even if it had, she'd have found some way to contact us. She'd never have left us not knowing where she was for two nights in a row.'

Tanner knew there was another possibility; that she'd run away, quite possibly with the boyfriend she'd neglected to mention.

'How have things been at home, recently?'

With it obvious that neither had understood the question, Tanner tried again. 'Have there been any arguments?'

The husband glanced briefly down at the table. 'Well, she was in the middle of doing her A-Levels, you see.'

Forced to assume that meant there had been, no

doubt something along the lines of her spending too much time chatting on her phone, and not enough with her head buried inside a book, Tanner returned his attention to the form.

'Have you been in contact with any of her other friends?'

'We've tried,' the man replied, 'but we don't know who most of them are.'

'So, it's possible that she could be staying with one of them?'

'It's possible, but again, she'd have called.'

'How about family?'

'None who live here.'

'Does she have a passport?'

'She's never needed one.'

Making a few more notes, Tanner asked as casually as he knew how, 'I don't suppose you brought in a photograph of her, by any chance?'

The man turned to his wife to mumble something in a language that sounded like some form of Arabic.

Nodding, the woman delved into a bag to bring out the requested item. With it held in her wrinkled brown hands as if it was a holy relic, she offered it for Tanner to take.

Doing so, Tanner stared down to see the face of a beautiful dark-skinned girl smiling back at him. It was difficult to imagine that she was the same person who'd been found hanging from the end of a rope at Horsey Mere, but with her small delicate chin, the distinctive shape of her nose and her gently curving cheekbones, deep down Tanner knew it was her.

The room fell into an anxious silence as Tanner's hand rested on the file he'd brought in with him. He'd put the moment off for long enough.

'Mr and Mrs Chadha, I don't know if you've heard, but a girl was found at Horsey Mere in the early hours of yesterday morning.'

Tanner watched as the husband bit down on his bottom lip. For a moment he wondered if he was going to translate what he'd said to his wife, but it was clear from the look in her eyes that she'd understood, enough at least to know what he'd meant.

'Now, I must stress that at this point in time, we don't know if she is your daughter.'

He let that sink in, before continuing.

'But we do have to accept the possibility that she might be.'

With them each giving him a nervous nod, Tanner continued.

'I'd like to show you some pictures of the jewellery the girl was found wearing, to see if you recognise anything. Would that be OK?'

They both stared into his eyes, their own wide with nervous apprehension.

'You don't have to, of course,' Tanner thought to add.

The husband placed his hand over his wife's before swallowing. 'We have to know...if she's our daughter.'

Taking that as permission, Tanner tentatively slipped out the first photograph he'd printed out. It was of an unpretentious gold-chain necklace.

A defiant smile flickered at the corners of the wife's mouth.

'It does not belong to her,' she replied, her accent thick, the tone defiant.

'And this?' Tanner continued, placing another piece of A4 paper over the top, this one picturing an unremarkable gold bangle.

'No,' the wife replied, shaking her head.

Tanner removed the two images to place back into his file. The way they were watching him do so, he could tell that they were desperately hoping he'd finished, meaning that the girl could not have been their daughter.

Taking in a breath, Tanner brought out the final image he'd printed out to slide gently over the table towards them.

'We found this on her as well,' he said, unwilling to say what it was.

Both parents stared down at the image picturing the tri-circular tattoo that had been found on the upper part of the dead girl's thigh.

There was no immediate response from either of them. They both just stared down at it, their eyes still and unblinking.

After a moment of harrowing silence, the wife lifted her hand to begin running her delicate fingers over the image, as if stroking the skin that was pictured. As she did, from the depths of her throat came a single word, spoken with such subdued reverence, Tanner was barely able to make it out.

'Anya.'

Speaking her daughter's name must have burst the dam that had been holding back her emotions. As her voice roared like thunder, torrents of tears began falling from her eyes to the table below, like rain from a fast-approaching storm.

- CHAPTER THIRTY ONE -

LEAVING THE PARENTS to spend a few minutes alone together, Tanner let Cooper know that they had a probable identity for the girl, and to arrange for either Vicky, Jenny or Sally to start looking into her life, with a focus on finding out where Zara Haddad lived. Their daughter may not have wanted to confide in her parents about where she was really going the night she went missing, but hopefully she would have told one of her friends.

He then headed for the kitchen, to make them a cup of tea.

'Can you tell me what she was like?' he asked quietly, after waiting for them to take a tentative sip from the mugs he'd presented them with.

'She was everything you could ask for,' the husband replied, parental pride ringing out in his voice. 'Kind, intelligent, attentive, dutiful.' His voice fell away as he stared vacantly down at the mug cradled in his hands.

'You said she had a friend, Zara Haddad. Does she live nearby?

'Just down the road.'

'How long had they known each other?'

'Since we first moved here. They met at school.'

'You mentioned she had some other friends.'

'There is another girl, but I can't remember her

name.'

Tanner deliberately paused for a moment. 'Have you ever heard her mention the name Carter?'

'Carter?' the husband repeated.

'Roy Carter?' Tanner replied.

'No! No boys! We told you before, Mr Tanner, she didn't have any boyfriends.'

'But she must have known some, from school, perhaps?'

'Not in that way.'

'Did she have any interests, outside of school, like cooking, or art?'

'She liked to read.'

'What sort of thing?'

'Classical fiction, mainly.'

'Romance?'

'Her favourite authors were Jane Austen and the Bronte Sisters.'

Tanner paused for a moment before deciding to change the direction of the conversation. 'The tattoo I showed you a picture of. Do you know anything about that?'

'It was a mistake.'

'A mistake?'

'One of her friends persuaded her to have it done. They told her it was only temporary; that it would wash off.'

Tanner raised a curious eyebrow, seriously questioning whether she could really have been that naive.

'Do you know if it signifies anything?' he continued, returning to his notes.

'As I said, it was just a foolish mistake, nothing more.'

'And do you know which one of her friends it was who "persuaded" her to have it done?'

'We don't.'

'But you did ask her, though?'

'We did,' the husband answered, glancing down.

Tanner moved his attention over to the wife, where he found the same look of regret he'd seen reflected in her husband's eyes.

It was becoming clear to Tanner that the picture they'd been endeavouring to paint, one of unified domestic bliss, where their daughter was the perfect child who'd been happy to spend her evenings at home, doting on her parents whilst her mind focussed on schoolwork and reading romantic fiction, was more likely to have been filled with the same bouts of furious arguments that tore through the fabric of most teenage family homes.

With the sense that their daughter had probably been leading an almost separate life, one which her parents probably had very little knowledge about, Tanner decided it was time to wind the interview up.

'Mr and Mrs Chadha, I'd like to thank you for coming in to see us today. We do have one or two things we'd like to ask of you before you leave, some of which will, on the surface, seem unnecessary. Firstly, I'd like to ask if one of you would be willing to help us to formally identify the body?'

Having deliberately directed the question at the husband, Tanner waited for some sort of a response.

Seeing him nod, albeit with obvious reluctance, he continued.

'Thank you. We'll also need to take a statement from you both, just so we know your whereabouts during the last few days.'

With neither responding, Tanner finished by adding, 'We'll also need to take fingerprints and DNA samples from you, as well as to arrange a suitable time for a police forensics unit to pay a visit to your home.'

- CHAPTER THIRTY TWO -

BACK IN THE main office, Tanner made a bee-line for the cluster of desks beneath the whiteboard, where he could see Cooper, Vicky and Sally all working quietly together.

'How've you been getting on with that extension request?' he asked Cooper, catching his eye.

'Just finishing it off now. How'd it go with the parents?'

'More interesting than I was expecting. I've asked Taylor to get a statement from them, along with the normal prints and DNA. I also want forensics to give their house the quick once over. Sally, can you organise that for me?'

'Of course,' replied the attractive young detective constable, batting her eyelids at him as was her custom. 'Are they looking for anything in particular?'

'Their daughter's blood,' came Tanner's stark response.

Vicky spun her chair around to face him. 'Do you think they may have killed her?'

'At this stage, I'd say that it's a distinct possibility, certainly not one I'm prepared to rule out. They were in there trying to make out like they'd spent the last few months playing Happy Families together, when I suspect the reality was anything but. If they did spend their time arguing, a fight could easily have got out of hand.'

'But – I thought the ME said the cause of death was from being hanged by the neck?'

'He also said she'd been hit over the head beforehand. Maybe they thought she was dead and decided to take her down to Horsey Mere, to make it look like she'd hanged herself, only to find out that she was still alive, just as they were hauling her up.'

'Jesus!' stated Vicky, staring up. 'Can you imagine if they had?'

'I'd prefer not to, but unfortunately, it's part of the job, which reminds me. Sally, when forensics go down there, can you make sure they examine their clothes for rope fibres, and check their shoes, to see if either of them had been anywhere near where her body was found. Oh, and get them to have a look for the girl's missing clothes, her shoes as well.'

With a click of his mouse, Cooper glanced up to announce, 'OK, that's Roy Carter's extension request done. Shall I send it off?'

'Not yet,' Tanner replied, checking his watch. 'I want us to get back to interviewing him first. Has anyone had a chance to start a background check on the Chadhas' daughter, Anya?'

'I asked Jenny to request access to her email, phone and social media accounts,' Cooper replied.

Hearing the name of his fiancée, Tanner glanced over to the door leading out to reception to see her huddled behind her desk. 'OK, that's fine. I'll ask her about it later.

'Another job for someone,' Tanner continued, digging out his notebook. 'We need to get hold of a girl called Zara Haddad. She was the person Anya was supposed to be staying with, the night she went missing. Hopefully she'll be able to tell us where she actually went to. We could also do with finding out how she really got on with her parents, and if she knows anything about our very own Roy Carter. Speaking of whom; Cooper, are you ready to head back in?'

- CHAPTER THIRTY THREE-

HAVING AGREED THAT Tanner should take the lead, they re-entered the interview room to find Roy Carter slumped at the table with his solicitor pacing up and down, his hands clasped behind his back.

'About time!' he spat, coming to a halt behind his client's chair.

'Sorry to have kept you,' Tanner apologised. 'We've just been collecting some last-minute evidence.'

His words had the suspect raising a pair of bloodshot eyes up into Tanner's, his freckled forehead creased with concern.

After formally re-starting the interview, Tanner kicked off the proceedings.

'No doubt you'll be pleased to know that we've found out who that girl was, the one discovered hanging by her neck at Horsey Mere, the same one you were so desperate to get a look at, who you said you definitely didn't know, even though you were too far away to see her face.'

Carter shrugged back a response, before staring down at his scrawny white hands clenched together on the table in front of him.

'Aren't you curious to know who she was?'

'Why should I be?'

'Her name was Anya Chadha.'

Tanner watched the youth's face for any sign that

the name had registered with him, but there was none, at least not one he could see.

'Are you sure you didn't know her?'

'I said so, didn't I.'

'I know, but you've said quite a lot so far, most of which hasn't been true; like denying the fact you threw a brick through that shop window, and that the petrol in the back of your van was in case you ran out, when the vehicle runs on diesel.'

'I never said that.'

'No, you said it was for the lawnmower and strimmer that you sometimes borrow from your dad, before changing your mind to say that you hired them instead.'

'If I couldn't use my dad's,' Carter added.

'Either way, none of that's of any particular importance. What is, however, was the forensics report that came in this morning. It says that the petrol we found in the back of your van is an exact match to the petrol used to burn the shop down.'

'Is that it?' the youth asked, glancing up. 'Is that the so-called "evidence" you were going on about?'

'In part,' Tanner replied, smiling.

'Just cus the petrol I had in the back of my van is the same as what was used to burn down that shop, doesn't mean shit. Loads of people must've bought the same stuff.'

Judging by the triumphant look in his eyes, it was clear that he'd been able to reach that conclusion at some stage since their last session, probably after his solicitor had suggested it.

'Very true,' Tanner agreed, 'but it does make it that much more likely that it was you who'd thrown it, being that you've already admitted to having put a brick through the window of the very same shop, just the day before.'

'But it's not much in the way of proof, though, is it.'

'Maybe not, but the petrol wasn't the only thing they discovered inside your van.'

'Let me guess, they also found my signed confession.'

'It actually concerns the girl; Anya Chadha.'

'I keep telling you - I don't know anything about her.'

'So you've said, but if you don't know her, and you've never met, I don't suppose you know how traces of her DNA could have ended up in the passenger seat?'

Any colour that was left in Carter's face drained away to leave a pale pock-marked surface.

'I – I – don't know anything about that.'

'You're saying you didn't know she'd been inside?'

'I – I didn't, no!'

'Fair enough. I suppose it's possible that she broke in one day in an attempt to steal your radio. Or maybe her intention was to take it for a joyride, but changed her mind when she found out what a disgusting state it was in.'

With Carter left searching for something to say in response, Tanner felt free to continue.

'I know! Perhaps you saw her hitchhiking by the side of the road one night and offered her a lift. When you attempted to have your disgusting way with her, she told you where to stick it, which wasn't inside her. So you hit her over the head, tied her up and drove her over to Horsey Mere with the intention of setting fire to her. But when you arrived, you realised you'd run out of petrol, having used it all to burn down that shop, so you decided to hang her by the neck instead. But my favourite theory is that you got so carried away with all the recent stories in the Norfolk Herald, you dragged her down to Horsey Mere to find out if she was a witch by throwing her into the water. When you realised she could swim, you came to the conclusion that she must have been, so you dragged her out, stripped her naked and then hanged her by the neck until dead, maybe with your dad lending a hand.'

'This is stupid!'

'We can bring him down here to ask him, if you like. I'm sure he'd appreciate that, being that he's only just started his campaign to become Norfolk's next MP.'

'Stop!'

'Stop what?'

'I didn't know her!'

'I don't believe you, and neither will a jury, not when you've been charged with vandalism, arson, manslaughter, and first-degree murder, all in the same day.'

'Alright! Alright!'

'And when your dad's standing in the dock beside you under a charge of aiding and abetting.'

'Will you shut up, for Christ sake!'

'I'll be happy to, just as soon as you tell us what Anya Chadha was doing in the passenger seat of your van?'

The room fell silent as the suspect's eyes fell back to rest on his hands.

With still no answer forthcoming, Tanner pulled out his phone. 'I don't suppose anyone's got Nick Carter's phone number, by any chance?'

'I – I was in love with her,' the youth muttered, so quietly, Tanner barely heard what he's said.

'I'm sorry?' he questioned, staring over at Cooper, who looked as surprised as he was.

'You heard.'

'You're trying to tell me that you two were going out with each other?'

'*Did I say that?*' the youth snapped; tears stinging his eyes.

Tanner was once again taken aback by his response.

'I thought you didn't like foreign-types?'

'Do you think I wanted to fall in love with her?'

'You're saying you didn't?'

'Of course I bloody didn't. I hated the fucking bitch.'

'But − you just said you were in love with her,' commented Tanner, struggling to make sense of what he was saying.

'Anya Chadera, or whatever her stupid name was; she was a witch.'

Tanner and Cooper both looked over at him. Even his solicitor was giving him a sideways glance.

Seeing the way everyone was staring, Carter laid his hands flat on the table. 'I wouldn't joke about som'ing like that.'

'Er, I'm fairly sure she wasn't a witch, at least not in traditional terms. But even if she was, I fail to see the relevance.'

'Don't you get it?'

'Frankly no, I don't.'

'The bitch cast a spell on me.'

'She cast a *spell* on you?'

'Her and her friends.'

'Please tell me you're not being serious?'

'One minute I hated her, the next I couldn't stop thinking about her. I couldn't sleep, I could barely eat. All I wanted to do was to be with her, doting on her every bloody word whilst she used me as some sort of free taxi service. It was as if I was possessed. That's why I petrol bombed that shop.'

'So, you admit it?'

'I had no choice. They were crawling around inside my brain. I had to get them out. It was the only way to shut them up.'

'But – that wasn't Anya's shop?'

'They told me that was where they met. They called it their coven. So I set the place on fire, to burn them all to Hell.'

- CHAPTER THIRTY FOUR -

THE ROOM FELL silent as Tanner, Cooper and the attending solicitor all took a moment to take in what Carter had openly confessed to; deliberately setting fire to a shop with the intention of killing all those inside. Tanner knew that the fact the owner's mother hadn't survived meant such an act would come with a charge of first-degree murder, even if she hadn't been the intended victim.

'Would it be possible for me to have a quiet word with you outside?' the solicitor asked, catching Tanner's eye.

Judging by the look of anxiety etched over his face, together with the conspiratorial tone of his voice, he'd clearly reached the same conclusion, and was looking to strike some sort of an early deal.

'By all means,' Tanner replied, pushing his chair back to stand. He was keen to take a break anyway, to give him a chance to decide how best to proceed.

With the interview suspended, Tanner propped himself up against a wall in the corridor, waiting to hear what the solicitor had to propose.

'On the basis of what my client has just confessed to, I'm going to have to insist that he undergoes a full psychological examination before you can take this any further.'

'Er, I'm sorry,' Tanner laughed, 'but that isn't

going to happen.'

'But you have to agree that he's not of sound mind. Not even close. Certainly not when he threw that petrol bomb. I mean, the guy believes a coven of witches cast a love spell on him, of all things.'

'So he says, but unfortunately, he hardly has a track record of telling the truth.'

'Which is why we need an expert's opinion.'

'Well, OK, but not until I've finished interviewing him.'

'I'm sorry, but I can't allow my client to sit there confessing to every major crime that's ever-taken place in Norfolk, when it's abundantly clear that he's a sandwich short of a picnic.'

'That's a legal term, is it?'

'You know what I mean.'

Tanner glanced down at his watch. 'Tell you what, we've only got another half an hour before we have to either charge him or release him. After that, you can do what you like.'

'You do know that you're wasting your time, don't you?'

'I'm not sure I do.'

'The minute a psychologist diagnosis him as being insane, whatever he's said in there will be inadmissible.'

'That's not true, and you know it.'

'His defence solicitor will easily be able to argue that his poor mental health meant that anything he confessed to couldn't have been the product of either his free will or rational intellect, nor could he have been aware of his legal right against self-incrimination.'

'That may be presented as an argument, but it doesn't mean a court would be swayed. He'd first have to be diagnosed as being mentally ill. At the moment, I'm far from convinced. Personally, I think he made up the whole thing just to give him an excuse for having petrol bombed that shop.'

'Then I'd at least like to have time to counsel him, before you go any further.'

'Presumably to advise him to keep his mouth shut.'

'As is his right.'

'Very well,' Tanner sighed. 'You've got as long as it takes me to make myself a coffee.'

- CHAPTER THIRTY FIVE -

DESPERATE FOR A coffee, Tanner arrived in the kitchen to find that not only was the carafe empty, but there was no more left in the cupboard for him to make himself anymore. Left with the choice of either an instant or a cup of tea, shuddering at the thought of both, he made his way out to reception to take a look in the storage cupboard located along a narrow corridor near the back of the building.

Turning in, he nearly walked straight into PS Taylor, escorting Mr and Mrs Chadha out to the carpark at the back. A bout of social awkwardness had him smiling around at them all to ask, 'Are you all done?'

'They've provided fingerprints, DNA samples and a statement, sir.'

Mr Chadha made a point of catching Tanner's eye. 'There was actually something we forgot to mention, Inspector, when you were talking to us before.'

Tanner found himself glancing down at his watch. With the progress they'd been making with Roy Carter, he was convinced they'd found their man. If what they had to tell him was to add to the evidence, so much the better, but if it wasn't, they'd simply be wasting his time. And with less than half an hour to go before they had to charge him, he didn't have much of it to waste.

'Is it not in your statement?'

'We weren't sure if it was relevant.'

'But you feel you need to tell me now?'

'We thought it might be important.'

Realising he was wasting time by just having the discussion, Tanner asked them to continue.

'It was the evening Anya went missing,' the husband began. 'We were sitting watching the TV together when she suddenly got up to announce that she was going out.'

Tanner waited for him to continue; one hand wrapped around his watch in an effort to highlight the fact that he didn't have very long.

'Was that it?' he eventually asked.

'Then she fainted.'

Struggling to see how either could have been relevant, he was about to tell them to give any information they had to Taylor when he heard the man continue.

'She fell over backwards, hitting her head on the coffee table.'

Tanner's mind stopped dead in its tracks.

'She hit her head?' he repeated, staring.

The husband nodded.

With Tanner wondering if the only reason they'd decided to mention this was because they knew a team of police forensics officers were about to descend down on their house, he thought for a moment before asking, 'Was she hurt?'

'She was bleeding a little.'

'And yet she still went out?'

'She said she felt OK.'

'Right,' Tanner replied, his tone overflowing with scepticism.

'To be honest,' the man continued, 'at the time we were more concerned as to why she'd fainted.'

With the growing suspicion that she hadn't done anything of the sort, and that they'd come up with the story to help explain what forensics were going to find, Tanner decided to play along.

'Had she ever done so before?'

'Not that we know of.'

'Maybe it was because she stood up too quickly. I understand that's often the cause.'

'That's what we thought, which made us wonder why she had. She wouldn't normally announce that she was going out like that, not after we'd settled down to watch TV together, and never so late, either.'

Curious to know where they were going with this, Tanner postulated, 'Maybe a friend messaged her, asking her to come out?'

'Her phone was in the kitchen.'

'OK. So...what was on TV?'

The man sent his wife a questioning look. 'It must have been the news.'

'It was the election,' the lady replied, with an affirming nod.

'I think it was,' the husband agreed. 'They'd just announced the by-election and were interviewing one of the candidates.'

With the realisation that the subject matter had swung all the way back to where the investigation had started, Tanner's eyes narrowed with curious intrigue.

'I don't suppose you can remember which candidate in particular?'

'I'm sorry, I can't.'

'So you're telling me that you were watching the news, about the by-election, when they started to interview one of the candidates, at which point your daughter suddenly got up, saying she had to go out?'

'And then she fainted,' added the husband, 'falling

backwards, onto the table.'

- CHAPTER THIRTY SIX -

TANNER'S MIND WAS a tangled mess of thoughts and ideas as he stood watching Mr and Mrs Chadha being led out through the station's discreet rear exit. At that moment in time he was unable to decide if their story was simply to provide them with a perfectly innocent excuse for what they knew forensics would find; traces of their daughter's blood on their living room floor, or if it had been genuine, and that something on the news had caused their daughter to faint before hurrying out the door, never to be seen alive again.

He stared down at his watch.

'Shit!' he cursed. It was already gone twenty-past. He now had less than ten minutes to decide what they were going to charge Roy Carter with.

Forgoing the coffee, he spun around, heading back towards the main office.

As he pushed his way through the double doors he saw Cooper charging towards him, his face flush with anger.

'Where the hell have you been?' the young DI demanded.

'I beg your pardon?' Tanner questioned, his temper flaring. Rarely had he been spoken to in such a disrespectful manner by a fellow officer, certainly not in the middle of the office.

'Roy Carter's walked!'

'What?'

'His solicitor just led him straight out the front door.'

'That can't be!' Tanner exclaimed, staring down at his watch. 'We've still got another ten minutes.'

'We only had until twenty-past.'

'You said half-past.'

'I said twenty-past!' Cooper yelled. 'And where were you, anyway? I've been looking bloody everywhere?'

'I was out the back, trying to find some more coffee, when I bumped into Mr and Mrs Chadha on their way out, and I'd appreciate it if you didn't speak to me in such a disparaging manner.'

'Why the hell shouldn't I? It's not as if you're my superior anymore.'

Cooper was right of course, and it took Tanner a good second to think of a suitable rebuttal. 'But I am the SIO!'

'You're right, you are,' Cooper sneered, 'but only because you told Forrester that I wasn't up for the job.'

'I never said that.'

'And now you've just let our prime suspect walk right out the front door.'

'You said we had until half-past,' Tanner raged, furious at being blamed for something that he honestly didn't think was his fault, especially by someone barely old enough to tie his own shoelaces.

'I told you what time he was due to be released, something you should have known for yourself, being that it's written as clear as day in the arrest report.'

With the two DIs yelling at each other in the middle of the open-planned workspace, it was only a matter of time before DCI Forrester came charging out of his office.

'What the hell's going on here?' he bellowed, the floor shaking as his vast physical mass stormed its way over the floor towards them.

'Tanner let Roy Carter walk, sir,' stated Cooper, stepping to one side to allow the DCI to face his fellow DI.

'You did what?'

'I did no such thing,' Tanner replied, baring his teeth at Cooper. 'There was simply a mix up with the time. I thought we had until half-past to charge him.'

'Didn't you check the arrest report?'

'Cooper told me it was half past, sir.'

'I did no such thing,' Cooper denied, staring over at Forrester. 'I was trying to find Tanner, to tell him that the suspect was about to go free, but apparently he was out the back, looking for coffee.'

Tanner was teetering on the edge of completely losing it. 'I was speaking with Mr and Mrs Chadha,' he seethed, 'as they were leaving through the back door.'

'Whilst Roy Tanner was walking out the front,' Cooper jibed.

'They had something to tell me, about the night their daughter went missing, which I believe could be vital to this investigation.'

Forrester took a moment to scowl over at them, before growling under his breath, 'Right, I want you two in my office, now!'

- CHAPTER THIRTY SEVEN -

FORRESTER STOOD BEHIND his desk, waiting for Cooper to close the door before starting.

'I suppose one of you had better let me know how you'd been getting on with Roy Carter, *before* he was allowed to walk out the front door?'

With Forrester's eyes resting on Tanner, the more senior of the two felt obliged to reply.

'He'd just admitted to having thrown the petrol bomb at the shop, sir, and that he knew Anya Chadha.'

'Who's Anya Chadha?'

'We believe she's the girl found at Horsey Mere, sir. Her parents came in earlier, saying their daughter is missing. They recognised the tattoo on her hip.'

'Christ!'

Forrester sank slowly down into his chair.

'I assume Roy Carter was still denying any involvement?'

'I was about to discuss that with him when the solicitor asked to have a word in the corridor.'

'About what?'

'He was demanding that his client be given a psychiatric evaluation before continuing.'

'Why on earth would he ask that?'

'It was because of the motive Carter had given for having petrol bombed the shop.'

'Go on.'

'Well,' began Tanner, with a degree of trepidation, 'he said he thought Anya Chadha was a witch, sir, and that her and her friends had cast a spell on him.'

'I see,' Forrester replied, still scowling. 'And he managed to say that with a straight face, did he?'

'He did come across as being surprisingly sincere.'

'So I suppose it was a witch's spell which made him throw the petrol bomb?'

'Not exactly, sir, no. He said the spell was to make him fall in love with her.'

'I don't think women need to cast spells on men to make them fall in love with them. A bit of makeup and a short skirt normally does the trick.'

A fleeting smirk lifted the DCI's face, before reverting to his previous scowl.

'But it doesn't explain why he petrol bombed the shop though, does it!'

'Carter went on to say that he thought Anya had been using the shop as what he called a "coven", sir, as that's where she'd meet with her friends. He said that burning it down would break the spell.'

'Then I think his solicitor was right. The guy *is* in desperate need of psychiatric help.'

'Yes, sir,' Tanner agreed, feeling able to relax his stance a little.

'Unfortunately for you, Tanner, that only means you've gone and let a dangerous psychopathic lunatic walk out the building scot-free!'

'Then we're just going to have to re-arrest him, sir.'

'Oh yes, of course. Silly me. Why didn't I think of that?'

Tanner knew what was coming next.

'Oh, hang on. I remember now,' Forrester continued, his words dripping with condescending sarcasm. 'Because somebody's going to have to find some *new* evidence before being able to do so!'

The room fell into an awkward silence.

'So, Tanner? What've you got?'

'As in new evidence, sir?'

'That's right,' the DCI confirmed, locking his sausage-shaped arms over his barrel-like chest.

'Well, sir, nothing yet, but...'

'Then how the hell are you going to re-arrest him?' Forrester yelled back, with such vehement fury that the windowpane rattled in its frame.

With no answer, Tanner made the sensible choice to remain silent.

'I suppose that also means he's likely to have been the one who strung her up?'

'I'm not so sure about that.'

'Oh, really, and why's that, may I ask?'

'It was what I was talking to Mr and Mrs Chadha about, sir.'

'Then you'd better enlighten me, hadn't you.'

'The night their daughter disappeared, they told me that they were all watching the news together when she suddenly got up to say that she had to go out.'

'Is that it?'

'They said that she then fainted, sir, falling back to hit her head on the coffee table.'

Forrester steepled his fingers together.

'So, you think they may have had a domestic, ending up with her dead?'

'There's more, sir. I went on to ask them why they thought she'd suddenly announced that she had to go out, given the lateness of the hour. It turns out they were watching the news, just after the by-election had been announced. Apparently, one of the candidates was being interviewed. That's when she suddenly stood up and fainted.'

'Do you think they could be telling the truth?'

'I don't know, sir, but I've asked for a team of forensics to head down to their house. If we can find evidence that they've been to Horsey Mere recently, then I think it may well have been a domestic argument that got out of hand, which they then attempted to cover up. If not, then perhaps their story is true; that there was something their daughter either saw or heard on the news that made her react in such a way.'

'Did they say which candidate was being interviewed when their daughter fainted?'

'They said they couldn't remember.'

Forrester thought for a moment.

'Where are we with the by-election candidates?'

'We're still digging into the Drummonds. As you know, we're particularly interested in having a look at their finances, but we've been unable to gain access, thanks to the private equity firm they use who are still refusing to release records without a court order.'

'I take it you're in the process of acquiring one?'

'We are.'

'How about Susan Sutton?

'We're still waiting to hear back from forensics, but at the moment she's at the bottom of the list, being that she seems to lack any sort of a sensible motive.'

'So that leaves our BNU candidate, Nick Carter, the person who just happens to be the father of the boy you allowed to walk out the door, the one who believes he's had a love spell cast on him which he's confessed to ridding himself of by burning down the shop he says they used as a coven. Tell me, Tanner, don't you think the fact that one is the father of the other is a little bit too much of a coincidence for us to continue to ignore?'

When put like that, Tanner knew he was right.

'Maybe we should bring Nick Carter in for

questioning?' suggested Tanner.

'With zero evidence that he's been involved in any of this?'

'Maybe not for the murder of Anya Chadha, but we do have that picture we found of him shaking hands with Patrick Hopkins, when he'd denied having ever met the man.'

'Jesus Christ, Tanner, is that really the best you can do?'

'It's a start, sir.'

'Is it?'

'Well...' Without simply repeating what he'd just said, Tanner closed his mouth.

Forrester allowed the room to fall into a sterile silence.

'I'm afraid I think that you're going to have to approach this from a completely new angle.'

'I'm happy to hear any suggestions, sir.'

'How about focussing your efforts on what *actually* seems to be connecting everything together?'

'I thought we were, sir, which is why we've been looking into motives surrounding the by-election.'

'I meant witchcraft, Tanner.'

With Tanner left looking unusually perplexed, Forester continued.

'Patrick Hopkins was found hanging over a five-pointed star, surrounded by glass jars containing parts of his body, all in an apparent effort to ward off some four hundred-year-old witch's curse. Roy Carter says he'd burnt down a shop that he thought was being used as a witches' coven in order to rid himself of an unrequited love spell, and Anya Chadha was found hanging by the neck above the grave of a 17th Century witch, after she'd been half-drowned, possibly in an attempt to find out if she was one as well.'

'I see what you're saying, sir, but I'm not sure how it helps.'

'How about having a word with the owner of that new age spiritualist shop, the one Roy Carter set fire to?'

'We've already spoken to her.'

'That was before Carter said Anya Chadha had been using it as a coven.'

'But, surely, sir, his real reason for setting fire to it was because it was full of foreigners, not witches.'

'It's also where Patrick Hopkins bought those glass balls wasn't it, and the book, which was why you went down there in the first place? And wasn't there something about the owner having a daughter?'

'She does, sir, yes,' Tanner replied, kicking himself for having forgotten.

'But I don't remember hearing anything about you having interviewed her.'

'We did ask her to give us a call.'

'And did she?'

'Not that I'm aware of.'

'Well, there you are then.'

Taking that as his cue to leave, Tanner turned to head out as Cooper cleared his throat.

'What about me, sir?'

Forrester took him in for a moment.

'I take it you don't want to go with Tanner?'

'Well, I'd, er...'

'No? Well, fair enough. Then I suggest you keep plugging away at the by-election candidates. We still need access to the Drummond's finances. We also need to know if there's any connection between Nick Carter and Patrick Hopkins, other than a picture of them shaking hands together. You never know, doing so may also help to unearth the new evidence we seem

to have found ourselves in desperate need of
regarding that love-struck psychotic son of his.'

- CHAPTER THIRTY EIGHT -

FTER THE MEETING, having looked up the name and location of the hotel where Janna Matar and her daughter had been put up by their insurance company, Tanner and Jenny jumped into the XJS to make their way over.

'Nadira Matar?' questioned Tanner, outside their hotel room about half an hour later.

He was staring into the dreamy brown eyes of the pretty young lady who was peering out at them through a half-open door.

'I am,' she confirmed, eyeing them both with suspicion before studying the IDs they pulled out to show her.

'Detective Inspector Tanner and Detective Sergeant Evans, Norfolk Police. I don't suppose your mother is in?'

'I'm afraid she's in bed.'

'Oh dear. I hope she's OK?'

'She still hasn't recovered from the fire, at least not fully.'

'Of course. We were actually there at the time. Before as well, when the window was smashed. Do you think she'd mind if we came in? We won't stay long.'

'I'm not sure.'

'We'd like to talk to you as well; if that's OK?'

The girl thought for a moment.

'I'd better let her know you're here. If you could wait there.'

A minute later, they were being shown through to an untidy room dominated by a large double bed inside which sat the owner of Tarragon, the new age spiritualist shop that had been burnt down, her unmade up face looking haggard and grey.

'Mrs Matar, we're sorry for intruding like this.'

'That's quite alright,' she replied. 'It's not as if I have anything better to do.'

'First of all, may we express our deepest condolences for the loss of your mother.'

'That's kind of you.'

Unsure how best to continue, Tanner thought for a moment before asking, 'How're you bearing up?'

'I probably look worse than I feel.'

'You look fine,' he lied, adding a reassuring smile. 'I hope your insurance company is taking good care of you?'

'Thankfully, yes.'

'And the shop?'

'Fortunately, we were only renting. We're having a look for somewhere else now, but I assume this isn't a social call?'

'We actually wanted to ask, both yourself and Nadira, if either of you know a young lady by the name of Anya Chadha?'

The mother glanced up at her daughter, standing by her side.

'I know her,' the daughter replied, with a quizzical look.

'Then I'm afraid we have some very sad news for you.'

'Why? What's happened?' she demanded; her voice tightening with anxiety.

'I'm afraid to say that her body was found yesterday.'

'Her...body?'

Tanner nodded.

'You mean...?'

'I'm afraid so.'

Lifting her hands to cover her mouth, Nadira sank slowly down to a chair positioned at the side of the bed.

Tanner allowed a moment of silence to follow.

'Did you know her well?' he eventually asked, keeping his voice respectfully low.

She nodded back a response.

'And you, Mrs Matar?'

'Only through Nadira. Was she the girl – the one they said had been found at Horsey Mere?'

'She was,' Tanner confirmed.

'How did she...? The papers didn't say.'

'We believe someone deliberately took her life.'

Tanner allowed the news to sink in for a moment before continuing.

'Do either of you know anyone who may have wished her harm?'

'I don't,' the mother replied, glancing over at her daughter.

'Miss Matar?' prompted Tanner.

'Nobody,' she mumbled, her voice barely audible.

'A name's been brought to our attention who we believe may have had something to do with it. I don't suppose you've ever heard of someone called Roy Carter?'

Tanner saw an unmistakable flash of recognition in the daughter's face.

'Do you know him?'

Instead of answering, she stared down at the floor.

'Darling, the policeman's asking you a question,'

the mother prompted.

Nadira's eyes flickered momentarily up at Tanner's.

'From school,' she eventually replied.

'Can you tell me what he was like?'

'Not very nice.'

'Did he bully you?'

'Something like that.'

'Did he do anything else?'

She shook her head. 'He'd just say stuff, you know, racial stuff.'

'He didn't...touch you, or anything?'

'Nothing like that, no.'

'What about Anya. Was she at the same school?'

Nadira nodded.

'Did he do anything to her?'

'Only the same.'

'What about after you left? Had either of you seen him since?'

The girl shrugged. 'It's not a very big place.'

'I take it that means you have?'

She shrugged again; her attention still directed down towards the carpet.

'Has he done anything to you since leaving school?'

There was no reply.

'Miss Matar?' Tanner prodded.

'Not to me,' she eventually replied.

'But he did do something to Anya?'

Nadira hesitated, her eyes glancing briefly over towards her mother.

'If he did something to Anya, darling, then you have to tell him.'

'It was a few weeks ago,' she eventually continued. 'We were at a friend's house for a sleepover; when her parents were away.'

'Who was the friend?'

'Zara.'

'Zara Haddad?' queried Tanner, glancing over at Jenny.

The girl nodded.

'Go on.'

'It was late when we heard a knock at the door. Zara opened it to find Roy Carter standing outside with some of his friends. When she asked what they wanted, they all barged in and started to break the place up.'

'Did you call the police?'

'We didn't have a chance. We were too busy trying to stop them.'

'OK, so what happened then?'

'Anya got hurt.'

'In what way?'

'Roy hit her.'

'Was she alright?'

'Just about. I don't think he used his fist. Then they fell about laughing, calling us names, like they always did.'

'And then?'

'Then they left.'

'And that was it?'

'We tidied the place up, as best we could, and went to bed.'

'Nothing else happened?'

She shook her head.

Tanner thought for a moment.

'When did you see him again?'

'I haven't.'

'What about Anya?'

'I've no idea.'

'So you don't know if Anya saw Roy Carter after that?'

She shrugged back a response.

'I suppose that means you don't have any idea what she may have been doing in the passenger seat of his van?'

Nadira's face flushed with blood.

'Shall I tell you what Roy Carter told us?'

'You've spoken to him?' she asked, glancing up.

'We arrested him yesterday. He admitted to throwing the brick through your shop window, and for having set fire to it as well. But it was the reason he gave us for having done so that made us decide to come over to see you.'

He watched as Nadira exchanged an anxious glance between himself and her mother.

'He told us that you and your friends had cast a spell on him.'

Tanner saw Nadira's mother turn to scowl silently over at her daughter.

'He said it was a love spell,' Tanner continued, taking in the mother's reaction. 'I don't suppose you know anything about that?'

'Oh, I'm sure my daughter wouldn't do something so stupid,' the mother replied. 'She knows all too well how dangerous such things can be, don't you, darling?'

'We only did it for a joke,' Nadira muttered, her voice barely audible. 'We didn't think it would actually work.'

'You're saying you *did* cast a spell on him?' questioned Tanner, exchanging a curious glance with Jenny.

The girl nodded.

'And you think it worked?' Tanner continued; his voice filled with sceptical incredulity.

'The next morning he came round looking for Anya. He said how sorry he was for having hurt her.

He then asked her out for a drink. When she said she'd think about it, he started offering to do things for her. That's when he began driving her around.'

As Nadira had been talking, it was clear that her mother was becoming increasingly agitated.

'Just how many times have I told you never to use magic for your personal amusement?' she eventually demanded.

'I'm sorry, mum. It was just a bit of fun. Besides, it didn't do any harm.'

'You stupid girl. Grandma Kayla is *dead* because of your "bit of fun"!'

With Nadira's face trembling as tears began falling from her eyes, Tanner couldn't help but feel sorry for her.

'I'm sure your daughter's so-called "spell" was in no way responsible for the actions of Roy Carter, Mrs Matar. He's had a long history of racially motivated anti-social behaviour.'

'What the hell do you know?' the mother spat; her anger bearing down on Tanner.

Tanner opened and closed his mouth, completely taken aback by her furious response.

'You've got no idea what we're talking about,' the woman continued. 'The power of Nature's law goes far beyond the realms of your narrow little policeman's mind. Even someone like you must know that every action has an equal and opposite reaction? My daughter certainly should!'

'Mrs Matar, I hate to burst your bubble, but magic and spells; they're not real.'

'I see, so perhaps you can tell me what is?'

'I'm sorry?' he asked, unused to having suspects throw questions at him, especially in such an openly philosophical vein.

'You just said magic and spells aren't real, so I'm

asking you what you think is?'

'I'm not having this discussion with you, Mrs Matar.'

'Because you don't know!'

Unable to stop himself rising to the bait, Tanner blurted out, 'What you can *see* is real.'

'You can't see a sound, Mr Tanner, but I assume you still think it's real.'

'You don't *see* sounds, Mrs Matar, you hear them.'

'So I suppose you'd say the same thing about air. Because you can feel it on your face, you know it's there, even though you can't see it.'

'Of course.'

'What about love?'

'Love?'

'Yes, love, Mr Tanner. Is that real?'

'That's different.'

'So, it's not then?'

'Not in the same way, no.'

'And why's that?'

'Because it's just a feeling.'

'Have you told your colleague that?'

'I'm sorry?'

'Miss Evans,' the lady continued, looking over at Jenny. 'Does she know that your love for her isn't real; that it's just a feeling?'

Tanner could feel Jenny's eyes boring into the side of his face, waiting for him to declare, right there and then, that his love for her was most definitely real.

'Anyway,' she continued, returning her attention back to her daughter, 'whether you believe it or not is irrelevant. The love spell Nadira and her friends cast will turn to hate, just as surely as night follows day. I fear the petrol bomb was just the start. I think you will find that it was Roy Carter who murdered Anya. I suppose we can at least be grateful that you were able to arrest him before he had a chance to do anything else.'

'Er...,' began Tanner, doing his best to digest the words she'd been saying, '...unfortunately, we had to release him.'

Mrs Matar shot him a look of panicked disbelief.

'What did you say?'

'We had to release him,' Tanner repeated.

'But – I thought you said he'd confessed to having burnt down my shop?'

'He did,' Tanner replied, wondering how he was going to be able to explain to her that the only reason Carter had been allowed to walk out the door was because he himself had lost track of the time. 'There was a legal technicality that his solicitor was able to take advantage of.'

'Then you're just going to have to arrest him again, aren't you?'

'Until we're able to find some new evidence against him, we're unable to do so.'

'You're telling me that a man who's admitted to deliberately burning down my shop, killing my mother in the process, who then murdered my daughter's friend, is walking around as free as a bird because of a legal technicality?'

'We don't know if he was responsible for what happened to your daughter's friend.'

'*You* may not, but I do!'

'As much as I may like to, we're unable to charge him with first-degree murder, or anything else for that matter, just because you happen to think he's responsible.'

'I don't think, I know!'

'Right.'

'What steps are you taking to protect my daughter?'

'Do you have any reason to believe she's in danger?'

'Haven't you been listening to a word I've been saying?'

'Yes, but -'

'Unnatural love will always turn to all-consuming hate. That boy's loathing of those who cast the spell will continue to fester and grow. It will only stop when the spell is broken.'

'Assuming what you're saying is true, how can the spell be broken?'

'It can't. Not until either he's dead, or those who cast the spell are.'

- CHAPTER THIRTY NINE -

A LTHOUGH TANNER OBVIOUSLY didn't believe Mrs Matar's story, that the supposed "love spell" her daughter and friends had cast would have turned Roy Carter into a hate-filled psychotic lunatic, one who'd stop at nothing until those responsible were dead, he could hardly rule out the possibility either. As she'd told him the first day they'd met, it wasn't what *he* believed that mattered. From what he'd seen, there was every possibility that Roy Carter was suffering from some form of clinical psychosis. If he really did believe that he'd been bewitched, and the only way to undo the spell was to kill those who'd cast it, then there was little reason to doubt that not only had he murdered Anya Chadha, but he was now planning on killing both Zara Haddad and Mrs Matar's daughter as well.

As soon as they were back inside the car, Tanner put a call through to Forrester.

'Sir, it's Tanner. We've just finished speaking to the shop owner, Janna Matar, as well as her daughter, Nadira.'

'How'd it go?'

'The daughter knows both Anya Chadha and the other girl, Zara Haddad. She also knows Roy Carter, from school, and confirmed what he'd told us, that they'd cast some sort of a spell on him.'

'Not this crap again!'

'It's utter nonsense, I know, however, if Roy Carter is under the impression that he's been bewitched, then I think we may have a problem.'

'In what form, dare I ask?'

'The mother was under the impression that the spell would turn sour, and that it would turn him into a raving psychotic lunatic.'

'I thought we'd already established that he was?'

'One who wouldn't stop until all three girls were dead, that being the only way for him to be released from the spell.'

'That's assuming such a spell could exist, which it can't.'

'Of course, but if Carter's so deranged that he believes it does, then the question of whether or not it's possible to bewitch someone with a love spell becomes largely irrelevant.'

'By what you're saying, I assume you think he's responsible for what happened to Anya Chadha?'

'At the moment, I'm more concerned with what he might try to do to the other girls. Fortunately, Nadira and her mother are relatively safe, as hardly anyone knows where they're staying; but just to be safe, I've asked the hotel's receptionist to change their rooms. I'd also like to request that a PC is stationed outside.'

'Is that really necessary?'

'I suppose that depends on whether we want another dead girl on our hands?'

'OK, well, I'll have to see if we can spare someone.'

'Then we're going to have to put Zara Haddad up in a safe house.'

'I think we'll need to have some sort of evidence that Roy Carter is actually intending to kill her before I'd be able to justify that to HQ.'

'Yes, although in fairness, if we had the evidence, we wouldn't need to, as we'd be able to arrest him.'

'You do realise that you're basing all this on what some holistic shop owner told you, one who would appear to believe in witches and goblins, probably vampires as well.'

'We already know Carter petrol bombed her shop, knowing there were people inside. If he did go on to murder Anya Chadha, then I believe there is every chance that what Mrs Matar said is true; that he's going to continue until all three girls are dead.'

The line fell silent for a moment before Forrester's voice eventually came back.

'Very well. I'll get someone to try and organise something. Meanwhile, I suggest you head over to see this Zara Haddad girl, to let her know what's going on.'

'Yes, sir. We're on our way over there now.'

- CHAPTER FORTY -

'JESUS CHRIST! NOT again!' Tanner raged, as he turned his Jag into the Glenwood Estate, a series of large 1950s council flats where Jenny had directed him.

Ahead they could see a thick plume of dirty grey smoke, rising ominously into the air. But this time it wasn't just a single building that was ablaze, it was an entire five-storey block, right in the middle of about half a dozen others.

Leaving the car nudged up on the pavement, Tanner and Jenny lept out to join a growing number of residents from the surrounding blocks, crowding around the building to gaze helplessly up at the dozens of families steadily emerging out onto the communal balconies, all screaming down for help.

'It's spreading fast,' he commented, staring about. 'Has anyone dialled 999?'

A nearby Asian man nodded. 'About five minutes ago.'

Tanner tried to tune his ears to the sound of an approaching fire engine, but with so many people screaming, he couldn't hear even the faintest sound of one.

'Is there no way for them to get out?' he asked, his question directed at the same man.

'It must have started in the stairwell.'

'Isn't there a fire escape?'

'The stairwell *is* the fire escape.'

'Shit!'

'The only other way down is for them to jump.'

Tanner thought fast.

'Do you know any of the people around here?'

'Most of them. Why?'

'We can't wait for the fire brigade, not if the cladding catches fire. Can you start asking around, to see if anyone's got a ladder? We'll need mattresses as well. As many as possible.'

With the man spreading the word amongst his neighbours, it wasn't long before ladders began being hauled out from garages and mattresses dragged out through doors. When those trapped inside the block saw what was happening, they too began heaving their mattresses out, tossing them out from the balconies to join a growing pile.

Finally hearing the sound of an approaching siren, Tanner worked with the men of the estate to push ladders up against the building's walls, whilst Jenny helped pile mattresses as high and as wide as possible, at the furthest edges of the balconies. With women and children from the first floor beginning to either tentatively take to the ladders, or to hold their breath before leaping down to the awaiting mattresses, as the block's outer cladding began to catch fire, the full horror of what awaited those trapped on the floors above was becoming all too apparent. None of the ladders the residents had could reach beyond the first floor, and the prospect of jumping from the second, some thirty feet up, was making people think twice, let alone from the floors above. For all the men, women and children trapped there, there seemed little hope.

Within what seemed like nothing more than the blink of an eye, the fire had become a raging inferno, leaping from one section of cladding to the next, driving those still trapped on the upper floors towards the farthest ends of the balconies. It wasn't long before those on the second floor must have reached the conclusion that they had no choice, they had to jump. As they scrambled over the railings, some on the floor above began to do the same, falling through the smoke and flames, thankfully landing mostly un-hurt before being dragged clear by those on the ground, allowing others to follow them down.

Although the sound of the siren was growing ever louder, it was nothing compared to how quickly the fire was spreading, as it surged ever higher, heading for the uppermost floors. There, distant faces could be seen staring down, each one no doubt frantically weighing up the risk of either a sixty-plus foot fall, or retreating back inside to pray in desperate hope of being rescued.

It was then everyone began pointing upwards, the women screaming as the men stared on in hopeless agony. Following their gaze, Tanner saw a woman on the very top floor, a baby held out over the side of the building. It was obvious what she was intending to do.

'A bedsheet!' Tanner shouted, catching the eyes of those nearest.

The call soon went up, and within moments, a large white sheet appeared. With no need for direction, a handful of people, Tanner and Jenny included, grabbed hold of its edges, and as a scream from the crowd had them staring up, they pulled it taut, just in time to catch the tiny child, it's face scrunched up as it cried, gasping at the air.

As the baby was carried safely away, the agonising sound of twisting masonry had the crowd staring up again to see a section of burning cladding break loose from its mounting to begin spiralling down towards them.

Grabbing Jenny's hand, Tanner pulled her clear, before hearing the cladding smack hard into the ground behind them as it exploded into a cloud of furious flames and billowing smoke.

The wrenching noise of the building's failing structural integrity was soon joined by the wail of the fire engine, finally turning into the estate. But a quick glance over his shoulder as everyone continued to run told Tanner that they were too late to save those still trapped at the top. Instead of faces he could only see flames, and in the place of tortured futile screams was nothing but the harrowing sound of silence.

- CHAPTER FORTY ONE -

DAYLIGHT FADED INTO night as the firefighters worked tirelessly to bring the fire under control, but it was over two hours before they were able to do so. Even then, the sky above remained filled with smoke, illuminated by shades of orange and red as the fire continued to burn from the very top of the building. Throughout that time, Tanner and Jenny had remained at the scene, transfixed by the agonising sight; unable to fully comprehend the terrifying and truly horrific fate of those trapped on the uppermost floors.

As they began taking statements from the surviving residents, it soon became clear that the young woman they'd hoped to speak with, Miss Zara Haddad, must have been amongst those who'd been lost. Her family's flat was on the very top floor, and there was a degree of certainty that they'd all been at home when the fire had started.

At some point after that, he'd called Forrester to update him. He couldn't remember when, or what he'd said; not exactly, but it had been something along the lines of what had happened, and that they believed the girl they'd hoped to speak to had been lost.

When he eventually saw the firemen rolling up their hoses, their tired angular faces streaked with sweat, Tanner left Jenny to continue taking statements whilst he crept over to the one who seemed to be in charge.

Showing him his identity, Tanner took a breath to ask, 'Were you able to pull anyone out?'

'Nobody alive,' the man replied, his voice reflecting the harrowed look in his eyes.

'Any idea how it started?'

'It wasn't an accident; I know that much.'

'Could it have been a petrol bomb?'

Tanner watched him gaze over at what was left of the building.

'It was some sort of an incendiary device,' he eventually replied. 'And we did find shattered glass at the base of the stairs, but I doubt a petrol bomb alone would have been enough. The fire investigation unit will give you a more detailed picture of what took place and why, but at a guess, I'd say someone poured petrol down the stairwell, starting from the top floor, all the way down to the bottom, before setting fire to it. With the amount of rubbish we found, especially on the landing areas, the use of cheap wooden doors, the total lack of fire alarms in any of the communal areas, and what is now classed as illegal cladding, the building just went up. To be honest, even without the petrol, the place was an accident waiting to happen. And then there's the heavy use of oil-based paint on all the walls, and the fact that there wasn't even a bloody fire escape. They didn't have a chance. We've been warning the council about this estate for months. The whole thing should have been knocked down years ago. At a minimum, it should have been put through a major refurbishment programme.' Taking in the surrounding blocks, he added, 'They all should have. But I guess that would cost too much money. Anyway, sorry, it's been a long day.'

'When will we know what type of petrol was used?'

'I've no idea. You'll probably have to wait for the fire investigation's report.'

'How long will that be?'

'With something like this, it could be months.'

'But you think it was deliberate?'

'Unless someone accidentally kicked an open petrol can all the way down all the steps before dropping a lit cigarette, I'd have to say so.'

As the fireman continued to help his team pack their gear away, Tanner turned to look for Jenny, eventually finding her wandering listlessly between huddled groups of people, scattered about on the circle of grass lying at the heart of the estate.

Replying to the questioning look in her eyes, he shook his head. 'They didn't find anyone.'

'What, nobody?'

'He said someone must have poured petrol down the stairs before setting fire to it. How've you been getting on?'

'I've spoken to a couple of people who said they saw a young lad running out of the block, just before the fire started.'

'Don't tell me; he was wearing a light grey hoodie?'

Jenny gave Tanner a single nod. 'Do you really think Roy Carter could have done this? I mean, he's only just been released.'

'Don't you?' Tanner demanded; his voice edged with fury.

'I suppose,' came Jenny's somewhat hesitant reply.

'Then I suggest we head over to wherever it is that he lives to have a little chat with him.'

Seeing him turn to stomp his way over to the car, Jenny called after, 'Can't it wait till tomorrow?'

'Not if he knows where Nadira is staying.'

'But – he can't, surely?'

Tanner stopped to spin back. 'How do you know?'

'I don't, but – even if he did, we made them change rooms.'

'Do you think that would stop him?' Tanner replied, gesturing over at the smouldering remains.

As much as she didn't want him to be, she knew Tanner was right. He could easily set fire to a hotel in much the same way he had done to the block of flats.

With Tanner storming off again, she had to run to catch up.

'I think we need to speak to Forrester first, before we go.'

'I already did.'

'About going round to see Roy Carter?'

'No, but it's the next obvious move. He'll know that.'

'Then how about we ask for backup? If he's as dangerous as we think he is, I'd be happier if we did.'

'I only want to have a word. I'm not planning on arresting him.'

'But even so.'

Reaching the car, it was only when he dug his keys out to find his hands were shaking that he was able to take a step back from himself. His mind was burning with uncontrollable rage, just as the building had been before. He'd barely be able to drive, let alone interview a suspect with anything close to the necessary dispassionate objectivity.

Seeing Jenny by his side, her eyes filled with heartfelt concern, he forced himself to take in a breath.

'Maybe we should wait until tomorrow?'

A surge of relief lifted the corners of her mouth, before melting away like dew before the morning mist. 'We should,' she agreed, 'but what if you're right? What if he does know where Nadira is staying?'

They both stood there for a moment, wondering what to do, when the muffled sound of Tanner's phone came from inside his crumpled black suit jacket.

Pulling it out to see it was Vicky calling, he stared down at it for a moment, hoping to God it wasn't news that the hotel where Nadira and her mum were staying had been burnt to the ground, with them and all the residents trapped inside.

'Tanner speaking.'

'I just thought you'd be interested to know that there's been a call about an anti-social disturbance on the Rockworth Estate, the one where Roy Carter lives.'

'Is it him, Roy Carter?'

'I don't know. Higgins and Jones have gone down in response. I just thought you might want to tag along?'

'OK, thanks Vicky. We were thinking about going there anyway.'

Ending the call, Tanner held Jenny's eyes.

'Looks like fate's stepped in again.'

'I didn't think you were a believer.'

Tanner shrugged. 'If he's going to give us an excuse to arrest him, I just may well become one.'

- CHAPTER FORTY TWO -

TWENTY MINUTES LATER, Tanner turned his XJS into the notorious Rockworth Estate to see PC Higgins and PC Jones standing on the pavement beside their squad car, its roof lights rotating around in portentous silence. Crowding around them were a group of skinny youths, hands hidden inside pockets, hoodies pulled up over their heads.

Unable to see their faces, Tanner pulled onto the curb to turn the engine off. Stepping out, he made his way over towards them, leaving Jenny searching her handbag for her ID.

As Tanner approached, the group of youths looked up, leaving their faces exposed to a streetlight on the other side of the road.

'What've we got?' he asked, his heart lurching into life as he recognised one of the hooded young men.

Higgins glanced around.

'At the moment; defacing public property, violent disorder, and harassment, but I have the feeling that we're just getting started.'

Tanner caught the eye of the youth he'd recognised. 'Good evening, Mr Carter. Isn't it past your bedtime?'

'Oh great, you again,' the lad bemoaned. 'Are you stalking me or what?'

'The word "stalking" would imply that I *want* to be

within ten feet of you, which I can assure you I don't.'

'Then why don't you and your chums just turn around and fu... hold on,' he stopped, craning his neck to see over Tanner's shoulder, 'who's your girlfriend?'

Tanner followed his eyes to see Jenny approach. 'Ah, yes. Roy Carter, meet DS Evans, one of Norfolk's finest detective sergeants. DS Evans, meet Roy Carter, someone whose life resembles a dog turd that's just been trodden on.'

'You're a funny man,' Carter sneered.

'You should see my stand-up routine.'

As Jenny came to a halt beside Tanner, Carter winked at her. 'All right, love? Fancy a quick one, do you? Just you and me? Your boyfriend can watch, if he likes.'

'Sounds good to me,' Jenny quipped. 'Your place or mine?'

'Blimey!' Carter exclaimed, turning his attention back to Tanner. 'She's a bit game, isn't she?'

'I suspect she's adopting a style of humour known as sarcasm, something that's probably a little beyond your intelligence level.'

'Nah, she's gagging for it. Types like 'er always are.'

'You can come back to my place if you like,' Jenny continued, placing her hand seductively down on her hip, 'but you'd better bring your mates with you, you know, for when you can't get it up. That *is* what everyone says, isn't it?' she asked, staring around at them all.

As Carter squirmed with embarrassed indignation, Tanner took the opportunity to re-join the conversation.

'I don't suppose you've been going around throwing any more petrol bombs recently?'

Looking relieved not to have to come back with a

suitably witty response to Jenny's remark, Carter sneered back at Tanner. 'Not recently, no.'

'But you were at the Glenwood Estate, about two hours ago?'

'Never 'eard of the place.'

'That's funny. Someone matching your description was seen running out of one of the blocks, shortly before the whole place went up in smoke, killing half the residents as it did; men, women, children, all trapped at the top.'

As Tanner spoke, the boy's eyes became increasingly wide as they darted between Tanner and the two uniformed officers.

'No way! No fucking way!'

'I take it that you're denying the fact that you set fire to the place, even though we have two witnesses who've said that they saw you there?'

'You can't pin that on me! I wasn't anywhere near the place! Swear to God!'

'Where were you then?'

'I was here, with me mates,' he replied, staring around at them. 'Wasn't I?'

'That's right, he was, *cunt*stable,' replied one of the taller ones, as the rest nodded in conspiratorial agreement.

'I'm not a constable, you muppet-brained moron, I'm a detective inspector.'

'You's lot all look the same to me. Anyways, it don't change the fact that Roy was 'ere, with us.'

'No doubt you'll all be willing to say that in court?'

'No problem.'

'Even though you'd be risking a seven-year sentence if you're caught lying?'

The lad shrugged.

'At least somebody seems to like you,' Tanner replied, returning his attention to Carter. 'I wonder what your dad would say?'

'Give 'em a call if you like. I've already told him what happened; that you arrested me for no good reason, proved by the fact that you were forced to let me go. You know, if I was you, I'd watch my back. The minute he becomes our next MP, he's gonna make sure you're given the boot, right up your arse.'

'You don't seriously think that your dad's going to win the election, do you?'

'Why not?'

'Er, I don't know, but it's probably got something to do with the fact that he's a xenophobic neo-Nazi, whose political ideology is to simply kick the living shit out of anyone whose skin isn't as pure and white as the driven snow, which is just about everyone in this day and age. Only the most extreme right-wing individual is going to vote for him, which fortunately excludes most normal people. Anyway, even if he did have a chance, which he doesn't, do you really think he'd stand by your side whilst you face a charge of not only first-degree murder, for that girl you strung up at Horsey Mere, but for manslaughter of the old lady at that shop in Stalham as well, something you've already admitted to, and now for the deaths of all those people at the Glenwood Estate. He's going to disown you faster than a paranoid rat deserting a submarine with a hole in it. The minute he finds out you've been charged, he'll probably hold a press conference to say that you're not his son, and that he's never seen you before in his life, just to save face in front of the Norfolk electorate.'

'He wouldn't do that.'

'Er, I think he would, and I reckon you know it as well. He's probably intending to do it anyway, especially if he wins,' Tanner laughed. 'I mean, why would he let his brand-new illustrious career as UK's latest MP be scuppered by a spotty useless twat such as yourself?'

'Cus he's me dad!' the boy declared, tears welling up in his eyes.

'Anyway, we've got more than enough evidence to re-arrest you, probably enough to have you put away for life, or as near to it as it won't make much difference.'

'I fuck'n dare you,' Carter sneered, pulling his hands out of his pockets.

'Mr Roy Carter, I'm arresting you on suspicion of...' Tanner paused mid-sentence to glance over at the two PCs, '...what was it again?'

'Defacing public property, violent disorder, and harassment,' Higgins replied, referring back to his notes.

'That's right. And I think we can add manslaughter and first-degree murder to that as well, don't' you?' Tanner continued, returning his attention back to Carter. 'Of course, you don't have to say anything, but it may harm your defence if you don't mention when questioned something you later rely on in court. Anything you do say may be given in evidence'.

Seeing the two uniformed police officers take an assertive step forward, one levering out a pair of rigid handcuffs from his duty belt, the young lad's face contorted into that of a raging psychotic lunatic. As the blade of a knife appeared at the end of his hand, from the depths of his throat came a taunting scream.

'C'MON ON THEN!'

Both constables took up a nervous defensive stance. Seeing one of them flick out an extendable baton, Tanner knew they had a rapidly escalating situation on their hands, one which he'd gone a long way towards creating. Knowing that neither Jenny nor himself were wearing stab vests, unlike their uniformed colleagues, he called out, 'Don't do anything stupid, Carter. If you get put away for killing a police officer as well, the guards are going to make your life a living hell.'

'My life's already a living hell!' he yelled, tears stabbing at his eyes. 'I can't get them out,' he continued, pressing a hand to the side of his head. 'The voices. They won't shut up. They won't fucking shut up!'

By that stage it was obvious to everyone there, even his mates, that the young man's mind was unravelling, right before their very eyes.

'It's alright, Carter,' Tanner said, his voice softening. 'We can help you.'

'You can help me? You can help me? How? By having me locked-up for the rest of my life?'

'We can make sure you get the right help, but you've got to put the knife down.'

'Yeah, right. I do that and you nick me for som'ing I never did.'

'That's not true. If you put the knife down, we'll get you the help you need. I promise!'

Through his eyes, Tanner could see him wrestling with the idea, one side pleading with the other to give himself up. But when the same eyes turned to fix themselves on Tanner, he knew the more reasoned side had lost.

'Bollocks,' he spat, his skinny body lurching forward, the knife's blade slashing violently at Tanner's side.

Caught completely by surprise, Tanner barely had time to step away before the knife came back again.

Moments before it buried itself into Tanner, Jenny lept to her man's defence, catching Carter's arm as she rammed into him with such force, they both fell hard onto the pavement.

A second later, Carter was back on his feet, leering at the policemen still watching him. As Jenny struggled to get back up, he grinned at them all before spinning around to bound away, his mates taking flight with him to become nothing more than a collection of scattering shadows, disappearing into the darkness of the night.

With the two police constables giving chase, Tanner was about to follow on when he saw Jenny stumble back to the ground, her hand clutching against her side.

'Are you all right?' he asked, taking to a knee.

'I think so,' she replied, her voice cracking with uncertainty. 'The knife. I think it might have caught me a little.'

Peeling her hand away, she held it out for them both to see.

In the estate's yellowing light, her palm seemed to be covered in what looked like nothing more innocuous than engine oil, dripping down from her hand.

Tanner fought against a sudden surge of rising panic.

'You'll be alright,' he said, forcing a smile at her before easing his head forward to take a look at the wound itself.

What he saw only made his heart thunder deep inside his chest.

'Is that blood?' she asked, her mind trying to understand what she was still staring at.

'You've picked up a slight injury,' he replied, hoping she wouldn't see the tears stinging at his eyes. 'Nothing more.'

'It doesn't hurt,' she said, her voice a whisper as her eyes stared vacantly down at her still open hand.

'That's good. If you roll this way slightly, and place

your hand back over the wound, like so,' he said, guiding it down to where her blood was spreading over her clothes with alarming speed, 'then press down hard, I'm going to call for help.'

- CHAPTER FORTY THREE -

I T WAS OVER an hour later, having followed behind the ambulance as it rushed Jenny to Wroxham Medical Centre, that Tanner found himself pacing up and down the reception area for what felt like an eternity. Nobody seemed to have any news for him, and every time he asked he seemed to be either ignored or told to sit down.

Eventually doing as he was told, he was perched on the end of a chair, his head cradled in his hands, when the sound of a voice floated down towards him. Glancing up, he saw a tired-looking middle-aged man in a white lab coat standing beside him, a clipboard in one hand and a pen in the other.

'Detective Inspector Tanner?' the man enquired.

'That's me,' Tanner replied, rising to his feet. 'Do you have any news? Is she alright?'

'My name's Doctor Marland. I understand you're a colleague of the patient?'

'I am, yes, but I'm also her.... Is she OK?'

'For now she is, but the wound is far deeper than we first thought. You wouldn't happen to know how we'd be able to get in touch with a member of her family, her parents for example? The number we have for them doesn't seem to be working.'

'Of course.' Tanner replied. 'I actually need to give them a call myself.' He'd put off telling them what had happened for far longer than he had any right to.

'They moved to a new house, about a year ago,' he explained. 'I've just been waiting to hear some news before doing so.'

'There's no need for you to call them, inspector, unless you want to, of course, but we are going to need their consent.'

'Their *consent*?'

'We're going to have to operate if we're to stem the internal bleeding.'

'Right,' Tanner replied, a section of his mind disengaging itself from the world around him.

'Unfortunately, doing so will mean that there's a high chance we'll lose the baby.'

'The b-baby?' Tanner stuttered, searching the doctor's face.

'Miss Evans is pregnant, inspector,' the doctor replied, in a clinically dispassionate tone. 'I take it you didn't know.'

Tanner stared off towards the corridor he'd seen her being taken down. 'I – I didn't. She hadn't...'

'It's possible she didn't know herself. The foetus is in the very early stages of gestation.'

The reception room fell silent, the only sound coming from a clock marking time against the wall.

'Anyway,' the doctor continued, 'we'll need her parents' consent before we can continue, unless she was married, of course?'

'Not married. Engaged. The wedding is in January.' Returning to look at the doctor, Tanner forced himself to take in a breath. 'I'm her fiancé.'

'Christ!' the doctor declared, staring over at him. 'I'm sorry, I'd no idea.'

'It's my fault. I should have mentioned something about it before.'

The man took a respectful moment, before posing the question he clearly needed an answer to. 'Are *you* willing – to give your consent?'

'Is there any time – to think about it?'

'I'm sorry, there isn't. We need to operate as soon as possible. If we don't, we're going to lose her.'

- CHAPTER FORTY FOUR -

W ITH HIS MIND fast closing down, Tanner signed the consent form that appeared from out of nowhere before watching the doctor turn on his heel to hurry away.

Collapsing back into the chair, he spent a few minutes doing nothing but stare down at the floor. The distant sound of an unanswered phone, ringing out from behind the reception desk, reminded him of Jenny's parents. However much he didn't want to, as both their future son-in-law and as Jenny's immediate superior, he had an obligation to let them know what had happened.

Digging out his phone, he quickly dialled their number before he had a chance to change his mind.

'Hi, Frank, it's John.'

'Hello John! Good to hear from you. Are you all right? You sound a little down.'

'I'm...' he began, his voice trailing away. He'd been about to say that he was fine, as that's what he'd have normally said, but to have said such a thing before going on to tell him what had happened to his daughter would have felt horribly wrong.

Wading through a mind that felt like a mud-filled swamp, he searched desperately for the right words. 'It's Jenny,' he eventually said. 'She's – she's been hurt.'

His words were met by silence from the other end

of the line.

'She's OK,' Tanner continued. 'She's at Wroxham Medical Centre, and is in good hands, but her condition is...'

More silence; followed by a question.

'What happened?'

Tanner found himself transported back to the scene.

'She was protecting me. Someone came at me with a knife. She grabbed his arm. They fell. Then, when she tried to get up...'

His voice came juddering to a halt.

'Can we see her – if we come?'

'I've been told that they'll have to operate. I've no idea how long it will take. I'm sorry,' he added, his voice cracking with emotion.

'Try not to worry, John. She may not look it, but she's as tough as old boots. Besides, it's not as if it's the first time.'

He was right, it wasn't, but this time it felt very different. When she'd been injured before, back in that god-forsaken windmill, he'd barely known her. Now she was to be his wife, the mother of his...

Remembering what he'd been told, about her being pregnant, he opened his mouth before closing it again.

'Anyway,' Jenny's father continued, 'I'd better let her mother know.'

'Of course.'

'If you could let us know the moment you have some news?'

'I'm staying here until she comes out of the operating room. I'll give you a call when she does.'

'Thank you. We'll speak again then.'

With the call ending, Tanner took in a breath. As his mind turned to think what to do next, the phone rang in his hands.

It was Forrester.

For a moment he considered letting it go through to answerphone, before finding himself taking the call.

'Hi, John,' came the DCI's voice. 'I heard about what happened.'

'Yes, sir.'

'Is she alright?'

'She's going to be!' Tanner said, as if stating a fact.

'And you? How are you coping?'

'I'm fine,' he lied, his jaw tightening.

'That's good. I just thought I'd check in.'

'Did they catch him?' Tanner heard himself asking. 'Roy Carter?'

'Not yet, no, but I've got everyone out looking for him. He won't get far. Not after what he's done. Anyway, try not to think about that for now. We'll catch up in the morning.'

With the call ending, Tanner put the phone away to again stare down the corridor she'd been taken, searching for a sign of the doctor, but there was nobody there. He checked the time on his watch, only to remember that it had been no more than ten minutes since he'd left to begin the operation. He'd no idea how long the procedure would take, but he knew it wouldn't be over any time soon.

Glancing out at the main entrance, through the glass doors at the carpark beyond, his mind contemplated the idea of heading out in search of the person responsible. Finding himself entertaining thoughts of what he'd do to him, were he to find him lurking down some dark alleyway, far away from prying eyes, with images becoming ever-more violent, he felt his chest tighten as his head began to spin. Realising his hands had transformed into fists, his knuckles as white as the bone underneath, he forced himself to take a calming breath. As much as he wanted to find Roy Carter, who he now knew, with absolute certainty, had killed so many people, and in such a short period of time, his first priority was Jenny. Only when he'd been told that she was going to be OK would he be able to take what he felt fully justified in being the appropriate course of action.

But what if she isn't? he asked himself. *What if the operation fails and she never wakes up?*

Shaking the thoughts from his head, he forced his eyes closed. With his hands clasped together in front of him, elbows resting on his knees, he hunched himself over, clearing his mind enough to begin doing something he'd never knowingly done before, to begin pleading with the God he knew Jenny believed in, silently asking for her safe return.

- CHAPTER FORTY FIVE -

IT WASN'T UNTIL two long hours had passed before Tanner heard his name finally being called.

Glancing up to see the same doctor approach, he leapt to his feet.

'How is she?' he asked, shadows of haggard expectation hanging from his face.

'The procedure was more complicated than we thought. The blade must have been twisted, either as it entered or when it was removed, leading to severe trauma of the surrounding tissue.'

'But she will be alright?'

'Hopefully, although she's yet to regain consciousness. We won't know for sure until she does. Until then, we're keeping her in intensive care.'

'And the baby?'

The man shook his head. 'I'm sorry, but as I said when we first spoke, it was unlikely we'd have been able to save it.'

Tanner nodded his understanding. 'Can I see her?'

The doctor frowned.

'Just for a minute?'

The haunted look of grim determination reflected in Tanner's eyes must have made it all too clear that he wasn't going to take no for an answer.

'OK, but only for a minute.'

After a nurse had led him through to the intensive care unit, Tanner sank down into the chair positioned beside the bed, his eyes resting on the gentle curves of Jenny's face. She was lying face up, her eyes closed, lips slightly apart. He took a moment to glance down at her hand. There, a needle had been taped in place, attached to which was a clear plastic tube. Following it up with his eyes, he found an intravenous drip, hanging from a hook above.

He returned to stare down at her face.

There were no outward signs that she was breathing, and the ashen colour of her skin had his mind fleeing from shadows fast closing in.

He'd only been there for what felt like a few seconds when he heard a woman's voice, calling him from the doorway.

'It's time to go.'

Tanner motioned to touch Jenny's hand, but he didn't dare. It seemed too fragile, like a crumpled petal clinging to the edge of a dying rose.

'Mr Tanner,' the nurse prompted, the inflection of her voice rising with impatience.

'Sorry, of course.'

Pulling his hand away, he pushed himself up from the chair.

'You will call me; if there's any news?' he implored, looking over at her.

'Of course. Now, come on. Miss Evans needs her rest, as do you, judging by the state of you.'

Back at his boat, refusing the temptation to drink, he gave Jenny's parents a quick call to let them know the situation; that Jenny was safely out of the operating theatre but had yet to regain consciousness. With Jenny's father once again reassuring him that she'd be OK, he forced himself to eat something before climbing into bed, only to end up sleeping in fits and starts, checking his phone whenever he found himself lying awake.

- CHAPTER FORTY SIX -

Thursday, 19th November

COME THE MORNING, when the hour was hospitable enough, he dragged himself out of bed to struggle through his normal routine, thoughts of Jenny never far away. As soon as he was ready, he was back in his car, driving down deserted country lanes towards where he'd been only a matter of hours before.

Back by Jenny's side, he found her lying in the exact same position as she had been the previous day. Nothing so much as a hair on her head seemed to have moved. It was as if he'd fallen back through time, and it was still the evening before.

Hardly daring to breathe, he remained there for a while, taking solace whenever he saw so much as one of her finger's twitch. As the minutes ebbed away, he found his thoughts drifting increasingly towards the person responsible. The more he thought about him, the more restless he became, until he reached a point where he couldn't stay there any longer.

Pushing himself up from his chair, he sneaked out of the room as quietly as he'd entered. After reminding reception to call him the minute there was any news, he strode out through the doors, down to his car to drive into work, with the sole intention of finding out which particular rock Roy Carter had chosen to hide himself under.

As Tanner pushed open the double doors leading through to the main office, conversations came to an abrupt halt, as everyone instinctively turned to glance over at him before looking away to carry on with their respective duties.

Fully aware of what they must have all been talking about; what had happened the evening before and the impact it must have had on him, Tanner's eyes naturally turned to take in Jenny's empty chair, before searching for what remained of his CID unit.

'We're all very sorry to have heard what happened,' commented Cooper, as Tanner approached.

'Is she OK?' Vicky asked, who looked as if she'd hardly slept herself.

'She had to have an operation,' Tanner replied, his words hollow and empty, 'but the doctors are optimistic.'

Catching his eye, Sally asked, 'Is there anything we can do?'

'Yes! Find Roy Carter! Has there been any news?'

'Nothing yet,' Vicky replied. 'We were out half the night looking for him. We all were,' she added, glancing around.

'Forrester told me. Thank you.'

'It's as if he's just vanished off the face of the earth.'

'Then someone must be hiding him. What about his dad's house?

'That was the second place on our list.'

'Did you look inside?'

'He wouldn't let us.'

'Have you applied for a search warrant?'

'I sent it off last night,' Cooper replied, hunching over to check his inbox.

'Anything back?'

'Nothing yet.'

Tanner checked his watch. 'It'll have to do,' he muttered to himself, before spinning around to head out the way he'd come.

'Where're you going?' called Vicky, rising from her chair.

'Where d'you think?'

'But...the search warrant...?'

Tanner was just passing his desk when Forrester's voice brought him to a reluctant halt.

'Tanner! A word; if you will.'

'Yes, sir,' he growled, his voice edged with hostile resentment. He knew what Forrester was going to say, and why he was going to say it, but it didn't matter. It wasn't going to stop him.

- CHAPTER FORTY SEVEN -

ENTERING HIS OFFICE to see Forrester levering his vast physical mass down into his executive's chair, Tanner closed the door to stand to attention, directly in front of him.

'You wanted to see me, sir?'

'Has there been any news?'

'Not since we last spoke.'

'I talked to Dr Marland last night,' began the DCI, 'after our conversation.' Leaning forward to rest his elbows on the desk, he took a moment to study Tanner's face. 'He said Jenny's injuries were more serious than they'd first thought and that she was still in intensive care.'

'I'm aware of that, thank you, sir.'

'No doubt you are, but it's not exactly what you told me last night though, is it!'

'I said she was going to be OK, sir, and she will be.'

'And you, Tanner? How are you holding up?'

'I'm fine.'

'So you said, but you don't look fine, and frankly, there's no reason why you should be. Not after what's happened.'

'That's as maybe, sir, but I am.'

'You do understand that whether you say you are, or not, won't alter what I'm going to have to say, don't you?'

Tanner didn't respond.

'I can't have you working on an investigation in which you've been emotionally compromised.'

'But I haven't been, sir.'

'Oh, really!'

'No more than everyone else.'

'I'm not a complete idiot, Tanner.'

'I never said you were.'

'Then stop talking to me as if I am!'

Again, Tanner remained silent as Forrester took a calming breath.

'Did they tell you?' the DCI eventually asked.

'Did they tell me what, sir?'

'About Jenny being... That she was...'

Tanner's face remained a mask of stone, but inside he could feel the emotional barriers he'd been attempting to hold in place begin to slip. He tightened his jaw with renewed resolution. If he could somehow prove to Forrester that he was no more affected by what had happened than everyone else at the station, then there was a chance, albeit a slim one, that he'd be allowed to remain working on the investigation.

'I don't think either of us knew, sir,' he eventually replied. 'It certainly wasn't planned. What's important is that Jenny is going to be OK.'

'Yes, of course.'

'Can I go now?' he enquired, becoming desperate to leave.

'I'm sorry, Tanner, really I am, but as I mentioned before, there's just no way I can allow you to remain leading this investigation.'

Tanner felt his heart thump deep inside his chest.

'If Superintendent Whitaker were to find out that I had,' Forrester continued. 'It's bad enough that one of my officers has been seriously injured on my watch. If I was to let you stay on as the SIO, it would be my job.'

Tanner shifted from one foot to the other.

'I suppose that means Cooper will be taking over?'

'Under the circumstances, I've reached the decision that it would be better for all concerned if somebody new was brought in.'

'Somebody *new*?'

'With that in mind, I've asked an interim DI to be sent over as soon as possible.'

'Then you may as well let me carry on until they get here.'

'Thank you, but that won't be necessary. I'm expecting someone this afternoon.'

'But – how is that even possible?'

'I made an urgent request last night, shortly after I heard what happened.'

'Even so!'

'I received a call from HQ this morning, confirming the placement of a certain...' Forrester turned to glance over at his computer screen, '...DI Morton, from the Metropolitan Police.'

Tanner was stunned into silence. Unable to speak, all he could do was to stare down at Forrester with his mouth hanging open.

'He comes highly recommended,' Forrester continued, still studying the screen as Tanner's eyes bored into the side of his face. 'Anyway, Tanner, the decision's been made. I suggest you look at it as a chance to spend some quality time with Jenny, whilst she recovers. No doubt it will also give you time to plan that wedding of yours. January, isn't it?'

'Yes, sir,' Tanner muttered, his teeth locked together, 'although, I must admit, it would be slightly easier to spend time planning our wedding together if the bride-to-be wasn't lying in an intensive care unit after having been stabbed by a psychotic racist xenophobe, the same person who's responsible for throwing a petrol bomb at a shop, killing the old lady trapped upstairs, hanging a young girl up by the neck until dead, and setting fire to an entire block of flats, murdering literally dozens of men, women and children in the process.'

'Who *YOU* let walk out the door!' bellowed Forrester, 'and for no other reason than you weren't doing your job properly!'

It took no more than a fraction of a second for Tanner to understand the full implication of Forrester's statement.

'You're saying that what happened to Jenny, and all those people trapped inside those flats, was *my* fault?'

'Of course I'm not.'

'I don't fucking believe it. You are!'

'You'd better watch your language, Tanner, else I'll be holding you on a charge of gross misconduct.'

'Go ahead! In fact, sod it. I've had enough of this shit. I'm out!'

'What?'

'I said I'm out. You've done as much anyway, so I don't see what difference it makes.'

'I haven't kicked you out, Tanner, I've merely taken you off the investigation.'

'What's the difference? You'll have my formal resignation by the end of the day.'

'No, please,' Forrester urged, as Tanner turned to leave. 'You're upset.'

'Damned fucking right I'm upset,' he muttered, wrenching the door open before slamming it hard behind him.

- CHAPTER FORTY EIGHT -

BURSTING OUT INTO the main office, acutely aware that every single person in the room was staring at him, Tanner fixed his eyes on the floor whilst making a bee-line for his desk.

Once in his chair, he logged into the Norfolk Constabulary's intranet whilst scrabbling around inside a drawer for an old USB flash drive he remembered seeing lurking there a few days before. Finding it, he slotted it into his computer's hard drive, just as his desk phone started to ring.

It was Vicky, calling him from the other side of the office.

Ignoring it, he navigated his way to the file containing all the information relating to their current investigation. With the phone still ringing, he copied it with the click of the mouse to go in search of the flash drive's file. He was about to paste everything over when he stopped. Given the fact that he'd just resigned, he knew that if he made a copy of all the files with the intention of taking them home with him, he'd effectively be breaking the law.

'Sod it,' he said, clicking down to watch the data begin transferring itself over.

With Vicky still trying to call, fully aware of what he was in the process of doing, and what he intended to do afterwards, he realised that it was likely that he was going to need at least one person helping him on the inside.

'Yes, Vicky?' he said, picking up the phone.

'Are you alright?'

'Not really.'

'What happened?'

'Forester's taken me off the investigation.'

'OK, but wasn't that to be expected?'

'So I quit.'

'You did what?'

'He told me it was my fault; what happened to Jenny, and all those people trapped inside those flats.'

'But – why?'

'Because I let Roy Carter walk out the door.'

'Oh, c'mon! That's hardly fair. You lost track of the time, that was all.'

'Yes, but -' Nudging his chair back he leaned forward, so that his head was resting against an arm laid along the edge of the desk. Staring directly down at the floor, as if it were a vast plunging abyss, one which he was on the brink of falling headfirst into, his voice cracked.

'He was right.'

The admission brought his emotional barriers tumbling down around him. As a wave of all-consuming guilt crashed over his head, he heard himself saying, 'It *was* my fault. If I *had* been doing my job properly, none of it would have happened.'

'I'm sorry, John, but that's utter rubbish.'

'If I hadn't allowed him to walk, all those people would still be alive, Jenny wouldn't have been stabbed, and we wouldn't have lost our...' his voice trailed away to be replaced by a high-pitched whine, resonating out through his nose as he physically forced himself not to start sobbing in the middle of the office.

'Jesus, John, you can't do this to yourself.'

Tanner sucked at the air through a series of short juddering breaths.

'It wasn't you who set fire to those flats,' Vicky continued. 'You certainly weren't the one wielding that knife.'

'You're right,' Tanner eventually replied, his voice stiffening with vengeful resolve. 'It was Roy sodding Carter.'

'OK,' began Vicky, the tone of her voice changing from that of parental chastisement to one of more motherly concern, 'which is why we're following the correct legal procedures to have him arrested.'

'Well, I'm off the Force, so thankfully, I don't have to follow those procedures anymore.'

'Have you formally tendered your resignation?'

'Not yet; no, but -'

'So, you're still a member of CID.'

'Well, I'm off the investigation, so I don't see what difference it makes.'

'It means that you can continue to work in an official capacity. Whether or not you're the SIO for this particular case is neither here nor there. Nobody will be able to stop you from investigating a case that just happens to share some of the same suspects, if not all of them.'

Tanner listened in quiet contemplation, as the pace of his breathing began to ease.

'And if you need any help, we're all still here for you. I'm sure Forrester is as well, even if he can't be seen to be. At the end of the day, we all want the same thing.'

'I'll think about it,' he eventually replied.

'You'll think about not resigning, or that you won't head straight out to find Roy Carter in order to beat the shit out of him?'

'I'll think about not resigning.'

'And Roy Carter?'

'Oh, don't worry, I'm still going to beat the living shit out of him, just as soon as I find him, which reminds me.'

- CHAPTER FORTY NINE -

HALF AN HOUR later, Tanner pulled into a quiet cul-de-sac on the outskirts of Lowestoft, at the far end of which he found Nick Carter's residence, a large pretentious house with two Romanesque-style pillars positioned on either side of the entrance.

Marching up to the door, he leaned forward to ring the bell, before stepping back to glance up at the windows, curious to see if his arrival had made any of the various net curtains twitch.

Unable to see any obvious signs of life, he lurched forward to ring the bell again, only for the door to be swung open, leaving him standing face to face with the leader of the BNU, Nick Carter.

'Detective Inspector Tanner, wasn't it?' Carter enquired, offering him a disingenuous smile.

Tanner got straight to the point.

'I'm looking for your son.'

'Well, I can't say you're the only one. I had more of your lot around here last night.'

'So they've told me. I understand you said that you didn't know where he was.'

'That's correct.'

'And now?'

'I'm still none the wiser, I'm afraid.'

Tanner tried to look over his shoulder, to peer inside the house, only for Carter to step to the side, preventing him from doing so.

'Do you know *why* we're looking for him?' asked Tanner, his eyes meeting Carter's.

'I've no idea.'

'Aren't you curious to find out?'

'Not really. Whatever it is, I'm sure he didn't do it.'

'He stabbed my colleague,' Tanner replied. 'The officer I was with when we first met,' he continued. 'Detective Sergeant Evans.'

'You mean, he *may* have stabbed your colleague.'

'No. I saw him do it, with my own two eyes.'

'Then it was probably nothing more than an unfortunate accident.'

'An *accident?*'

'They do happen, you know.'

'Your son launched an unprovoked attack against me. He then stabbed my colleague when she came to my defence.'

'Or maybe it was you who launched an unprovoked attack against him, and your colleague just happened to get a little hurt when she decided to force him to the ground.'

'She's fighting for her life in intensive care.'

Carter shrugged.

'She's also lost the life of her unborn child.'

'I've got no idea what that has to do with either me or my son.'

Tanner could feel his blood boiling with primordial rage as his heart thundered hard inside his chest.

'You callous, un-caring bastard!'

'I'm sorry, but why should I give a shit about something that happened to some stuck-up tart of a policewoman. If she knew she was pregnant, she should have been more careful.'

'She didn't know she was pregnant.'

'Then it's no great loss, is it. Besides, I'd have thought being knocked about a bit would have come with the job. If she didn't fancy the idea, she should have thought twice before joining the police. To be honest, it sounds like she'd have been better suited to a career in teaching. One thing I do know, if you go around attacking people when they're doing nothing more threatening than using a knife they'd just found to remove a stone from the bottom of their shoe, you're asking for trouble.'

'You know where he is, don't you?'

'I've already told you I don't.'

'But you have spoken to him though; since last night?'

'What makes you say that?'

'Because it's blindingly obvious that he's gone to some length to tell you what happened, and that you've already managed to come up with a story together to help explain it.'

Carter shrugged again. 'He may have called, at some point.'

'Then he would have told you where he was.'

'I didn't ask, and he didn't say.'

'Bollocks!'

'Look, I'm sorry about what happened to your colleague, but you'll just have to accept that it wasn't my son's fault.'

Tanner drew in a calming breath.

'Your son's presumed innocence is going to be a matter for a court to decide, not you. But that aside for now, it's not the only thing we want to talk to him about. There's also the small matter of him throwing a petrol bomb at a shop, with the intention of killing everyone inside, and setting fire to a block of flats, murdering half its residents in the process. And not forgetting, of course, the girl found hanging by her neck at Horsey Mere.'

'And I suppose he also tried to blow up Parliament as well, did he, maybe having a go at stealing the Crown Jewels whilst he was at it?'

'Not that I'm aware of, but I'd be more than happy to ask him about it.'

The sound of something heavy being knocked over near the top of the stairs had Tanner trying to glance over his shoulder again, before once more being prevented from doing so.

'He's inside, isn't he?'

'That was my wife,' Carter replied. 'She's sorting through some stuff upstairs.'

'I thought you said you were divorced?'

'Well, I am, but -'

'ROY CARTER!' Tanner bellowed, taking a half-step back to stare up at the house. 'I KNOW YOU'RE IN THERE!'

'I've already told you, he's not here.'

'You do know you're full of shit, don't you?' Tanner said, stepping forward to try and pass the man, only to be blocked once again.

'Where the hell do you think you're going?'

'I'm going inside to question your son.'

'Sorry, I didn't realise you had a search warrant.'

'I don't need a search warrant.'

'Oh, really. That's a first.'

'When in active pursuit of someone we believe has committed a serious crime, we have every legal right to enter a private residence, such as yours, without the need of one.'

'Fair enough, but I'll have to check that with my lawyer before I can allow you through.'

'Please, go ahead.'

'Well, I would, but unfortunately he's on holiday at the moment. Two weeks in Bermuda. But do feel free to come back when he returns.'

'I've had enough of this,' Tanner muttered. 'I suggest you stand aside.'

'Or what?'

'Or I'll be charging you with perverting the course of justice by harbouring a known criminal.'

'But I'm not though, as there's nobody in there.'

'Apart from your wife, of course, the one who you said walked out on you when you were inside, never to be seen again.'

'Anyway, there's no way I'm letting you go in, not before I've either had a chance to speak to my lawyer, or you can provide me with a valid search warrant.'

'As I said before, I don't need one.'

'You also said you were only allowed to enter if you were in active pursuit of someone.'

'Which is exactly what I'm doing.'

'So, you were chasing him just now, were you?'

'We don't have to be physically chasing after someone to be in active pursuit.'

'OK, but that's something else I'll need to check with my lawyer. In the meantime, I suggest you turn yourself around and toddle off to wherever it was that you came from.'

The sound of an approaching siren had Tanner glancing around at the other houses. One of the neighbours must have overheard their argument and called the police. Under normal circumstances, their imminent arrival would have been most welcome, but not when he knew the man standing directly in front of him was unfortunately correct. He had no legal right to enter the house, as he had no proof that Roy Carter was inside. But if he could prove he was.

Knowing he didn't have long, Tanner surged forward in a desperate attempt to barge past the man, only to be shoved back.

'That's assaulting a police officer, right there!' Tanner shouted, with growing frustration.

'Er, no. That's called self-defence. You're the one who just attacked me!'

With the siren growing ever-closer, Tanner could feel his self-control fast slipping away. Lurching forward again, this time he threw a punch, straight at Carter's face, sending him stumbling back against the door, one hand clutching at his nose as he crashed into the house.

'You – you hit me!' the man stuttered, blood spurting out from between his fingers. 'You fucking hit me!'

'That's what you get for assaulting a police officer,' Tanner muttered, stepping over the man to charge up the stairs, heading for the floor above.

- CHAPTER FIFTY -

REACHING THE LANDING, with the prospect of either Nick Carter coming up after him, or his colleagues from the Norfolk Constabulary, he dived from room to room, conducting the most rudimentary of searches.

With the blaring sound of sirens coming ever-closer, Tanner threw open the last door to find himself inside a large bedroom. At the far end was a small bookcase, lying at an angle against the end of the bed, its contents strewn over the floor. Beyond that was a window that had been left wide open.

'Shit!' Tanner cursed, rushing inside to jump over the books and stare out of the window to see the flat roof of an extension, only about ten feet below.

He took a firm hold of the window frame as he stared furiously down. In hindsight, it was blindingly obvious what Nick Carter had been doing; stalling for time, giving his son the best possible chance to make a run for it.

'I should have hit the bastard sooner,' he lamented, gazing out at the network of houses and gardens beyond, wondering where he was most likely to have fled.

From the front of the house came the wail of the siren, turning into the cul-de-sac to approach the house. When it was finally turned off, Tanner listened to the uncomfortable silence that followed, broken moments later by the dull thud of two car doors being slammed. The sound of distant voices forced Tanner to begin contemplating the actions he'd taken. Not that he cared all that much, but a detective inspector punching a law-abiding member of the public squarely in the face, for no justifiable reason, was going to have consequences, especially given who that person was. Tanner couldn't imagine that he wouldn't press charges, if for no other reason than for the publicity such a story would generate towards his election campaign. But Tanner knew that such a case would eventually come down to Carter's word against his, and Tanner wasn't the one who'd done six months for GBH.

The only thing he was upset about was for having been stupid enough to let Roy Carter slip away – again! If only he'd had the patience and temperament to have waited for the search warrant, and then to have stood aside whilst his team conducted a legal search of the premises, making sure to cover all means of escape before doing so, they'd have caught Roy Carter skulking inside. Instead, he'd allowed his heart to rule his head, and not for the first time, leaving him with nothing more to show for it than an open window, an over-turned bookcase and an expected charge of assault.

He pivoted around to lean back against the window ledge. There he spent a minute or two coming up with a suitable story for having punched the home's owner before gaining illegal entry to his property. With something in mind, he skirted around the books still lying over the floor, heading for the landing and the staircase beyond.

'That's him!' Carter shouted, gesticulating madly over at Tanner the moment he emerged from the house.

'That's the man who assaulted me!'

Ignoring both the accusation and the person who'd made it, Tanner nodded casually over at the two uniformed officers standing beside him.

'Higgins, Jones,' he said, nodding over at them.

'Afternoon, sir,' Higgins replied, with the merest hint of a smirk. 'Mr Carter, here, says you assaulted him. Is there any truth to that?'

'None whatsoever.'

'You lying sack of shit!' Carter bleated, spots of blood flying out from his mouth.

'I'm afraid it was Mr Carter who assaulted me,' Tanner continued, 'when I was endeavouring to question him about the location of his bastard son. The state of his face is the unfortunate result.'

'That's utter bollocks!'

Tanner turned his head to glance back at the house. 'It was then that I heard the sound of a disturbance coming from inside, so I felt formally obliged to enter the property in order to investigate.'

'Did you find anything?' Higgins questioned, his attention turning to the notes he was making.

'You're not seriously listening to this?' interrupted Carter.

'Only an open bedroom window with the bookcase underneath having been knocked over. It was probably an opportunistic burglar, taking advantage of the fact that Mr Carter and I were otherwise engaged outside the property. If that was the case, my timely intervention must have deterred them, but I suggest Mr Carter has a look around, just in case anything of value is missing.'

'That man broke my fucking nose!'

Higgins glanced up to catch Tanner's eye. 'Would you like us to arrest Mr Carter, for assaulting a police officer, sir?'

'WHAT!' Carter raged, staring at the two uniformed police constables with unhinged incredulity.

'Not really,' Tanner replied, with a shrug of indifference. 'Anyway, I'd better be off. Unlike some people I could mention, I don't have time to stand idly around all day.'

'You complete and utter bastard!'

'If I were you,' Tanner continued, glancing over at Carter to take in the state of his face, 'I'd get someone to have a look at that nose of yours. I'll be honest with you, from where I'm standing, it doesn't look good.'

- CHAPTER FIFTY ONE -

ETREATING TO THE only place he had any real interest in being, Tanner made his way back to Wroxham Medical Centre to sit quietly beside Jenny, still lying unconscious within one of their intensive care units.

There he remained for several hours until the combination of hunger, thirst and a tyrannical nurse forced him out, the latter promising that he'd be told the minute there was any news.

Emerging to find day had turned to night, with the sense of being utterly alone, he headed for home, stopping at a local petrol station on the way for something decent to drink.

Twenty minutes later, a hand wrapped around the neck of a bottle of Jamaican Rum, he was ambling down the footpath towards his yacht, staring down at the unlit footpath passing beneath his feet, when a voice from ahead had him looking up with a start.

'Tanner? Is that you?'

He didn't need to see the person's face to know who it was. The voice was distinctive enough.

'DCI Forrester, sir?'

'I hope you don't mind?'

Tanner shrugged. 'I didn't know you knew where I lived.'

'I asked Vicky.'

'I didn't know she knew, either.'

'I just wanted to stop by, to make sure you were OK.'

'I've been better,' Tanner replied.

Forrester glanced down to see the bottle clutched in his hand.

'I do hope you're not thinking about drinking all that in one go?'

'Don't worry,' Tanner replied, 'I'll be using a glass.'

Brushing past Forrester's vast physical mass, Tanner tucked the bottle under his arm to begin unclipping the canvas entrance.

'I heard about a disturbance involving Nick Carter, outside his house earlier.'

'Oh yes?' Tanner mused, stepping on board to begin rolling up the entrance.

'He says you assaulted him.'

'Uh-huh.'

'I sincerely hope you didn't!'

'I seem to remember telling Higgins what happened.'

'And I read his report.'

'So, there you are then.'

'But it's in complete contradiction to what Carter said.'

'I suppose that means you'll have to decide which one of us you're going to believe,' Tanner continued, turning to glower back at Forrester, 'me, or some xenophobic Neo Nazi.'

'Yes, well -'

'Was that it? Can I go now?'

'Look, Tanner, I didn't come to talk to you about that.'

'No?'

'Well, not only that. He *is* threatening to press charges, but he's probably only doing so in an attempt to drum up some media attention for what I suspect has become a somewhat faltering by-election campaign.'

'So, why are you here?'

'I wanted to ask you to reconsider what you said earlier, about resigning.'

Without replying, Tanner finished securing the top of the rolled-up canvas to step in through the entrance, into the blackness of the yacht's rich mahogany cockpit, leaving Forrester standing outside.

'I was hoping you'd changed your mind,' he heard him call out, as he set the bottle down on the table to light the cockpit's oil lamp. As its soothing mellow light pushed gently back against the surrounding darkness, he turned to duck his head back out through the entrance.

'May I offer you a drink?'

'Oh, er, I really shouldn't,' the DCI replied, before adding, 'Maybe a small one.'

'You can come on board; if you like?'

'Who, me?' Forrester questioned, gazing along the curvaceous lines of the forty-two-foot 1930s Broads cruiser, an expression of serious misgiving creasing his face. 'I'd probably sink it.'

'Somehow, I doubt that.' Seeing him continue to hesitate, Tanner added, 'At least you'd be able to sit down.'

'OK, well, I suppose you only live once.'

Smirking, Tanner watched as Forrester lifted a tentative foot onto the side of the boat. Half-hopping on the other, he bounced himself onboard, only to find the boat tilting suddenly under his enormous weight. As he began falling backwards, Tanner caught hold of his outstretched arm to pull him forward, keeping a hold of it whilst he clambered his way down into the cockpit.

'I thought you said I wouldn't sink it.'

'I must have underestimated just how much you weigh.'

Forrester scowled at him through the oil lamp's rich orange light.

'Anyway,' Tanner continued, handing him an empty glass tumbler, 'a drink for your efforts?'

Spinning the top off the brand-new bottle of Jamaican Rum, he poured out a generous measure of the deep cinnamon-coloured liquid into first Forrester's glass, then his own.

Thanking him for the drink, Forrester glanced around. 'It's certainly cosy.'

'We like to think so. I'm only sorry Jenny can't be here to give you a guided tour. My knowledge of what everything is has improved, but not by much. Anyway, take a seat.'

As they eased themselves down onto the opposing benches, Forrester took the opportunity to ask, 'Has there been any news?'

'Nothing,' Tanner replied, fishing out his phone to stare down at the screen before laying it down on the table directly in front of him. 'I've just come from the medical centre. Her condition hasn't changed.'

'Well, don't worry. I'm sure she'll be back on her feet in no time.'

Downing the drink in one, Tanner poured himself another. 'Have there been any developments at work?'

'We've had a forensics report back on the petrol used on the Glenwood Estate. It wasn't the same used for the petrol bomb thrown at the shop.'

'I'm not surprised. I doubt if even Roy Carter is stupid enough to have bought the exact same brand from the exact same petrol station.'

'Possibly not, but it doesn't help to support the

theory that he was the one who set fire to the place.'

'Apart from the two witnesses who said they saw him run out, just before it started.'

'They only said they saw someone wearing a grey hoodie, which in fairness could be half the teenage population of Norfolk.'

'Who else would have had the motive, being that Zara Haddad was trapped at the top?'

'We still don't know that she was, at least not officially.'

'I think she'd have come forward by now if she hadn't been. After all, that was her home, where her entire family lived. But whether or not she was makes no difference. The fact that she lived at the top gives Roy Carter motive for having set fire to it.'

'Because he believed she was one of three witches who cast a spell on him, killing them being the only way to break it?' questioned Forrester, his voice drenched in doubt.

'As that shop owner, Mrs Matar, keeps telling me, probably her daughter as well, it's not what *we* believe that's important. Speaking of whom, I assume they're both still OK?'

'We've still got a squad car parked outside the hotel.'

'What about the murder of Anya Chadha? Has anything been found to link Roy Carter to the scene at Horsey Mere?'

'Nothing yet.'

'I don't suppose anyone's found him?'

'I'm afraid not.'

'And what about my replacement?'

'He arrived this afternoon.'

'Any good?'

'It's early days, I suppose.'

'Sounds like you're not sure.'

'He spent the afternoon reviewing the files before coming to the conclusion that Roy Carter probably didn't have anything to do with either the fire at the Glenwood Estate or the murder of Anya Chadha.'

'Seriously?'

Forrester shrugged. 'And I think he could be right. The evidence just isn't there.'

'But the motive is. Who else could have wanted both girls dead?'

'We don't know, at least not yet. Anyway, the new DI says he's going to have to start all over again. Apparently he's put in a request for more manpower to be sent up from London.'

'He went over your head?'

'Yes, well, as I said, he's going to take a little getting used to. Fortunately, he's only with us on secondment.'

'You never told me how he was able to take up the position so quickly?'

'He's in the same position as you. He was pulled off an investigation due to a conflict of interests.'

'But why would he want to move up here?'

'He's got family in the area.'

There was a lull in the conversation, leaving Forrester swirling his drink around whilst Tanner stared vacantly down at his phone.

'You never answered my question?' Forrester eventually asked.

'I know.'

'OK, well, as I said before, I sincerely hope you're able to re-consider.'

They both jumped at the sound of Tanner's phone, buzzing on the table.

Tanner stared down at it for a moment, before glancing up at Forrester.

'Well, it's not for me,' the DCI replied.

Tanner laid down the glass to pick up the phone. 'Hello?'

The boat's cockpit fell into a sullen silence, as Forrester leaned in towards the table.

Within a few moments, Tanner opened his mouth, his voice cracking with emotion. 'OK, thank you. I'll be straight down.'

DAVID BLAKE

- CHAPTER FIFTY TWO -

BACK INSIDE WROXHAM Medical Centre's reception area, seeing Dr Marland approach, Tanner leapt up from the chair he'd been waiting on.

'How is she?'

'She's still very weak.'

'But she is awake?'

'She regained consciousness about an hour ago. We're going to keep her in the intensive care unit for the time being, but hopefully she's through the worst.'

'Have her parents been told?'

'They have. They said they'd come over in the morning.'

Tanner paused to send the doctor a look of pleading desperation. 'Can I see her?'

'She's still heavily medicated.'

'Please?'

'Well, under normal circumstances I'd say no, but as long as you only stay for a few minutes. And you'll need to keep the conversation light. No talk about work, or wedding plans or anything.'

'Of course. Thank you.'

As he was about to be led away, Tanner caught the doctor's eye. 'May I ask how much she's been told?'

'Only that she had to have an operation, and how long she's been unconscious for.'

'I assume nobody's mentioned anything to her

234

about – about the baby?'

'No, and I'd urge you not to either, at least not yet.'

Tanner entered the dimly lit private room to immediately stare over at Jenny, sitting up with her head resting back against a pillow; her eyes firmly closed. Gravely concerned to see her face was still a milky ashen grey colour, he closed the door as quietly as he could before turning to approach.

'John,' he heard her croak, her eyes flickering open.

'Hey, Jen. The doctor said you were awake. How are you feeling?'

'Probably better than I look.'

'Are you sure about that? I mean, you look pretty bad.'

'Thanks a lot.'

They smiled gently at each other, as Tanner sank slowly down into the now all too familiar chair. 'Seriously though, you look fine.'

'Liar.'

'OK, you could probably do with a touch of foundation. Maybe a little blusher as well, and some eyeliner, a dollop of mascara, and a generous portion of lipstick. Your hair's a bit of a mess too, but nothing a digital perm couldn't sort out.'

'You've been reading my Cosmo again.'

'Not much else to do, really,' he shrugged, 'what with you being away, and everything. I better warn you that boiler suits are set to make a comeback, as are floral-patterned dresses. It's also worth knowing that the latest trend is to wear a blazer with cycling shorts. I'm not sure how Forrester will react, but I'm keen to give that last one a go.'

Jenny's face cracked into a painful looking grin before fading away as quickly as it had appeared.

'What's been happening at work?'

'Oh, you know, the usual.'

'You mean, there's another psychotic serial killer on the loose?'

'I'm afraid the doctor told me not to talk shop with you.'

'So there *is* another psychotic serial killer on the loose!'

It was Tanner's turn to smile.

'It's probably no great surprise to learn that I've been taken off the investigation.'

'Because of what happened to me?'

Tanner nodded.

'They're not blaming you; I hope?'

'Nothing like that, no.'

'I suppose that means Cooper is the new SIO?'

'Thankfully, Forrester thought better of it.'

'So, who's leading?'

'He brought in a new DI, on secondment from London.'

Jenny raised an eyebrow. 'I bet that went down well.'

'He arrived this afternoon.'

'That was quick!'

'He has family in the area and had been kicking around with nothing much else to do; a bit like me, really. I've yet to meet him so I don't know what he's like, but Forrester doesn't seem keen. Apparently, he went over his head to request additional support from London. He's also dismissed the idea that Roy Carter had anything to do with either what happened to Anya Chadha or the fire at the Glenwood Estate.'

'Even though he was seen running out, just before it started?'

Tanner nodded. 'It probably didn't help that forensics found the petrol used was different from that used on the Tarragon shop.'

'How about the murder of Patrick Hopkins. Has he had any "revelations" about that?'

'I haven't asked.'

Realising he'd so far being doing the exact opposite of what the doctor had told him, Tanner endeavoured to move the discussion away from work. 'Anyway, so, how are you feeling, really?'

'I'm OK, I suppose. Just tired.'

'It's probably the painkillers.'

'The doctor told me that I've been unconscious for a while, which I thought was strange.'

'Why strange?'

'I didn't think people were supposed to have dreams when they were.'

'I assume you had?'

'The same one,' she nodded, 'over and over.'

'Can you remember what it was about?'

Jenny nodded. 'I was a child again,' she began, glancing down, 'playing outside my home with my brothers and sisters. Other children as well.'

'I didn't think you had any siblings?'

'I don't, but it wasn't my home either. I was in some sort of village, in the middle of a desert. But it felt like it was, if that makes any sense, just as it felt as if they were my family.'

'What happened then?'

'We were all playing together when there was a noise, like an explosion, and I found myself being carried away, still watching everyone behind me.'

Jenny stopped, her eyes trailing away.

Finding himself drawn into the story, Tanner was about to ask her to continue when Jenny shook her head, as if to clear thoughts crowding her mind. 'That's when it happened,' she eventually continued. 'A soldier came into the village holding a machine gun. The children I'd been playing with, my brothers and sisters, they were all murdered, one after another. And after they had been, the man came looking for me.'

'Jesus Jen!'

'He dragged me out into the middle of the courtyard, the bodies of my family lying scattered around, placed the gun against my head, said something in a language I couldn't understand and pulled the trigger. Then I'd wake up to find myself playing with the children, as if nothing had happened, only for it to start all over again.'

By the time she'd finished, there were tears spilling over the edges of her eyes.

'Sorry,' she apologised, lifting an arm to wipe at them with the sleeves of the hospital gown she was wearing.

'There's nothing to apologise for.'

'The worse thing about it was that I always felt like I knew what was about to happen, when I was playing with the children, but there was never anything I could do to stop it.'

'You've been through a hell of a lot, Jen. I'm sure the dream was just your mind's way of helping you come to terms with it.'

'And all the time I thought I knew who the man was, but his face was always just out of view. Every time I tried to look, he seemed to know, and would deliberately look away.'

'It was just a dream, Jen.'

'I know, but it felt real.'

'Don't they always?'

'I suppose.'

There was a gentle rap on the door, followed by the head of a nurse.

'I think it's time to give Miss Evans a chance to get

some more rest, don't we think?'

'I'm feeling fine,' Jenny argued.

'Even so,' the nurse responded, giving Tanner a look that told him he had to leave.

'Right, yes. Of course. I'd better be off,' he replied, climbing to his feet.

'But – we haven't had a chance to talk about the wedding,' Jenny said, taking a hold of his arm.

'Don't worry, I'll be back first thing tomorrow. We can talk about it then.'

- CHAPTER FIFTY THREE -

B ACK AT HIS BOAT, Tanner spent the evening trying to stop himself from worrying about his fiancée, whilst doing his best not to drink too much in the process.

After cooking dinner, he first attempted to settle down with a book, but reading proved to be impossible. His mind kept drifting away, halfway through each page. Instead, he put the radio on to begin attempting to fix some of the things he was supposed to have done many months before, but had never quite found the time.

As the hour grew late, with his mind being constantly drawn back to Jenny's side, he eventually decided to turn in for the night. It was either that or stay up till the early hours, drinking himself into a senseless stupor.

Friday, 20th November

The stark caw of a crow had him blinking his eyes open. The cabin was still shrouded in darkness. What he could see of the sky through the yacht's oval-shaped portholes was a luminous midnight blue, lit by either a sinking moon or the sun as it climbed inexorably up towards Norfolk's never-ending horizon.

Lifting his arm, he checked the time on his watch. It was just gone half-past six. He rolled his head over to stare at the pillow where Jenny's head should have been, wondering if he'd be allowed in to see her at such an early hour. Deciding it was worth a shot, he rolled out of bed to begin making himself decent for a somewhat early hospital visit.

'Hi,' he said, somewhat sheepishly, as he approached the medical centre's reception desk.

With the unfamiliar face of a female nurse staring up at him, he cleared his throat. 'I don't suppose it's too early to visit a patient who's being looked after here?'

'I'd say it was at least one hour too early,' she replied, with a disapproving scowl.

'It's just that she only woke up last night, after an operation, and I'd hardly had a chance to say hello before I was asked to leave.'

'Are you a friend or a relative?'

'Both, I suppose.'

The lady continued to stare at him, apparently waiting for a more precise answer.

'I'm her fiancé,' he eventually replied.

With the nurse's eyes still fixed on his, Tanner added, somewhat awkwardly, 'We're due to be married in January.'

'The patient's name?'

'Jenny. Jenny Evans.'

The nurse blinked a couple of times before returning her attention to her computer, as if she'd recognised the name.

'If you could take a seat, Mr...?'

'Tanner. John Tanner.'

'I'll see if someone is free.'

'But – I know which room she's in.'

'If you could take a seat,' the nurse repeated, with an insistent smile.

Apologising, Tanner left the nurse to pick up a phone on her desk as he turned to slink over to the all-too familiar row of chairs.

Within in a space of just a few short minutes, the enquiring voice of a woman came floating over towards him.

'Mr Tanner?'

Pushing himself up from his chair, he found himself staring up into the tired but confident blue eyes of a middle-aged woman wearing a white lab coat, again someone he'd not seen before.

'I am.'

'My name's Doctor Phillips,' she said, holding out her hand.

Taking it, Tanner glanced over her shoulder. 'Isn't Doctor Marland around?'

'He's not on duty at the moment. Would it be possible for us to have a quick chat?'

'I was hoping to see Jenny Evans.'

'It won't take long.'

Turning her shoulders slightly, she added, 'If you could follow me?' before leading the way over towards a corridor, just beyond the reception's desk.

Entering a small side office, she stood to one side to hold the door open for him.

'What's all this about?' Tanner asked, remaining stubbornly where he was.

'Just in here,' the doctor insisted.

The moment he crossed the threshold, he felt her close the door behind him before watching her pivot around the desk.

'Do have a seat,' she said, taking one for herself.

Tanner stared down at the chair being offered to him with a growing sense of unease. 'Is there another form you want me to fill out?'

'If you could take a seat,' the doctor repeated, using a mouse to close various computer files that she must have inadvertently left open.

Realising that he was been given little choice, Tanner sank cautiously down into the chair.

The moment he had, the doctor left her computer to rest her eyes gently onto his.

'Mr Tanner, I'm truly sorry to have to be the bearer of such unfortunate news, but I have to tell you that Miss Evans died in the early hours of the morning.'

'I'm sorry?'

'I've been told that she experienced problems during the night. The decision was made to conduct a further laparotomy operation.'

'You must have the wrong person.'

'Unfortunately, she didn't survive the procedure.'

'But I – I saw her last night. She was sitting up in bed. The doctor told me she was through the worst.'

'Sometimes when dealing with serious internal injuries, there can be unexpected complications.'

'No, you're wrong!'

'As was the case last night.'

'I'd like to see my fiancée now, please!' he demanded, rising to his feet.

'I'm very sorry, Mr Tanner.'

'You're not listening to me. I want to see Miss Evans!'

Breaking eye contact for the briefest of moments, the doctor reached into a drawer.

'If I may, I'd like to give you this,' she continued, pushing a leaflet over the desk towards him. 'It provides details of the bereavement services we're able to offer.'

Seeing his hand reach tentatively out towards it, he yanked it away.

'You're wrong!' he repeated, his attention returning to the doctor. 'Jenny's fine. I saw her last night. She was getting better. The doctor said she was. Besides, someone would have called me if she wasn't.'

'We prefer to do these things face to face, whenever possible. There's a helpline number on the back,' she continued, turning the leaflet over to bring Tanner's eyes down to it.

A silence that was as cold as the grave descended down over the room.

'Again, I'm most terribly sorry,' she eventually added, her voice filled with empathic warmth. 'If there's anything we can do, anything at all, please don't hesitate to ask.'

- CHAPTER FIFTY FOUR -

TANNER BLUNDERED OUT into the carpark to stare vacantly about. Seeing his car, he began drifting over towards it, only to stop halfway. It was supposed to take him somewhere, but he didn't have anywhere to go.

Glancing down, he saw his car keys draped over the palm of his hand. Unable to remember having taken them out, he stared down at them, wondering what possible use they could be to him now.

The sound of his phone ringing from deep inside his jacket had him pulling it out to hear the sound of a woman's voice, talking at him from the other end.

'Tanner, hi, it's Vicky.'

'Vicky?' he questioned.

'Er – from work?'

'Sorry, yes.'

'Are you OK? You sound a little...distant.'

'Do I?'

'I just thought you'd be interested to know that we think Roy Carter has been spotted. A call came in from a corner shop on the outskirts of Lowestoft. Someone matching his description was reported robbing the place this morning, assaulting the owner in the process.'

Instead of replying, Tanner's eyes drifted back to his car.

'I was thinking that if it was him,' Vicky continued,

'he couldn't have gone far. His van's still with forensics.'

There was still no response from Tanner, leaving Vicky to say, 'I just thought you'd be interested to know,' her voice edged with uncertainty.

'I suppose you'd better send someone over,' came Tanner's eventual response.

'Well, I would, but the new DI wants our focus to remain on Professor Bamford.'

'Who?'

'You know, the guy who did the genealogical research on the Hopkins family for the Norfolk Herald. He thinks he's the person most likely to have killed Patrick Hopkins, as he has the most obvious motive; that his wife ran off with him, only to die in a car crash, with him behind the wheel.'

'Revenge for the death of his wife,' Tanner commented, turning to gaze back at the medical centre.

'He thinks he's a more likely suspect than the Drummonds. The private equity firm who manages their family's estate finally came through with full disclosure. They're worth well over thirty million, so money can't be an issue, and he thinks it's unlikely he'd have killed Hopkins simply to trigger a by-election, else he'd have done it sooner.'

With Tanner falling silent again, Vicky was left to say, 'So anyway, do you want me to send you over the address of that corner shop?'

'Sorry, what corner shop?'

'The one that said someone matching Roy Carter's description had robbed the place this morning.'

'You're telling me someone's seen Roy Carter?' Tanner demanded, shadows of rage bursting out into his conscious mind.

'Someone matching his description,' Vicky

confirmed.

'Then of course I want you to send me the address!'

'Right. OK. Sorry, sir, but – are you sure you're alright?'

'If I find Roy Carter I will be,' Tanner muttered, but too quietly for Vicky to have overheard.

- CHAPTER FIFTY FIVE -

'I'M LOOKING FOR the owner?' said Tanner, approaching the counter of the corner shop Vicky had directed him to.

'And you are?' queried the stern face of a middle-aged woman, her mouth struggling to pronounce the words.

'Detective Inspector Tanner, Norfolk Police,' he replied, pulling out his ID.

A relieved smile flickered briefly over the lady's face before disappearing.

'We called you a long time ago.'

Tanner ignored the remark. 'Are you the owner?'

She shook her head. 'You need to speak to my husband. Follow me, please.'

Doing as he was told, he allowed himself to be led down a narrow aisle, one side stocked high with wine, the other burgeoning with household necessities.

'The police are here,' the woman announced to a man stooped over one of many piled up boxes in the loading bay at the back.

As he stood to turn around, Tanner saw the skin around one of his sunken dark eyes was broken and bruised.

'Detective Inspector Tanner,' he said, the ID still in his hand. 'Are you OK?'

The man reached up towards his eye. 'I've probably had worse,' he replied, with just the hint of an accent.

As the lady spun around to head back inside the shop, Tanner exchanged his ID for his notebook. 'I take it you're the owner?'

'I am.'

'May I have your name?'

'Kassim Hassan, Kassim with a K.'

'I assume it was you who reported the incident this morning?'

'About an hour ago,' the man replied, glancing down at his watch. 'It was a young man wearing one of those hoodie-type things pulled up over his head.'

'Can you describe him?'

'Thin. Not very tall. Very white skin.'

'Did he have red hair?' Tanner enquired, glancing up from his notes with an expectant look.

'I think so.'

'And the hoodie?'

'Light grey.'

As Tanner returned to his notes, the man continued.

'I can't say I thought anything of him at first. We often get youngsters in here with their hoods pulled up over their heads, and he seemed to be actually shopping, instead of wandering up and down pretending to be. He even had a basket. It was only when he reached the counter and placed all the items down that he pulled out a knife, demanding the cash from the till.'

'What happened then?'

'I refused.'

Tanner lifted his head to raise an eyebrow at him.

'That's when he punched me.'

'Go on.'

'That was about it, really. I gave him the cash and he left.'

'How much did he take?'

'Just over two hundred pounds.'

'What about the items in the basket?'

'What about them?'

'Did he take them?'

'Sorry, he did, yes. He even had me put everything into bags for him.'

'Can you remember what they included?'

'Just the normal. Milk, bread, sandwiches; a few snacks.'

'I noticed when I came in that you have CCTV cameras,' said Tanner, still taking notes.

'We do.'

'Do they work?'

'Of course! I can show you the footage; if you like?'

Following the man up an unkept staircase, Tanner found himself being shown into a grubby little office near the back of the shop. There the owner levered himself down into an old office chair to turn on a large somewhat dated desk-top computer.

'You can see him coming in here,' he said, squinting at the screen.

Tanner spent a minute or two watching the grainy colour image being presented to him.

'Do you have anything that shows his face?'

'I should do,' he replied, using the mouse to open the footage from another camera, angled down at the front of the shop from behind the counter. Rewinding the video he paused it, just as the same hooded youth glanced up.

A grin crawled its way over Tanner's face. It was Roy Carter. There was no doubt about it.

'You know, now that I think about it,' the shop's owner continued, 'I'm fairly sure I've seen him here before, with some other boys.' With the mouse still in his hand, he navigated to another folder. 'I remember thinking that they may have been shop lifting, but I couldn't be certain, so we let it go.' As he started speeding through some footage from a previous day, it wasn't long before he froze the image once again. 'Here, look. Isn't that the same man?'

'Looks like it,' agreed Tanner, making a quick note of the date and time highlighted at the bottom of the screen. 'I don't suppose you know which way he went; after he left?'

'I saw him heading up towards the old Hatchmead Estate.'

'Are you sure?'

The man nodded. 'It's the only place that road leads to.'

- CHAPTER FIFTY SIX -

TANNER KNEW THE area the shop owner had referred to, both by name and reputation. It was an old 1960s concrete estate, dominated by a single wide block of flats, all of which had been abandoned at least two years before. The intention had been for the site to be transformed into an ultra-modern housing development, filled to bursting point with so-called "luxury" two and three-bedroom flats. But the holding company who'd purchased the site had gone into receivership shortly after taking ownership, leaving behind a concrete monolith that was not only a crumbling eyesore, but a major health and safety hazard as well.

It hadn't taken long before the name of the estate began to be broadcast over the police radio frequency, as a growing number of drug dealers and their customers sought to frequent the building, making the most of the privacy the abandoned estate offered them. But after two boys were killed when a section of the building gave way underneath them, crushing them to death under hundreds of tonnes of corroded concrete, most people in their right mind had the good sense to keep well clear.

But Roy Carter wasn't in his right mind. Taking into account the items he'd stolen, along with the cash, Tanner was convinced he was using the estate to hide up in.

Leaving his car where it was, Tanner stomped his way along the road he'd been told Carter had taken, up a gradual incline towards the estate at the end. When he got there, he cast his eyes over the seven-foot-high security wall, plastered over with long-faded artist's impressions of what the site was supposed to have been transformed into, searching for some sort of a way in. It didn't take him long to find one. The bottom of a large section of plywood had been levered away from the supporting post behind it. With a quick glance over his shoulder, he crouched down to take hold of it to heave back. Making sure not to catch himself on any of the rusty steel nails sticking out, he eased himself cautiously through the gap.

Standing on the other side he stared about, taking a moment to find his bearings. He'd been inside the estate a few times before, in response to various callouts, but he'd only ever entered through the main entrance. From where he was, everything looked different. One thing was clear, though; the place was huge. Far bigger than he remembered. The chances of him being able to find a lanky red-headed youth, one who didn't want to be found, certainly not by him, was going to be a tall order.

As his eyes swept over the estate, he momentarily considered the idea of calling Vicky, to ask for backup, before remembering what she'd already told him.

'It's probably better this way,' he muttered to himself.

With his jaw locked he lurched forward, heading for what was left of the estate's tower block. If Roy Carter was hiding there, that's where he was most likely to be.

- CHAPTER FIFTY SEVEN -

I T WAS THE rattle of an empty can, glancing off someone's foot near the top of the crumbling ten-storey block, that alerted Tanner to Carter's whereabouts. Turning towards the sound, he managed to catch a glimpse of red hair, stark against the endless background of battleship grey, before seeing it disappear behind a rusty green railing.

'Gotcha!' he muttered, quickly counting the floors down to the ground.

As he ducked through an uneven gap between the entrance doors, the vile stench of urine had him reeling back. Forced to choke down the bile that arrived unwelcome at the back of his throat, he pushed himself forward into the abandoned building's gloomy damp lobby. A quick glance over at the graffiti covered lift doors had him turning to the concrete stairs, lurking in the shadows to his right.

Taking them two at a time, doing his best to avoid the disgusting remnants of human detritus that littered every step, it wasn't long before he was breathing hard, middle age bringing him to an eventual standstill as he clawed his way up to the seventh floor.

Taking a much-needed moment to catch his breath, he let his eyes follow the heavily rusted metal handrail that ran along the top of the balcony's boundary wall, to where he'd seen the face disappear.

But it had taken him a good few minutes to scramble his way up. Assuming it had been Carter he'd seen, it would have given him plenty of time to have moved up to the balcony above, or to have even crept down to the one below.

Tanner remained where he was, slowly gaining control of his breathing as he tuned his ears to the slightest of sounds. But other than the distant chatter of a magpie, and desiccated leaves being shuffled along the balcony's floor by the cold autumnal air, there were none.

He turned his head to stare along the balcony on the opposite side. It was the same story there; nothing but swirling litter and flaking paint.

A faint shuffling sound behind his head had him spinning around, his heart leaping inside his chest. But it wasn't Carter emerging from out of a dark corner, the blade of a knife glinting in his hand. It was a monstrously proportioned rat, staring down at him from the flight of stairs above, whiskers twitching as it sniffed cautiously at the air.

'Jesus Christ,' Tanner muttered, placing his hand over his chest. 'You scared the crap out of me.'

The rat dropped its head to disappear around the edge of the stairs, leaving Tanner staring after it, up to the floor above. It was no use. Carter could have been anywhere by then, probably hiding in one of what must have been over a hundred deserted flats. It would take him hours to search each one, and as he did, the youth could simply slip silently into another.

There was nothing for it. He was going to have to try to flush him out, the old-fashioned way.

'Roy Carter!' he bellowed. 'It's DI Tanner, Norfolk Police!'

He stopped to listen, but the only thing he could hear was his own voice, echoing its way around the stairwell.

'I know you're here,' he continued. 'The owner of the shop you just robbed told me you were.'

Still nothing.

'Backup will be here any minute.'

Becoming desperate, he added, 'There's nowhere to hide.' His own words left him cringing. Anyone with half a brain must have known the opposite was true.

The unmistakable sound of someone sprinting up the stairs above allowed a self-satisfied grin to stretch out over his face.

Taking off after him, he was soon approaching the uppermost floor when he heard a door slam directly above his head.

Thinking Carter must have dived into one of the long-deserted flats on the floor above, Tanner stopped where he was, trying to work out if the noise had come from the right balcony or the left. But he could have sworn it was neither. More like straight ahead.

With the sudden realisation that Carter may have found his way onto the roof, where he was fairly sure there was a fire escape leading back down to the ground, Tanner once again took to the stairs, pushing hard to find himself on the very top floor. There he saw another short flight of stairs, directly ahead, at the top of which was a small wooden door marked by a corroded sign stating, "No Unauthorised Access."

Bursting through it, he emerged into the sharp brightness of day to find himself standing on a wide flat roof. As he squinted against the light, he gazed frantically about before stopping to pull himself up. Roy Carter was at the farthest corner of the building behind him, one hand latched onto the rail of the dilapidated metal fire escape.

As Tanner began stomping his way over, he saw the youth send him a look of panicked desperation, before placing a tentative foot down onto the edge of the crooked steel gantry.

Seeing the structure lurch to one side, Tanner called out, 'I wouldn't risk it if I were you.'

Carter stared back at him, his eyes wide with fear. It was obvious he was thinking the same thing.

Tanner drew closer.

'There's not even any point,' he continued. 'A squad car has just pulled up outside the main entrance. Even if the fire escape doesn't give way, they'll be there to pick you up when you arrive at the bottom.'

It was a complete lie, of course, one Carter should have easily seen through; the total lack of sirens being the most obvious giveaway. But Tanner had to hope that it would be enough to deter him. If he did reach the ground in one piece, he'd be gone.

'I didn't do it!' the red-headed youth suddenly cried. 'I didn't set fire to that block of flats, and I didn't murder that girl!'

'None of that matters anymore,' said Tanner, coming to a gradual halt just a few feet away.

'I suppose you're going to tell me that you've arrested the person responsible, and that the only reason you want me to come quietly is so that you can buy me a pint down the pub?'

'I'm sorry, but I'm afraid the opposite is true. The policewoman you stabbed on Wednesday. She's dead.'

He'd heard the words come out of his mouth, but it was as if they'd been spoken by somebody else, about a person he'd never met.

Carter's eyes dived between Tanner's.

'I – I didn't stab no policewoman!'

'Oh, you must remember. We were at the Rockworth Estate. You were there with all your mates, about to be arrested for God knows what when you came at me with your knife.'

'I didn't!'

As Tanner began re-living the moment, he took a step closer.

'She did her best to defend me, taking you to the ground, only for you to run off like the pathetic coward you are. But not before burying the knife you'd been threatening us with into her side.'

'It was an accident!'

Tanner took another step closer, uncontrollable primordial rage surging through his veins.

'Her name was Jenny Evans.'

His face contorted into a mask of vengeful fury, as what had happened to Jenny, and the fact that she was gone forever, finally began to filter down into his conscious mind.

'She was only twenty-nine years old,' he continued, lips drawing back to reveal a savage grimace. 'She was also my fiancée, the mother to my unborn child, the girl I loved with all my heart, body and soul, and it was you – YOU who took her away from me.'

'But – I – I didn't,' Carter spluttered, his second foot inching its way to join the other on the twisted structure that was already creaking under the burgeoning weight.

'There are at least three witnesses who'll testify otherwise, myself being one of them.'

'I didn't do it! It was an accident!'

'The murder of a police officer will mean you'll be spending the remainder of your days stuck inside a cell; prison guards beating you to a bloody pulp during the day, your fellow inmates gang-raping you at night. Sounds like fun, don't you think?'

By that time, Carter's whole body had begun to shake. Glancing over his shoulder, he stepped back, transferring the full weight of his body onto the fire escape. But it was too much. As the top of the gantry ripped itself away from the uppermost edge of the building, Carter lunged forward, ready to leap back to where Tanner was standing. Then he looked down at the gap. It was too wide for him to jump, not without the risk of falling a hundred feet to the ground below.

'Help me!' he screamed, a hand stretched out for the detective inspector to take.

But Tanner remained stubbornly where he was, burying his own hands down into the depths of his pockets.

'I suggest you jump,' he eventually offered. 'You never know, you might even make it.'

'Take my hand first,' Carter pleaded, his scrawny body trembling with fear.

Tanner took a cautious step forward to peer over the edge of the building.

'Nah,' he eventually said, pulling back. 'Looks a little too high for my taste. You're on your own, I'm afraid.'

Carter's lips began to quiver as tears cascaded down the sides of his face. 'But – you can't just leave me!'

Tanner watched him for a moment, his mind taking him back to when Jenny had been lying on that pavement, staring down at the blood oozing from the wound left by this scrawny little shit's knife.

His heart turned to stone.

'An eye for an eye,' he eventually said, the words creeping out through a smile full of vengeful malice. 'Isn't that what the bible says?'

'Please!' the boy sobbed, 'I'll do anything! I'm

begging you!'

'Tell you what. If you can bring my fiancée back to me, I'll be more than happy to give you a hand.'

'But – you know I can't do that.'

Tanner glared over at him. 'Then you're of no use to me.'

As the words came out of his mouth, the entire structure shifted violently to one side, but this time it didn't stop.

'NOOO!' Carter screamed; his eyes wide with terror as he reached desperately out for help.

But Tanner did nothing but to remain where he was, watching as Carter's scrawny body plummeted down into a torrent of twisted steel, shattered masonry, and all-consuming concrete dust.

- CHAPTER FIFTY EIGHT -

TANNER CONTINUED TO stand on the roof's crumbling edge, staring out towards Norfolk's vast open horizon. Having seen the person who'd murdered his fiancée die before his very eyes, he was expecting to have experienced some sort of emotional release. But his thirst for vengeance remained, just as it had before, boring relentlessly down into the darkest depths of his soul.

His head dropped to take in the twisted remnants of the fire escape, shrouded in a ghostly layer of swirling dust. He took a half-step closer, so that both his feet were resting on the building's edge. It would be easy enough for him to follow Carter over. He'd only need to lean forward, just slightly.

With a jolt, he forced himself back, shaking his head as he did. He'd nearly gone, but there wasn't a chance in hell he was going to, not if it meant ending up lying next to the person who'd already taken so much from him.

It was then that a thought slid its way into his mind. None of this had started with Roy Carter. He'd only been a cog in a much bigger wheel, one that had begun turning inextricably around ever since that MP, Patrick Hopkins, had been found hanging by his neck. That's when the hostility towards immigrants had begun, fuelled by the Norfolk Herald's stories about that 17th Century witch, and the supposed ancient curse she'd placed on the MP's family name. For the sake of Jenny's memory, and for the redemption of his soul, he could see he had been left with little choice. He was going to have to find out who'd killed Hopkins. Before he did that, he had to report what had just happened. If he neglected to, when Carter's body was eventually found, and the shopkeeper told his colleagues that he'd directed him up to the Hatchmead Estate, he knew he'd immediately be suspected of having murdered him.

With those thoughts filtering down through his mind, he dug out his phone to alert the station to his location, and the events that had taken place.

- CHAPTER FIFTY NINE -

FINISHING THE CALL, he remained where he was until the sound of distant sirens could be heard drifting through the air towards him. Only then did he return to the roof access door and the ten flights of concrete stairs beyond. When he eventually reached the bottom, he ambled his way over to the estate's main entrance. There he assisted the first squad car arriving at the site, helping them to cut through the estate's security gates' chain before heaving them open, allowing for what soon became a steady stream of incoming emergency traffic.

'So, you chased him up the stairs, onto the roof,' said PC Higgins, reading from the notes he'd been writing whilst taking another of the DI's statements. 'Then he climbed onto the fire escape to begin making his way down. That's when it gave way underneath him?'

'Pretty much,' Tanner confirmed.

'OK, thank you, sir. I'll type that up when I get back to the office.'

As the young police constable spun away, Vicky's auburn hair came bobbing into view.

'Are you alright?' she asked, her forehead creased with concern.

'I'm fine,' Tanner replied, struggling to hold her eye.

'Are you sure it was him? Roy Carter?'

'No question.'

'How did you find him?'

'The owner of the corner shop saw him running up the road towards the estate. There weren't any other places he could have been. It was then just a question of flushing him out.'

Vicky paused for a moment. 'Forensics aren't going to find anything, are they?'

'Anything, as in?'

'You know; that you -'

'That I threw him off the top of the building?'

'Well, after he'd put Jenny into intensive care.'

'Don't worry. I didn't so much as breathe on him.'

'I'm sure, of course,' Vicky responded, her face blushing slightly. 'It's just that, well, it's a shame you were here on your own when it happened.'

'I didn't see much point in calling for backup. Not after what you told me about the new DI.'

'Speaking of whom,' Vicky muttered, stealing a glance over at a square-jawed middle-aged man dressed in a pristine charcoal grey suit, swaggering his way over towards them.

'DI Tanner, I presume?' the man called out.

DI...?' began Tanner, staring vacantly over at him. 'Sorry, I don't seem to know your name.'

'Morton' the man replied, taking Tanner in with a condescending glare. 'DCI Forrester told me you were taken off the Horsey Mere investigation.'

'That's correct.'

'So may I ask what it is that you were doing chasing after one of the suspects?'

'I was responding to this morning's report of a robbery. Apparently, nobody else could be bothered.'

'It may surprise you to learn that we have other slightly more pressing matters to attend to, at least we did until you managed to kill one of the people involved.'

'I sincerely hope you're not accusing me of murder?' Tanner asked, his inner rage finding a new channel of focus.

'Not yet, no, but I will be recommending that the matter is handed over to Professional Standards. What with your much documented anger management issues, plus the fact that the victim, Roy Carter, is alleged to have stabbed your girlfriend, I wouldn't be at all surprised if you dragged him up there with the deliberate intention of shoving him off the top.'

'If you'd been doing your job properly, you'd have been over here yourself. He'd already confessed to the attempted murder of Nadira Matar, by throwing a petrol bomb at her mother's shop. It was subsequently blindingly obvious that it was him who set fire to the Glenwood Estate as well, killing literally dozens of innocent people in the process, including Nadira's friend, Zara Haddad. When you add in the fact that Anya Chadha's DNA was found in his van, the girl found hanging at Horsey Mere, anyone would have to be a brainless moron not to have arrested him at the first opportunity they had.'

'And you think his motive for having done all that was because some teenage witch had cast a love spell on him?'

'In part.'

The new DI laughed. 'And you're the one calling me a moron?'

'Er, no. I called you a brainless moron, and I was being generous.'

Morton leered back at him. 'From what I can understand, it was thanks to your total inability to do your job properly that he was allowed to walk free in the first place. Had someone been feckless enough to have done that in the MET, they'd have been strung up for gross incompetence, especially in light of the fact that he went on to stab your girlfriend. By the way, I hope you've apologised to her, being that it was your fault that she was attacked in the first place. And whilst I'm on the subject, being that you're her supervising officer, it was your responsibility to have made sure she was wearing a stab vest before allowing her anywhere near someone wielding a knife.'

Morton had hardly had a chance to finish the sentence when Tanner snapped, throwing first a punch, then himself at the interim DI.

As the man immediately began fighting back, a voice exploded over the top of them.

'Just what the *hell* is going on here?'

Breathing hard, Morton shoved Tanner off of him before drawing himself up to straighten his tie.

'Your DI just physically assaulted me, sir, as witnessed by everyone here.'

'For Christ sake, Tanner. What in God's name are you doing here?'

'I found Roy Carter,' he replied, his eyes remaining fixed on the interim DI.

'So I heard, and only a few minutes before he just happened to fall off the roof of a ten-storey block of flats.'

'That was hardly my fault.'

'But the fact that you were in active pursuit of him was, though, wasn't it?'

Tanner didn't respond.

'Have you told everyone about Jenny?'

With Tanner not even looking as if he was listening, it was left to Vicky to ask, 'What do you mean? What about Jenny?'

Realising he hadn't, Forrester stopped. 'Look,

Tanner. Just go home, will you.'

'Er, excuse me?' questioned Morton, staring over at Forrester with incredulous indignation. 'That man just assaulted me. You can't just let him go home.'

'What's happened to Jenny?' Vicky repeated, her voice changing in tone to that of a demand.

With Tanner's countenance remaining unchanged, Forrester let out a remorse-filled sigh.

'She passed away,' he eventually replied, his eyes dropping.

The air fell into a cold, lifeless silence.

Vicky's eyes darted between Forrester's and Tanner's. 'But – I – I don't understand.'

'I called the medical centre this morning,' Forrester continued, his voice no more than a whisper. 'Her condition deteriorated last night, leaving them with no choice but to undertake a second operation. She didn't survive.'

'But – she – she can't be.'

With pleading eyes she gazed over at Tanner, only to find his head slumped forward, his eyes fixed on the ground.

'John?' she questioned, her voice cracking with emotion. 'Tell me it's not true?'

Every fibre of his being longed to tell her that it wasn't, that the doctor had been wrong; Jenny was making the full recovery he'd been promised. But that wasn't what had happened. It was only then that his mind was fully able to accept the truth. She was gone, and there was nothing he could do to get her back.

His bottom lip shuddered as he searched for an answer. But instead of words came an outpouring of raw, unchecked emotion. Sinking to his knees, his head held in trembling hands, he began rocking backwards and forwards, openly sobbing as he did, with neither malice, embarrassment, nor shame.

- CHAPTER SIXTY -

IT TOOK OVER an hour for Tanner to become emotionally stable enough to climb back into his car. After driving aimlessly around with no sense of time, the desire to climb inside a bottle eventually led him back to his boat. It was only when he was standing on the grass verge, opposite its rounded wooden bow, that he realised it was the last place he needed to be. Every single part of it, from the small triangular flag fluttering at the top of the mast, to its smooth curved steel tiller reminded him of Jenny. He didn't trust himself to step on board, not when thoughts of tying one of its ten-kilogram mud-weights around his waist to drop himself over the side were already clawing their way through his mind.

He was just about to turn back to his car, to see if he could find a Travelodge to check into for the night, when he saw something had been left under a stone on the cabin roof. Curious, he stepped over to find a letter, the handwritten envelope addressed to him.

It was from Jenny's father.

He sucked in a juddering breath, questioning whether or not he had the mental fortitude to read it. What if it was accusing him of having murdered their daughter? If it was, then he'd have been right.

With a part of him almost hoping it was, he lifted it up to read.

He wasn't long into it when he realised the

opposite was true; the words urging him not to feel he was responsible in any way, that Jenny always knew the risks of having chosen such a profession.

It was the last paragraph that had him fighting back the tears.

Please don't be a stranger. Our door is always open.

He was about to tuck the letter away when he saw a postscript had been added.

We have something of Jenny's that we need to give to you. Maybe you could drop by this evening?

Tanner's eyes drifted over towards where he'd left his car. He visualised stepping up to their front door, wondering what he could possibly say; if he'd be able to say anything at all.

Realising that he'd not spoken to them since he'd been told the news, a wave a guilt crashed over his head. How utterly selfish had he been? He'd spent the entire time thinking about nothing more than *his* loss, *his* remorse, *his* grief. No matter how difficult it would be for him, he had to see them, if for no other reason than to offer them his condolences.

He pulled himself up straight as he tucked the letter safely away to turn on his heel, heading back to the car he'd only just climbed out of.

- CHAPTER SIXTY ONE -

IT WAS JENNY'S father who opened the door, his skin grey and lose, his eyes tired and red.

'John!' he exclaimed, a smile cracking his face.

'Hi Fred. I'm sorry I haven't been in touch since – since... It's just been...difficult.'

'There's no need to apologise; no need at all.'

'I just came to offer my deepest, most heartfelt condolences for the loss of your daughter.'

Tears began welling up in the eyes of both men.

'Is Mary around?' Tanner forced himself to ask, glancing over Fred's shoulder.

'To be honest, she's been finding it rather hard to come to terms with what happened. The doctor gave her some sedatives, to help her rest, but I'll be sure to tell her you came over. She'll appreciate it.'

Silence followed, as both men searched for something more to say.

'Did you get my letter?' Fred eventually asked.

'I did. Thank you.'

'I meant what I said - that our door is always open. I know the wedding didn't...that you never...but as far as we were concerned, it was only a formality. To be honest, I always felt – I always felt...' he bit down on his lip. 'Well, it's going to sound overly-sentimental, but I always felt that you were the son we never had. I know Mary felt the same.

'Anyway,' he continued, tearing his eyes from

Tanner's. 'We have something of hers which we need to give you.'

Reaching back inside the house, he lifted a padded envelope off a table in the hallway to hand over to Tanner.

'It's her police notebook,' he added, by way of explanation. 'It came with her personal effects. I was going to take it into the station, but I thought it would probably be better if I gave it to you, in person.'

- CHAPTER SIXTY TWO -

JENNY'S FATHER'S KIND words of parental love proved to be a much-needed cathartic experience, giving Tanner the emotional support he needed to be able to return to his yacht.

Once onboard, he tried desperately hard to keep himself busy, doing his best to be grateful for the precious time he'd had with the woman he'd been so hopelessly in love with. But it didn't take long for his mental resolve to falter, leaving him reaching for the bottle he kept tucked away underneath the seat out in the cockpit.

With the contents virtually gone, he was left a sobbing drunken mess, unable to do anything other than to crawl down into the cabin, drag a blanket over his shoulders and pass out.

But sleep was to offer him little respite. As soon as his eyes were closed, a seemingly endless series of harrowing dreams began creeping their way through the darkest recesses of his tormented mind. The most disturbing of these had him being buried alive whilst three naked teenage witches were hauled up by their necks directly above him. With their feet twitching until they were finally dead, he was forced to watch as their bodies began to decompose, just as a stupefying stream of haunting incantations began tumbling out through their putrefying purple lips.

Saturday, 21st November

Waking with a start, Tanner's lungs choked at the air as his mind was forced to endure one final haunting image. It was of Jenny's worn black police notebook, tumbling down from one of the hanging girl's maggot-riddled hands.

He rolled over in his bed, only for a wave of nausea to crash down over his head, leaving the brain inside splitting with agonising pain.

Forcing himself up, he scrabbled around the cabin for some painkillers before lurching out into the cockpit in desperate search of a glass of water.

With the pills swallowed, he found himself slouched at the table, head buried in his hands as he tried to peel away the nightmare's harrowing images that seemed to have been burned into the backs of his retina. Only when he began to feel the effect of the pills did he dare to move, and that was only to put the kettle on.

Back at the table, he saw the padded envelope he'd been given by Jenny's father the evening before. He must have left it there when he got back. With the nightmarish images still haunting his mind, he picked it up. Pausing for the briefest of moments, he broke the seal to let Jenny's police notebook slip out.

He stared down at it, his mind a tangled mess of fractured emotions.

Drawing in a fortifying breath, he picked it up to begin tentatively leafing through its pages. As he did, a particular date and time seemed to jump out at him. Looking more closely, it was when the Glenwood Estate had been set fire to. He could have sworn he'd seen the exact same date and time somewhere else, but for the life of him, he couldn't remember where.

With the kettle boiling, he pushed himself up to make himself a much-needed coffee. As he did, he remembered where he'd seen it, or at least he thought he did.

Coffee made, he dug around for his own notebook to find his last entry. It was the one he'd made when speaking to the owner of the corner shop. There it was, the same date, the same time. It was what he'd written when being shown the footage of Roy Carter and his mates supposedly helping themselves to the contents of the shelves a few days before.

If Carter had been in the corner shop when the Glenwood Estate fire had started, there was no way he could have been responsible.

This left Tanner with a disturbing question. If Roy Carter hadn't set fire to it, who had, and perhaps more importantly, for what reason?

Curious to look back through the estate's CCTV footage covering the time in question, he found his laptop to log into the Norfolk Constabulary's intranet, only to find his access to the relevant files had been revoked.

Cursing, he got back up to dig around for the memory stick he'd used to copy the files on to, but the footage wasn't even on there.

He pulled out his phone to call for help.

'Vicky, hi, it's me.'

'John! How are you?'

'OK, I suppose. Listen, are you in the office?'

'Well, I can't think where else I'd be, given that it's the weekend.'

Tanner smiled. He'd forgotten it was Saturday.

'Can you do me a favour? I need to take a look at the CCTV footage from the Glenwood Estate, around the time the fire started.'

'What are you looking for?'

'To be honest, I'm not sure.'

'Can't you access them on the intranet?'

'I can't get in. Someone's blocked my access.'

'No doubt that will be DI Morton. Tell you what, give me ten minutes and I'll email them over to you.'

- CHAPTER SIXTY THREE -

A S SOON AS the email came through, Tanner opened the first of three video attachments to fast-forward to the part when a skinny youth could be seen hurrying out of the block's communal entrance, his face obscured by the hoodie worn over his head. Despite the fact that his physique and posture was the same as Roy Carter's, at the end of the day he had to admit that it really could have been virtually anyone. There was also no reason to believe that he'd had anything to do with starting the fire. All he was doing was running out of the building, a few minutes before it was reported to have started.

Knowing that they'd already been through the footage, searching in vain for evidence of someone actually setting the building ablaze, or at least looking as if they had, he let out a heavy sigh. He may have had evidence to prove that Roy Carter couldn't have started it, he was still none the wiser as to who had.

Unable to think what else to do, he stared absently off into space. With his mind slipping into neutral, he could feel himself spiralling down a hole filled with nothing more welcoming than self-pity and depression. He shook his head clear. Whatever he did, he had to keep busy.

Forcing his attention back to the laptop, he rewound the video to begin watching it from the very beginning.

An hour later, his eyelids blinking themselves closed, he sipped tentatively at the steaming edge of his third coffee of the day. He was on the last video and had so far seen nothing that could have been described as even vaguely suspicious; just the random comings and goings of those living on the estate.

He was seriously beginning to question what he was doing when someone caught his eye. It was a smartly dressed woman entering the building's lobby, wheeling a suitcase behind her. He'd already seen her from another angle, but had simply assumed her to be a resident returning from some sort of work-related business trip. However, there was something about her that didn't quite fit. It wasn't just the clothes. He'd seen other women coming and going dressed in formal business attire. It was the way she carried herself that caught his attention. Everyone else he'd seen, both men and women, walked with their shoulders hunched, their heads tilted towards the ground. This woman carried herself as if she owned the place.

Tanner leaned in towards the screen to try and see her face, but the combination of the sunglasses she was wearing, the angle of the camera and the video's grainy colour image left him unable to see any of her features with any clarity.

With the vague memory that he'd seen the same woman leave the building, he began fast-forwarding through the footage. He didn't have to go far before he saw her again as she made her way out. He checked the time stamped on the screen. She'd only been in the building for eight minutes. She hadn't dropped the suitcase off either, as she was still dragging it along behind her.

Still unable to see her face, he made a quick note

of the times she'd entered and left before going back to re-open the first video he'd watched, where the camera had been pointing down towards the entrance from the outside wall. But that was even worse. He couldn't see her face at all.

Knowing the final camera presented a much wider view of the block, from the other side of the road, his heart sank. Unless she'd approached the building from that side, looking up at the camera as she passed, the footage would be of little use.

With the forlorn hope that she might have, he opened the video to find the relevant section.

There she was again, the woman with the suitcase. But she was approaching the building from the other side, nowhere near the camera.

With growing frustration, he continued to watch as she stepped up to the curb, heading towards the entrance. There she had to stop to heave the wheels of the suitcase over the curb before heading through the doors.

Fast-forwarding again, eight minutes later, he saw the same lady leave. As she did, she glanced up, revealing her face for the first time. Tanner hit the pause button to lean in towards the screen. But doing so only made the image more distorted. He tried pulling away, blurring the image by squinting his eyes. For a moment, he thought there was something familiar about her, but without being able to accurately see the contours of her face, she could have been any one of a million smartly dressed women. There was also nothing about her demeanour to suggest that she'd just set fire to the stairwell inside. She was simply walking out in the same confident manner in which she'd entered.

Realising that the only reason he'd had for suspecting her was that she looked slightly out of place, he was about to slam the laptop closed and head back to bed when he decided to at least see where she ended up. It was only then that he noticed the bonnet of a car, nudging into the shot to the far left of the screen. It was a Mercedes, but not the sort of beaten-up old one you might expect in such an estate. It had the distinctive sweeping design of the very latest model, making it look about as out of place as the lady. Furthermore, she was heading straight for it.

He squinted at the screen again, desperate to make out the number plate. It wasn't clear, but it was a short personalised one, and the letters and numbers could have only presented four, maybe five different combinations.

With renewed hope, he lept up to find a pen and paper before returning to write them all down. Once done, he logged into the Police National Computer to pull up the vehicle registration database to begin entering the variations in.

It only took a matter of minutes for a surname to appear on the screen that had his heart pounding as he went in search of his car keys.

- CHAPTER SIXTY FOUR -

HALF AN HOUR later, Tanner was turning his XJS into the vast opulent driveway of the Drummond's family estate.

Ringing the doorbell, he heard a dog bark from somewhere inside, immediately followed by the sound of a viciously chastising voice.

With the door being opened to reveal the distinguished face of the property's owner, Tanner pulled out his ID.

'Sorry to bother you, Mr Drummond.'

'What is it?' the man replied, staring out at him with a look of bewildered impatience.

'DI Tanner, Norfolk Police. I was here a few days ago, if you remember, about that unfortunate incident involving Mr Patrick Hopkins.'

'Yes, of course,' Drummond nodded, taking a more relaxed stance. 'How can I help?'

'Is your wife around?'

'My *wife*?'

'The lady who was here last time. That was your wife, wasn't it?'

'Of course it was.'

'Is she in?'

'What do you want to see her for?'

'Nothing important. I just have something I need to ask her.'

'Can't you ask me instead?'

Tanner replaced his ID for his notebook. 'I was looking to establish her whereabouts on Wednesday, between the hours of one and three in the afternoon.'

'And you expect me to know?'

Tanner could feel his patience beginning to ebb quickly away.

'I'm not asking you, Mr Drummond. I was simply giving you the reason why I need to speak to your wife.'

'Well, I'm sorry, but I've got no idea where she is.'

'Could you at least tell me if she's at home?'

Drummond paused before answering, his eyes searching Tanner's. 'It probably depends if her cars here,' he eventually replied.

'Am I correct in thinking that she drives a Mercedes; a silver S-Class Cabriolet, to be exact?'

'Look, what's all this about?'

'I don't suppose you have any idea what she may have been doing at the Glenwood Estate at the time in question.'

'None at all.'

'Would it help to know that a young lady by the name of Ms Zara Haddad lived in one of the flats at the top?'

Drummond continued to stare out at Tanner, his expression a mask of uninterested indifference.

'Would it also help to know that she's believed to have died in a fire there, the result of an arson attack, one which took the lives of dozens of men, women and children?'

Although his expression remained unchanged, his eyes began jumping erratically between Tanner's.

'And that your wife was caught on no less than three separate CCTV cameras,' Tanner continued, 'both entering and exiting the building, and only minutes before the fire was reported as having started?'

The colour fast drained from Drummond's face.

'If you know something, Mr Drummond, then you need to tell me.'

'I don't know anything. Why should I know anything?'

'OK, but if I think, for any reason, that you're deliberately withholding information from me, then you should know that I have every right to take you to Wroxham Police Station to continue this conversation down there. I also have the right to have you arrested for obstruction of justice. So, unless you want to be filmed by half the nation's press who seem to be permanently camped outside, being dragged out of the back of a squad car wearing a pair of handcuffs, I suggest you tell me what you know.'

At first, Drummond didn't reply, but just continued to offer the detective inspector a defiant glare.

'OK,' began Tanner, digging out his phone. 'If that's the way you want to play it.'

'Alright. Calm down. What do you want to know?'

'Do you have any idea what your wife may have been doing there?'

'I honestly don't.'

'But you recognised the girl's name, Zara Haddad?'

Drummond hesitated.

'We either do this here or under caution down at the station.'

'I've heard her name before,' he eventually replied, his weight shifting from one foot to the other.

'In connection to what?'

'I received a hand-delivered letter on Monday evening; from her and two others.'

'The two others weren't Anya Chadha and Nadira

Matar, by any chance?'

'Possibly. They were endeavouring to blackmail me.'

'*Blackmail* you?' Tanner repeated, raising an incredulous eyebrow.

Drummond shrugged.

'I take it you didn't report it?'

'Of course not.'

'Was there any particular reason why you didn't?'

'Honestly, if I called the police every time I received a threatening letter, one that was either demanding money or threatening to have me killed, I'd have you lot on speed dial.'

'I never knew you were so popular.'

'I'm sure it's the same for anyone in a position of power. Par for the course, I'm afraid.'

'But you're not though, are you?'

'Perhaps not yet, but the moment I threw my name into the hat for the by-election, it was only a matter of time.'

'What did the letter say?'

'Same old, same old.'

'I don't suppose you could be more specific?'

'I'm not sure I can remember.'

'Oh, I'm sure you can.'

'If you must know, it was something to do with me having attempted to have my way with them at some party.'

'Was that it?'

'The claim was that they were neither consenting, nor of suitable age. It was all nonsense, of course, as these things always are.'

'Were they asking for money?'

'That and the expectation that I'd rescind my candidature for the forthcoming by-election.'

'Or else?'

'They'd take their story to the press.'

Tanner thought for a moment. 'Do you still have the letter?'

'I threw it away.'

'Your wife. Did she see it?'

'She opened it by mistake. I told her not to give it a second thought.'

'And did she?'

'Did she what?'

'Give it a second thought?'

'How the hell should I know!'

- CHAPTER SIXTY FIVE -

WITH MICHAEL DRUMMOND left standing at his door, Tanner hurried back to his car to dig out his phone.

'Forrester, sir, it's Tanner.'

'Tanner! Good to hear from you. How've you been holding up?'

'I know who set fire to the Glenwood Estate,' he blurted out, ignoring the need for social pleasantries.

'I'm sorry?'

'The person who set fire to the Glenwood Estate,' he repeated. 'I know who it was.'

'I thought we'd agreed that it must have been Roy Carter?'

'It wasn't him, sir. I know I thought it was, but it wasn't.'

'What are you talking about?'

'He was caught on camera, shoplifting from that corner shop, at the exact same time the estate was set fire to.'

'But – we have CCTV footage of him coming out of the building, just before the fire started.'

'It may have looked like him, sir, but it wasn't.'

'Then who did?'

'Alison Drummond, sir.'

'Who?'

'Michael Drummond's wife.'

'Now, hold on a minute there, Tanner.'

'I went through the CCTV footage from the estate again this morning. She was there, Alison Drummond, wheeling a suitcase inside the building. It must have contained some sort of petrol canister because she came out with the exact same suitcase only eight minutes later. Then I saw her walk back to a Mercedes parked outside. I ran the number plate through the database. It was a brand-new S-Class Cabriolet, one registered in her name.'

'But – what possible reason could she have had for wanting to set fire to an old council estate?'

'For the same reason I thought Roy Carter had. To kill Zara Haddad!'

'OK, I think you need to stop there, Tanner. Ignoring the fact that you're not even supposed to be working on this case anymore, I've already approved DI Morton's report; that Roy Carter was responsible for both setting fire to the Glenwood Estate and for the murder of Anya Chadha.'

'Well, sir, he's wrong. Zara Haddad was trying to blackmail Michael Drummond.'

'Blackmail?'

'So were her friends; Anya Chadha and Nadira Matar.'

'I see. And may I ask what possible reason you could have for having reached that frankly bizarre conclusion?'

'Because I'm currently standing in Michael Drummond's drive, having just finished discussing the matter with him.'

'Please tell me your joking!'

'They wrote to him a few days ago, demanding he takes his name off the ballot in the forthcoming by-election, each one claiming that he'd tried to rape them at some party, when they were all underage as well. The accusation would effectively make him a suspected pedophile. He shrugged it off, saying the letter was just one of many, but not before his wife saw it. I think she took it more seriously.'

'Are you honestly suggesting that Michael Drummond's wife murdered Anya Chadha before setting fire to the Glenwood Estate in order to kill Zara Haddad, all because of some letter?'

'That's exactly what I believe! She married a Member of Parliament, one who went on to become the Foreign Secretary, only for him to be unceremoniously booted out at the next election. That would have effectively left her the wife of an unemployed nobody. I don't think she was prepared to take any chances of him not being able to win the forthcoming by-election, especially if that would mean he'd be left labelled a child molester by the tabloid press.'

'I assume you're about to tell me that she murdered Patrick Hopkins as well?'

'I don't have any proof that she did, but I wouldn't put it past her.'

'You don't have any proof that she killed those two girls, either!'

'Her car places her at the scene of the Glenwood Estate fire, and she has motive.'

'It's not enough, Tanner. Not by a long way!'

'I'm sorry, sir, but I disagree.'

'Does Michael Drummond even still have the letter, to prove that they were trying to blackmail him?'

'He said he threw it away.'

Tanner could almost hear Forrester shaking his head.

'I can ask the other girl,' Tanner proposed. 'Nadira Matar. She'd be able to confirm it.'

'Do you seriously think she'd admit to having been

part of an attempt to blackmail the former Foreign Secretary?'

'If we questioned her under oath, she might.'

There followed a long pause from the other end of the line, before Forrester's voice eventually came back to ask, 'Where's Drummond's wife now?'

'He says he doesn't know. Her car's not here.' It was Tanner's turn to stop to think for a moment. 'I assume you still have a squad car parked outside the hotel Nadira and her mum are staying at?'

'Well...no,' came Forrester somewhat hesitant response. 'With Roy Carter dead, we didn't feel it was necessary.'

- CHAPTER SIXTY SIX -

HALF EXPECTING TO find it a blazing inferno, Tanner screeched his XJS to a halt outside the hotel Mrs Matar and her daughter had been put up in by their insurance company. Relieved to find that it wasn't, he jumped out to stare about at the many cars crammed into the carpark, searching for a silver Mercedes cabriolet. Unable to see one, he hurried inside, only to find the reception desk deserted.

'Hello!' he called out, ringing the bell. 'Is anyone there?'

He stared impatiently towards the door leading through to the dozens of rooms beyond, and was about to step over to see if it was locked when a young lady finally appeared.

'Sorry about that,' she apologised, smoothing down her skirt. 'How can I help?'

'DI Tanner, Norfolk Police,' he replied, briefly presenting his ID. 'I need to check on a couple of your residents; a Mrs Matar and her daughter. They've been here for a while now.'

'What's their room number?' the receptionist asked, plonking herself down on the chair to take hold of a mouse.

'I'm not sure. They switched rooms a couple of days ago, for security reasons.'

'Are you referring to Mrs Janna Matar and Miss

Nadira Matar?'

'That's them.'

'Well, they haven't checked out, if that's what you're asking.'

'Can you tell me which room they're staying in?'

The lady glared over at him. 'I'm sorry, inspector, but it's against company policy to give out residents' room numbers. May I ask why you need to know?'

'As I said, I just have to check to make sure they're OK.'

'Can't you phone them?'

'I've already tried. It went through to voicemail.'

'Well, I'm sorry, inspector, but I'm not allowed to tell you which room they're staying in.'

'I don't believe this,' Tanner muttered, glancing back at the same door, only to see a familiar face push herself through.

'Mrs Matar!'

'Inspector Tanner!' she replied, surprise lighting up her eyes. 'What are you doing here?'

'I just came to make sure that you're OK.'

'We're fine; but thank you for your concern. It's appreciated.'

Tanner cast his eyes over her shoulder, into the corridor beyond. 'Is Nadira still in your room?'

'She popped out to buy some milk.'

A shadow of concern fell over Tanner's face. 'When was that?' he enquired, turning to look back at the entrance.

Mrs Matar glanced down at her watch. 'Fifteen, maybe twenty minutes ago. I was just coming out to see where she was. There's nothing wrong, is there? The policemen parked outside, they told me the boy you were looking for, Roy Carter, that he'd been killed in an accident.'

'He was,' Tanner confirmed, peering absently out

through the hotel's glass doors. 'Where did she go, to buy the milk?'

'There's a garage, on the other side of the carpark.'

'OK. She's probably just stuck in a queue. Wait here. I'm going to take a look.'

'But -?'

'I just want to make sure she's OK, that's all.'

Without wishing to alarm her any more than he probably already had, Tanner heaved open the door to jog his way over to the garage. But he could find no sign of Nadira there, either waiting in the queue or anywhere else.

Sprinting back, he burst into the hotel's reception.

'She's not there,' he announced, gulping in air.

'Then she must have wandered off somewhere,' said the mother, checking her watch again.

Tanner turned to face the receptionist.

'Has anyone else been here, asking about either Mrs Matar or her daughter?'

'Well, yes, but that was over an hour ago.'

'Who was it?' Tanner demanded.

'She said she was a magazine editor, looking to interview them for a story. She asked for their room number, like you. When I refused to tell her, she started ranting and raving, going on about the freedom of the press, eventually storming out, but not after saying some quite awful things to me.'

'Was she thin; immaculately dressed?'

The receptionist nodded.

'Shit!' Tanner cursed. 'Call the police,' he continued, turning for the door. 'Tell them what's happened – that Nadira Matar has gone missing.'

'But...!' Mrs Matar exclaimed, sending an imploring look to the back of Tanner's head. 'You told me Roy Carter was dead!'

Tanner stopped where he was, his hand resting on

the door handle. 'He is,' he replied, glancing back. 'But I was wrong. It wasn't Roy Carter who killed your daughter's friends. I think it was someone far more dangerous.'

- CHAPTER SIXTY SEVEN -

FLINGING HIMSELF THROUGH the doors, with night already closing in, Tanner leapt into his car to wheelspin his way out. With the certain knowledge that it had been Alison Drummond pretending to be a magazine editor, and that she'd left the hotel to wait outside, hoping for an opportunity to grab Nadira Matar, there was only one place he could think she may have taken her to.

Twenty minutes later, his headlights on full beam, Tanner was braking hard to swing his car right at West Somerton before roaring off down the dark empty road.

It wasn't long before he saw the single Hawthorne tree, black against a luminous band of fading yellow light that rippled gently on the water of Horsey Mere beyond.

Unable to see if there was anyone underneath it, he started to panic when his headlights caught the metallic silver paintwork of the only car left in the carpark.

Skidding in, he slammed on the brakes to leave the car rocking back and forth in a cloud of hovering dust, directly opposite the one he'd seen from the road. It was the Mercedes cabriolet he'd been looking for.

With his car's lights left on, he leapt out to stare over towards the tree in the darkness ahead. He'd hoped his headlights would have been powerful enough to penetrate the shadows beneath, but it was just too far away.

Cupping his hands around his mouth, he bellowed out, 'Mrs Drummond! It's DI Tanner, Norfolk Police!'

He stopped to listen, but all he could hear was his own voice, echoing through a steadily rising mist.

'I know you're out there; that you've got Miss Nadira Matar as well. Whatever you're thinking of doing to her, it's too late. Your husband told me about the letter; that the girls were trying to blackmail him. I also know that it was you who set fire to the Glenwood Estate.'

Tanner listened again, desperate for his words to have the desired effect; to persuade her to leave the girl unharmed and give herself up. But there was nothing in the night that suggested they had.

'Shit,' he cursed to himself.

Pulling a torch from the glovebox, he yanked the keys out from the ignition to begin pelting along the well-trodden grass path that followed the contour of the mere. It wasn't long before his eyes were able to penetrate the shadows underneath the tree.

'Mrs Drummond!' he shouted, still running.

It was only then that he saw the body of a girl, hanging by her neck, hands bound, feet twitching.

'Jesus Christ!'

Hurling himself forward, he tried desperately to push her up, hoping to ease the tension of the rope, but her body was too high.

He forced himself to remain calm. Torch in hand, he traced the rope up to a branch from where it plunged down to another, near the tree's base. Seeing that's where it had been tied off, he leapt over to begin grappling with the knot. But the rope was soaking wet, and his fingers struggled to find a purchase.

Ditching the torch, he took to a knee. With a combination of his fingers, nails and teeth, the knot finally gave way.

Pulling it loose, he took a firm hold of the rope before dropping the girl to the ground, just as the dull thud of a car door being closed floated over the thickening mist.

As the sound of an engine roared into life, he grabbed his torch to shine down into the girl's bulging brown eyes. But her pupils remained fixed, unmoving, making her swollen face look like a discarded plastic doll.

He peeled the beam away to try again, but they didn't move. He was too late. The girl was dead.

- CHAPTER SIXTY EIGHT -

T HE DISTANT WHINE of the Mercedes' engine reversing at full tilt had Tanner leaping to his feet. He knew that if he had any chance of being able to prove that Alison Drummond had murdered the girl, he'd have to catch her in the act of trying to escape. He couldn't rely on forensics to come up with anything. The girl's mud-smeared body combined with the soaking wet rope meant she'd shoved her into the mere before hauling her up, just as she had with Anya Chadha. Surgical gloves and a hairnet would have been enough to prevent them from finding either her prints or DNA. The only evidence he had that she'd killed the three girls, as well as all those people trapped at the top of the Glenwood Estate, hinged on the CCTV footage of her entering and leaving the building, and as Forrester had already said, it wasn't enough.

With those anguished thoughts rattling through his head, he sprinted back along the grassy path, his eyes fixed on her still reversing car, hoping to God that something would happen to stop her.

That's when he heard her grind the car's gears into first before it juddered to a halt.

In her panic to escape, she'd managed to stall it.

Having gained precious seconds, Tanner dug deep, pushing his body to the limit to sprint as hard and as fast as his lungs would allow.

Ahead he heard her start the engine again, piling on the revs only for it to once more come to a grinding halt.

She'd done it again!

Do that once more, Tanner prayed, gaining precious ground.

But she must have learnt her lesson, as Tanner heard her re-start the engine to keep the revs low enough to allow the gearbox to engage.

With the Mercedes' wheels digging into the loose gravel, Tanner leapt over the carpark's low wooden barrier to wrench open his car door and jump inside.

Keeping one eye on the Mercedes as it pulled out onto the road, he threw the car into reverse. Turning the steering wheel first one way, then the other, he was able to wheel-spin his way out to the carpark's exit before she'd even made it to the first corner.

Desperately hoping she'd make another mistake, he turned the car onto the road before burying the accelerator deep into the footwell's carpet. As the tyres caught on the cold wet tarmac, the car surged forward, quickly gaining speed as its over-sized V12 engine began growling through the gears. Forced to brake as he threw it into the first bend, he accelerated again, just in time to catch the Mercedes' taillights in the distance, braking hard to round the next corner.

Knowing the T-junction at West Somerton was less than a half a mile further on, and that if she made it there, the idea of her fleeing the scene of a crime would be difficult for any jury to accept, Tanner tore into the next bend far faster than he should. As he rounded the corner, he felt the back of the car lurch violently towards the curb. Fighting to keep control, he emerged out on the other side with his heart pounding. He'd made it, but only just.

Another fleeting glimpse of the taillights up ahead

and he knew he'd risked his car, possibly his life as well, for nothing. He hadn't gained. If anything, she was pulling away.

As her taillights disappeared again, he heard a sound erupt from around the next corner that was so singular, so distinctive, he knew what had happened without having to see it.

Taking his foot off the accelerator, he eased the car around the road, peering out through the windscreen as he did.

Ahead was the underside of what was left of the Mercedes. She'd lost control as she'd rounded the bend, just as he nearly had. From what he could make out, the car had clipped the edge of a wall before being flipped onto its side, smashing hard into an awaiting lamppost.

Leaving the XJS at a safe distance, Tanner flicked on his hazard lights before stepping cautiously out.

The scene presented to him was eerily quiet, just the ticking sound of the Mercedes' engine as it began to cool.

He took a tentative step closer, only to be brought to a standstill by the overpowering smell of petrol. Glancing down at the road he saw the smooth sheen of a cold clear liquid, spreading out around a shattered brake light that sparked intermittently with ominous portent.

A sound drew his eyes to the top of the car. There he saw the driver, clawing her way out through the shattered driver's side window.

He remained where he was, watching as she perched herself on the top of the door before turning to tug at something.

Another spark from the broken brake light had her head whipping around to stare down. She must have seen the petrol, as she turned to stare over at him, her face a mask of glistening blood.

'My leg,' she muttered, her voice nothing more than a faltering whisper, 'It's caught on something. Help me, please.'

Tanner was about to step forward when he stopped. If the spark came into contact with the petrol, he knew what would happen, just as she did. But that wasn't what was preventing him from coming to her aid. The woman staring over at him, her eyes imploring him to help, had not only taken the lives of three teenage girls, but all those families trapped at the top of the Glenwood Estate as well, and all for no other reason than to elevate her social standing. But there was another reason he remained where he was. He needed to know if she'd also murdered Patrick Hopkins, so triggering the chain of events that ultimately led to the death of the woman he was still so desperately in love with.

'I'll help you,' he began, 'but I'm going to need a confession first.'

She didn't reply.

'I need to hear you admit to having murdered those girls. I also need to know if it was you who killed Patrick Hopkins?'

He waited for her to speak, but her mouth remained closed.

Another spark had her staring down to the back of the car, her eyes wide with fear.

'You know what will happen if the petrol catches fire?' posed Tanner, taking a half-step away.

She turned her head back to face him.

'You're only going to help me if I confess?'

'If you tell me the truth!' he insisted.

'Well, *fuck you!*' she spat, returning to heave frantically at her leg.

A lifeless thud had them both staring down.

There, spreading out around the back of the car was a flickering circle of blue.

The petrol had ignited.

'Tell me!' Tanner demanded, desperation rising in his voice. 'Did you kill Patrick Hopkins?'

'Help me, please!' she cried, her face contorted in pain as she tugged frantically at her leg.

Desperate not to lose her before knowing if she had, Tanner launched himself forward, just as a wall of heat smacked into his chest, sending him flying back against the side of his car.

As an ear-piercing whine drilled itself down into the depths of his brain, he forced himself onto an elbow to stare out into a heat that was so intense, he could feel it scorching the skin of his face.

The car had exploded, turning the Mercedes into a blazing inferno, flames stretching their way up to where Alison Drummond still sat, tugging at her leg, as if blissfully unaware that her entire body was burning with uncontrollable rage.

- CHAPTER SIXTY NINE -

H E MUST HAVE passed out at some point after the car exploded, as the next thing he knew he was surrounded by the wail of sirens as doors were slammed whilst people screamed out instructions. As he felt his body being lifted into the air, a woman's voice came drifting down to him from somewhere far above.

'Is he going to be alright?'

'Jen?' he croaked, lifting his head, his eyelids fluttering open to find himself in the back of an ambulance.

'It's Vicky; DS Gilbert, sir. Are you OK?'

Tanner let his head fall back, screwing his eyes closed against a flood of unwanted memories.

'Do you know who was in the car?' came Vicky's voice again.

'Alison Drummond,' Tanner replied, feeling himself beginning to come round. 'Michael Drummond's wife.'

Remembering the girl at Horsey Mere, he opened his eyes to find Vicky's arm. 'Did you find the girl; Nadira?'

'Was she in the car as well?'

'She's at Horsey Mere. I tried to save her, but I was too late.'

'OK, hold on. I'd better let someone know.'

Letting her go, he watched as she exchanged places

with a paramedic before disappearing out through the back of the ambulance.

Tanner rested his head back down to stare up at the roof, leaving the paramedic to begin an examination. He'd just been told that he'd been given a heavy dose of pain killers when he found Vicky back by his side.

'I've asked Cooper to go down with Sally to take a look.'

'What about the new DI?'

'He's not around.'

Tanner sent her a questioning look.

'He had a row with Forrester earlier. I suspect he's on his way back to London by now.'

'He didn't last long.'

'No, well; he wasn't right. Not for the Broads, at least. He wouldn't stop telling everyone how to do their jobs, even Forrester!'

The image of the twitching feet of the girl he'd tried to save flashed into Tanner's mind.

'It was Alison Drummond,' he muttered, his mind turning to visualise her tugging at her leg on top of the burning car. 'I tried to get her to confess?'

'I assume she didn't?'

Tanner shook his head. 'We're not going to have enough to prove that she did it.'

'Maybe you should try to get some rest?'

'I asked her about Patrick Hopkins as well.'

'What did she say?'

'There wasn't enough time.'

Tanner took a moment to clear his mind. 'I assume nothing was found regarding that professor? What was his name?'

'Bamford,' Vicky replied. 'That was what Forrester and Morton were arguing about. The motive was there, but not much else.'

'No new leads?'

'Only one.'

'What was that?'

'You remember Hopkins was in the Army, before going into politics?'

'Uh-huh.'

'Well, we managed to find out why he left.'

'I thought he'd retired.'

'He'd *been* retired, but only after being court martialled. From what we've found out so far, he had a complete mental breakdown when he was serving in Iraq, ending up with him rampaging through a village with a machine gun.'

For some obscure reason, the story reminded Tanner of Jenny, but for the life of him he couldn't think why. Then he remembered the dream she'd described to him, the very last time they'd talked together; how she'd been playing with children in the middle of a desert village when they'd all been massacred by a soldier.

'If that's true,' he eventually said, 'how come we've only just found out about it? Surely he must have ended up doing time?'

'Military convictions don't appear on criminal record checks. It was Cooper who thought to take a look at his Army background.'

'I assume you're thinking that someone may have found out what he'd done, deciding to take justice into their own hands.'

'Something like that,' Vicky replied.

Once again, Tanner found himself back by Jenny's bed, listening to her retell the story of her dream, as if she was talking to him from beyond the grave.

As goose bumps crawled their way over his skin, his whole body shook.

'Are you OK?'

'Help me up, will you?'

'I hope you're not thinking about going somewhere?' she questioned, taking a hold of his outstretched arm.

Perched on the edge of the stretcher, he grimaced in pain as he searched through his pockets. 'I just need to check something,' he eventually said, pulling out a well-used police notebook.

'That's not yours, is it?'

'It's Jenny's,' Tanner replied. 'It was amongst her personal effects.'

Vicky watched in silence as Tanner began leafing through its pages.

'Do you know when it happened; when Hopkins went on that killing spree?'

'It was in 2003,' Vicky replied. 'I'm not sure of the exact date.'

'We found someone's prints at the scene of Hopkins's murder,' Tanner continued, 'but we never considered the person they belonged to as being a suspect.'

'Why wouldn't we have done that?'

'Because the items originally came from her,' Tanner replied, still turning the pages. 'I'm just trying to find out if Jenny made a note of when she told us she came to the UK.'

Stopping at a page, he stared down at it for a moment before snapping it closed.

'Do me a favour, will you?' he asked, replacing Jenny's notebook with his own to quickly scrawl something down. Tearing off the page, he handed it to her as he eased himself off the stretcher. 'Find out everything you can about this person, especially in relation to her life before she came to the UK.'

'But...where are you going?' Vicky questioned, staring down at the name he'd written.'

'I need to give a concerned mother the news that her daughter is dead.'

- CHAPTER SEVENTY -

TANNER FOUND JANNA Matar where he'd left her, in the hotel's reception area, perched on the edge of a chair, staring expectantly down at her phone.

Straightening his tie, he pulled open one of the glass doors to take a single step inside.

The woman jumped to her feet to send him a look of imploring desperation. 'Did you find her?'

Tanner remained where he was, his demeanour calm, his face resolute.

'*Did you find her?*' Matar repeated, her voice haemorrhaging emotion.

'Why did you come to the UK?' he eventually asked, his eyes fixed on hers.

'What?'

'You told me you were originally from Iraq. What made you want to leave?'

'What's that got to do with my daughter?'

'Was it because of something that happened to your family?'

The woman froze, as if her whole body had been turned to stone.

'We've found out that your father, brothers and sisters were all murdered by a British soldier, right in front of your eyes.'

Colour fast drained from her face.

'I think you came here to try and forget; to start a

new life with a family of your own, but that all changed when a man walks into your shop. You'd probably seen him on TV before, but you only recognised him when he stood directly in front of you to stare down into your eyes. Only then did you realise what you had to do. For the sake of your family, their lives, and the life he'd taken from you, you were left with no choice. You had to kill him.'

The distant wail of approaching sirens had the woman sinking back into her chair.

'But as I heard you tell your daughter, actions have consequences, Mrs Matar. The death of Patrick Hopkins set in motion a chain of events you could have never foreseen. The need to hold a by-election leads three girls to send the Conservative candidate a letter. It demands that he rescinds his candidacy, or they'll take their story to the press; that he'd once tried to have sex with them at a party, when none of them were either consenting or of legal age. But his wife opens the letter by mistake. Knowing such a story would ruin her husband's chances of being re-elected, so destroying any chance she had of resuming her previous elevated position in society, she decides to take matters into her own hands. She kidnaps Anya Chadha to leave her hanging by the neck at Horsey Mere. She then sets fire to a block of flats, killing Zara Haddad trapped at the top. She then goes in search of your daughter.'

Tanner paused as a series of blue lights began circling the room.

'Meanwhile, Patrick Hopkins's murder fans the flames of racial bigotry. In steps Roy Carter, who begins to taunt your daughter and her friends, just as he used to do at school. One night he punches one of them in the face, leading them to take their revenge by casting a spell on him. But the spell leads him to madness. He throws a petrol bomb at your shop, the resulting fire claiming the life of your mother. Later, when we try to arrest him, he stabs my fiancée, Jennifer Evans; the woman I loved with all my heart, body and soul.'

Tanner's voice began to shake as the sound of voices could be heard outside.

'And now she's dead. She's dead, Mrs Matar, because of what *you* started!'

Glancing over his shoulder to see two uniformed police officers step up to the entrance, he turned back to face her.

'Mrs Janna Matar, I'm arresting you for the murder of Patrick Hopkins. You do not have to say anything, but it may harm your defence if you do not mention when questioned something which you later rely on in court.'

'But...Nadira...?' she asked, her voice trembling as tears began falling from her eyes.

'Anything you do say may be given in evidence.'

'You haven't told me what happened to my daughter!'

'She was hanged by the neck until dead, Mrs Matar. That's what happened to your daughter!'

- EPILOGUE -

TANNER STEPPED TO one side to allow the two police constables in through the doors. Gesturing down at the suspect, he watched in bitter silence as she was lifted to her feet for her hands to be handcuffed behind her back. He then followed them out into the night to watch as she was bundled into the squad car parked immediately outside.

He knew what he was supposed to do next. As the arresting officer, his job was to follow the car back to the station to hand her over to the duty sergeant for formal processing. But how could he? Despite the fact that it had been her actions that had ultimately led to Jenny's death, all she'd done was to murder the man who'd slaughtered her family. Having done so, she'd already paid a terrible price. Alison Drummond had seen to that.

As he watched the squad car drive slowly away, he knew he had no intention of doing so. He'd had enough, and not just of the job. He'd lost too much to go on. The murder of his own daughter had left him on the brink. It had been Jenny who'd kept him back from the edge. With her gone as well, there was nothing left to keep him from stepping over.

With the sudden all-consuming desire to embrace his own death, he drifted over towards his car. He knew it wouldn't be difficult. He'd already decided how. He'd simply scuttle the boat after locking himself inside the cabin with a suitably large bottle of Jamaican Rum.

The sound of his mobile phone ringing brought his mind back to the land of the living. Glancing up to find he'd already reached his car, he ignored the phone to start digging around for his keys. By the time he'd found them and had levered himself inside, the phone had stopped, only to start again a second later.

Out of general irritation he pulled it out.

It was Forrester.

His thumb hovered over the screen, unable to decide if he should take the call or not. Eventually, his sense of loyalty got the better of him.

'Tanner speaking.'

'Tanner, it's Forrester.'

'Yes, sir.'

'I just got off the phone to Vicky. She told me what happened; about Michael Drummond's wife and the girl you found.'

'I – I wasn't in time to save her, sir.'

'Maybe not, but at least you tried. She also mentioned to me that you're on your way to arrest that shop owner, Mrs Matar, for Patrick Hopkins's murder?'

'I already have.'

'Oh, right. I see. So, you're sure it's her then?'

'One hundred percent.'

'OK, good.'

A moment of silence followed before Forrester's voice came back over the line.

'I assume you heard what happened to DI Morton?'

'Vicky told me.'

'Yes, well, it's always been tricky to find good people, like yourself. I think I can speak for everyone here when I say that we're all looking forward to your return. We can expect you back, can't we? After you've had a few days off, of course.'

He didn't reply.

'OK, well, look. Feel free to take as much time off as you need. At the end of the day, you're a damn fine DI, Tanner. I know you've been through hell and back over the last few days, what with what happened to Jenny and everything, but I need you here. We all do.'

'Yes, sir.'

'So, we will be seeing you then, after you've had some time off?'

'I – I don't know.'

'There's no need to decide now, of course. Take as much time as you need.'

More silence.

'Tell you what, how about if I drop by in a few days, to see how you're doing? Maybe you could take me out in that old boat of yours?'

'I can't really sail, sir. That was always Jenny's thing.'

'Then perhaps that's something you could work on. Take yourself off sailing for a few weeks. I'm sure it would help take your mind off things.

'Anyway, I've gone on enough. Do please take care of yourself, Tanner. And if you need anything, even if it's just someone to talk to, you can always give me a call.'

With the conversation ending, Tanner tucked his phone away to reach down and start the car's engine.

Jenny would like that, he thought to himself, easing the car forward. *Me, going sailing, on my own. She'd find it hilarious, of course, but she'd definitely like it.*

*DI John Tanner
will return in
The Wherryman*

- A LETTER FROM DAVID -

Dear Reader,

I just wanted to say a huge thank you for deciding to read *Horsey Mere*. If you enjoyed it, I'd be really grateful if you could leave a review on Amazon, or mention it to your friends and family. Word-of-mouth recommendations are just so important to an author's success, and doing so will help new readers discover my work.

It would be great to hear from you as well, either on Facebook, Twitter, Goodreads or via my website. There are plenty more books to come, so I sincerely hope you'll be able to join me for what I promise will be an exciting adventure!

All the very best,

David

- ABOUT THE AUTHOR -

David Blake is an international bestselling author who lives in North London. At time of going to print he has written eighteen books, along with a collection of short stories. When not writing, David likes to spend his time mucking about in boats, often in the Norfolk Broads, where his crime fiction books are based.

Printed in Great Britain
by Amazon